EXILE

Alex Stephens

For Pumpkin, Taffy, and Joe.
Cats can't read, but if you could, I'm sure
you'd like this book.

Outer
Sea of Falencia
E
Verhan
Haxothron
Semmerfall
Nored
Excutatem
Felfort
Crimine
Tiherra Vendir
Wulland
Isles of Penelopen
Moar
Tuyin Matma
Me S
Samme
Perheath
Tazgrad
Ramothus
Sitika
Minor Channel
Gold Sea
Port Hameth
West Aathoris
Outer

Ocean
Jennira's Pass
Illiera
Aural
Grand Channel
Senim
Highlands
Sacred Lands
Yilioo
Galfbena
Mésura Lake
Tontéres
Minesra
dian
Rive
Sileolis Lowlands
Sea of Elethèl
ea
Leorn
Epona
N
W
E
S
Ocean

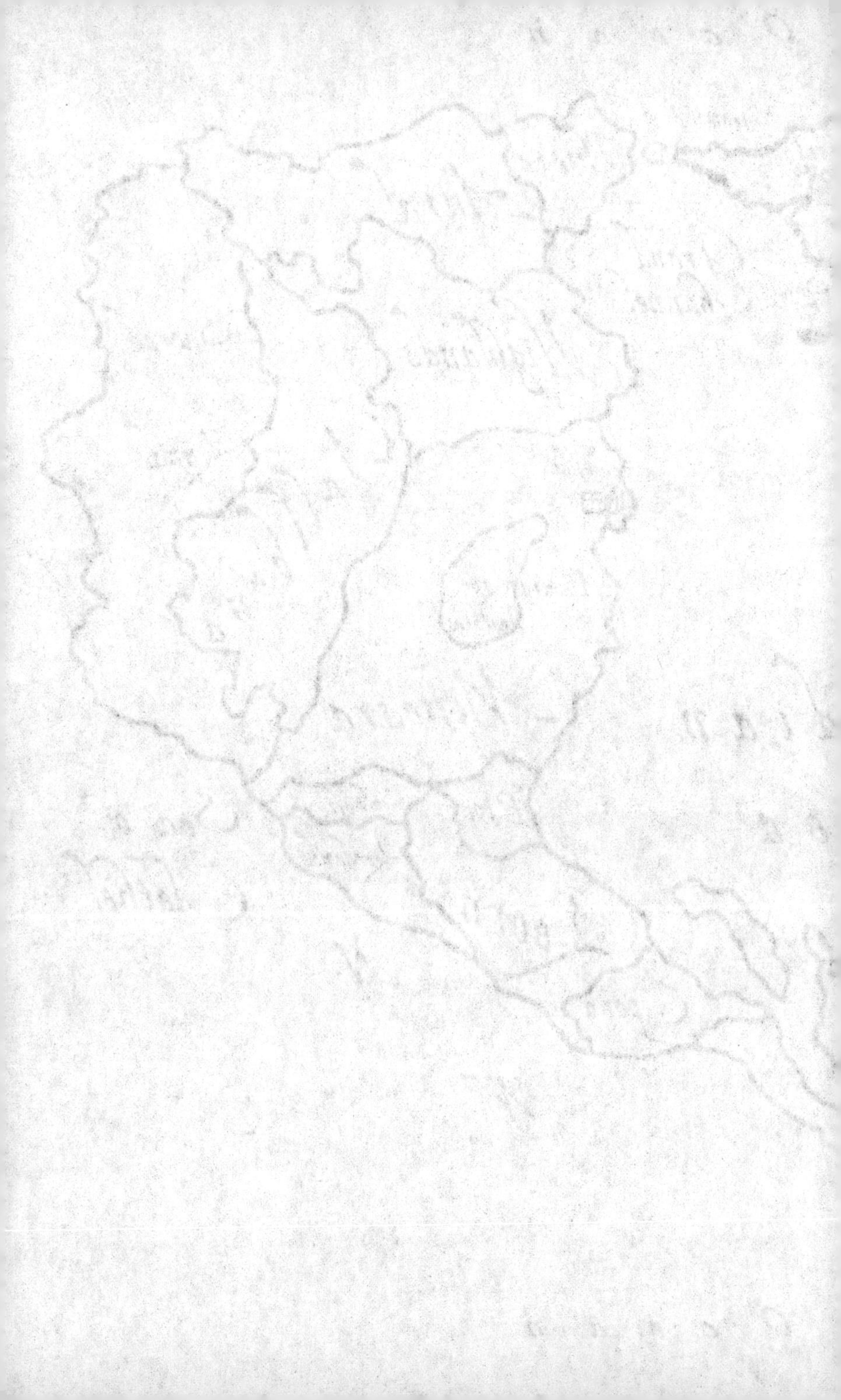

PART I

Chapter One

The last snow of the year fell along with my empire. I wouldn't know it, though, as I watched the flakes of ice drifting down to the castle courtyard.

"Prince Damion?"

I turned around to face the servant standing in the doorway. He continued, "It is almost time. Shall we return to your chamber?"

I glanced back to the garden, the frost dusting the bare branches of the rose bushes. I would rather stay, but it wouldn't be worth my father's reprisal if I showed up late. Taking a deep breath of brisk, cold air, I returned to the door and stepped back inside. The hall was hardly any warmer, and the servant was quick to drape a coat over my shoulders as he followed me down the corridor.

I took my time walking through the halls and up the staircases to my room. I was in no rush to get there — it's not like I had any *real* role at the Assembly besides ceremonial support for whatever nonsense my father was proposing. I had learned over the past twenty years not to let it bother me for the sake of my sanity.

We came to the door, and I paused to let the servant open it. He seemed to fumble a bit with the lock, and I realized I didn't recognize him. Was he new? I didn't think I had seen him before. He swung open the door and stepped aside, bowing as I entered. It was a little much. Definitely new.

Once inside, I held out my arms as he slid off my warmer, more practical coat and replaced it with the ceremonial one. I hated this thing more than I hated Assemblies — it was thick as blubber and made my shoulders ache just looking at it. I adjusted it as comfortably as I could, but it was always a losing battle.

As he continued swapping my boots for dress shoes, securing my belt, and patting my hair into place, my gaze wandered outside my window. The climb up the stairs to my room was always exhausting, but the view made up for it: The Edden river directly below wound parallel to the castle, toward the bay where ships cruised in and out of the docks. Beyond the river, the entire city of Exceres, capital of Excutatem, spread out for miles. The skyline was jagged with chapels, towers, and plumes of fireplace smoke, all contrasted against the dark shadow of the mountains in the distance. From up here, the crowds seemed to morph together into one single being which flowed through the streets hypnotically. I almost didn't hear the servant when he told me I was ready.

We withdrew from my chamber and began to retrace our steps through the halls and down the stairs. I was caught off guard when he suddenly broke the silence.

"Lord Damion, may I ask you a question?"

I didn't slow or look back, but my brow furrowed. It was definitely not customary for an attendant to ask something like that — or to talk at all, for that matter. I didn't really want to answer any questions, but the break of standard protocol made me curious.

"About what?" I asked monotonously, masking my intrigue behind forced disinterest.

He started to respond, but I could hear the words catch in his throat. He paused. "It's nothing. Pardon me, I shouldn't have said anything."

He fell back into silence, but he should have known better than to pique my curiosity and then change his mind.

"*About what?*" I pried. Finally, he gave in.

"Forgive me if this is foolish, I really don't mean to waste your time, but there are rumors around the castle of a *change* in the war. I don't believe it, of course, but…"

"You wanted to know if I knew anything?" I surmised.

"Well, yes, I–"

"If you're going to waste my time saying 'pardon me' again, don't. You can't believe everything you hear. Where did this even come from?" When I could sense him tense up at the question, I added, "I'm not going to turn them in for making up rumors. I just want to know."

He still didn't appear completely at ease. Hesitantly, he replied, "One of the caterers. She said she overheard Emperor Jourdan and General Assix preparing for the Assembly, but surely she heard wrong."

I had nothing to say to that. It was more bold of a rumor than we usually heard around here, but it wasn't any of my concern if the staff were losing sleep over it. I let the topic drop as we turned onto the corridor which led to the assembly hall.

At the end of the long stretch towered two massive doors held open by a series of pulleys, allowing members of the Politicians' Guild to descend onto the room in droves. Dozens of old men, each trailed by a small cohort of wives and servants, shuffled into the assembly chamber.

Gradually, they took notice of my approach — a few stepped aside to make way for me, followed by those closest to them, until the chain reaction had the entire crowd parted. They fell silent as I passed. Though I was a seventh of the age of the youngest among them, they'd all been pining to win my favor since I was born.

Once inside, I marched up the aisle, past rows of chattering nobles, toward the platform in the forefront. I took my seat to my father's right as he silently scrutinized the incoming audience. To his left was an empty throne, next to which was the throne occupied by my grandmother. After her was my sister, Rema, though it always seemed strange to me to place a girl of barely sixteen on the same stage as the past, present, and future rulers of the empire. Surely there must be some noble kids' table for her to rule over. To my right stood Acturas Assix.

Despite being almost fourteen years older, and having led the palace guard before I was old enough to even understand why we *needed* guards, I regarded Acturas more as an older brother than as an agent of my father whose loyalty I'd eventually inherit as king. Since the outset of the war, and the *fall* of his predecessor, he'd held the title of Commander-in-Chief under my father. It got his family back in the spotlight — literally, in his case, as he looked out from the stage onto the rows and rows of nobility taking their seats.

Once most assemblymen were seated, the servants delicately set the gavel in front of my father, and he less delicately took to hammering it at once. The room fell into silence. He stood and began the same rehearsed opening I had heard a million times at a million Assemblies. I distracted myself by flipping through the stack of papers laid out before me: four pages of my father's speech transcripts I wouldn't be reading; a seating chart, so I didn't accidentally misaddress the Baron of Reiley as the Duke of Bey, lest I cause the biggest scandal of the week; and finally, an envelope?

I turned it around and found it was signed *From Acturas, READ ALONE.* I glanced to my right, trying to make some sense of why he would sneak this in here, but he seemed fixated on the door to the chamber. I followed his gaze. The sentinels were slowly unwinding the wheels, sending the doors creeping shut almost silently. Just before closing, they seemed to give up with any sense of care, releasing the wheels and sending them swinging shut with a resonant boom that roused the assemblymen from their bored stupors. All eyes, including mine, turned to my father.

His crown caught the chandelier light above us, casting a golden glow around the shadow over his face.

"Now, we shall start upon the business of the day," he began, followed by a pause which left the room in intrigued silence. "Firstly, we would like to address the unfortunate context in which Excutatem finds itself. Our efforts to spread our borders to our rightful territories abroad have been decisively successful for many years, by the grace of the Elementals and our righteous leadership. But, as you all are well aware, our forces have stalled in the Elven Highlands of the mid-East. There are reports of elven mages on the front lines. Even dragons."

There was a sharp gasp from a good portion of the audience. I just sat in silence, staring at the wall opposite to me with my brow furrowed. I hadn't been told anything about this — though, I never asked. I'd assumed it would just be another mundane exercise in how high they can raise grain taxes before we all got beheaded, or another assurance to the barons that all those farmers were actually *lucky* to be sent as soldiers to the front lines in the Eastern Continent.

Where is this going?

"These claims are largely unfounded, though, and we don't believe the elves *even in their desperation* would be foolish enough to go to those lengths. Still, it remains a fact that our current strategies cannot seem to overcome the elves' defenses north of Minesra. We had hoped to breach their borders by last week, but it is now in question whether we will ever see our forces march on their capital of Mésura. This is not because of the situation in the East, though; our new development is much more urgent."

I swallowed. Despite my usual disinterest in the war effort, something about this felt *off*. His tone, the resolve… there was none of the passion typical of his speeches.

He continued solemnly, "A handful of you have already heard the rumors. As it turns out, one of our kitchen maids has decided to tell stories she never should have heard, and she has already been dealt with. In any case, we regret to inform you all that these rumors are true. The elves are pushing back."

Confused whispers broke out at various points around the floor, but he raised his hand, silencing them all. "We are far from finished. They are pushing back, but not in the Highlands, nor in the East at all. Our treacherous neighbor Illiera has conspired with them all along, and a battalion waged an attack on Jennira's Pass two days ago. They're in the West."

A beat of silence. Everyone seemed to process his words at the same rate. Then, as they did: chaos.

The whole chamber erupted — furious whispers, unintelligible shouts, chairs collapsing as people leapt to their feet in panic. My father issued a glance at Acturas, who was already directing the guards to control the crowd. As the last assemblymen uneasily returned to their seats, the king continued.

"Now, under normal circumstances, a single battalion would be nothing of a threat. We are afraid, however, that these are far from normal circumstances. Our western forces are focused in the deserts in the South, and we have only just begun to call back our armies in the northern tundras. Worse yet, the Isles of Penelopene have once again united in rebellion, and the elven navy has monopolized their waterways. Our success thus far has relied on the condition that the enemy would be too occupied in defense to mount any retaliation, allowing us to direct most of our forces abroad. Clearly, this is no longer a given. If we don't react now, the tide may turn against us."

He let the words simmer. There was no more chaos from the crowd. Everyone held completely still, waiting for him to finish.

"But we did not summon you all here to fearmonger. The Hall of Elements will defend the city, and the Elementals will reinforce us with divine protection. The elves pose no threat to us united behind the capital's walls, and so we must *stay* united. There will be no surrender. There will be no negotiation. Excutatem is the most powerful empire the world has ever known, and no elf, no army, can reach its heart. Do not let panic lead you astray from your emperor and Elementals."

I let myself exhale. I knew it was nothing serious — he was probably just being dramatic to build support for his next waves of tax raises and military drafts. Still, I couldn't help but feel it was all a little much. My father continued his discourse, but at this point, I was barely listening.

An attack *in* Excutatem?

There was no way that could happen.

Chapter Two

I was shaken awake the next morning. I squinted up at a dark figure silhouetted against the morning light. I probably should have been more panicked, but after my post-Assembly bender last night, I could hardly keep my eyes open, much less fend off a potential attacker.

"Damion, get up," Acturas whispered. I felt an ounce of relief sink in, though it was quickly diluted by a wave of irritation.

"Leave me alone, I'm too tired for this," was what I intended to say, but it must've been borderline incomprehensible in my current state.

"We have to leave. There are bags for us in the kitchen. Get dressed."

Leave? What was he talking about? I could hardly gather my thoughts enough to sit up, but Acturas didn't waste time waiting for me. He haphazardly flung boots, a deer hide cloak, and my wallet to me from my closet. I tried to go for a more stylish, albeit less weather-appropriate coat, but he grabbed my arm and dragged me into the hallway.

I wanted to ask him what all this was about, but it wasn't easy to get words out while being aggressively shepherded through the empty halls of the castle. He brought us to a stop at a door, pushing it open to reveal the kitchen, which only added to my confusion. He pulled me inside, closing and locking the door behind us.

"Shouldn't there be people here?" I asked as he opened a cupboard. Inside were two bags and a small sword. He pulled them down and handed a bag to me, plus a small knife from the kitchen counter, while he kept the major weapon to himself.

"I sent in an anonymous tip to the guards that someone on the kitchen staff is conspiring against the king. They'll be delayed until the interrogation is over. Still, we shouldn't push it. Better to get on the road as soon as we can."

Then Acturas bent down under a counter, the sound of stone grinding filling the silence. He resurfaced holding a large porthole cover.

"I'll go first, you follow."

I stood for a second, not getting his point. What did he– oh. Oh, no, that wasn't happening. I knelt down to confirm my suspicions, and sure enough, a hole was built into the floor under the counter.

"This leads to the drainage gutters," he elaborated, not at all helping his case. "It's just rain water. Maintenance barely comes down here anymore, so we should be all clear."

My stupor faded away at once with the suggestion. "Acturas, what are you going on about? You want me to go down into a *drainage pipe?* Are you stupid?"

He seemed irritated. "You didn't read my note, did you?" Judging my answer from my expression, he pressed his fingers to his temples and continued. "Do you remember what your father said yesterday? The thing about how the elves were in the West?" I nodded, suddenly anxious at the reminder. "Well, *as I tried to tell you*, they're not at the Pass. They're past it. And the gates. They'll be here soon, and our armies won't have a chance of catching up. Your father ordered me to take you and escape before they get here — in secret, hence the tunnel."

I stared at him. I remembered what the servant had mentioned yesterday — this *had* to be just another rumor. But if anyone knew what the truth was, it was my father, and I knew he wouldn't order anything like this if the situation wasn't dire. No matter what he thought, though, I had to have some explanation before I went along with a plan like *that*.

"How is that even possible? For them to cover, like, a hundred miles in a day?"

"They've got something we didn't account for — I mean, we couldn't have known Remius Neiphorous is leading the battalion."

The name plunged the room into a bucket of ice. Neiphorous was a name I, and all human nobility, knew all too well; the family of humans who defected to the elves, forsaking their homeland, betraying their country. They had competed with my family for centuries for political control, working their way back into the court only to sabotage our war effort and flee east. Remius was the most revered among them, the patron of the Neiphorous Manor and former Commander-in-Chief of our army. If he was back, there was only one thing he'd be here for: to replace my father as king.

"But the Hall of Elements… what about them? Are they in any condition to fight?"

Bitterness flashed on his face. "The Hall is spread too thin. Our Elementalists are scattered across the continent, there are only a few left in the city. And to make matters worse, there are reports that Neiphorous has a rogue Elementalist who can conjure *fire*."

My heart dropped. There was only one person that could be — I hadn't seen him since he betrayed my father and deserted the Hall of Elements. If Neiphorous had an Elementalist of Infernus, one of the Cardinal Elementals, then the odds suddenly seemed stacked much higher against us.

"So…" I stammered, barely having any time to rationalize this news, "you're sure there's nothing we can do? We're just leaving?"

Acturas's expression darkened. I got the impression he wasn't appreciating my questioning of his leadership. "Good lords, Damion, will you just listen for *once?* Do you think if there were any other way to protect you, I would be leading us down into a *drainage pipe?* This is the only option, end of story. Now, *go*."

I was not arguing with that.

The hole wasn't as deep as I expected, but the real horror rested in the pipe itself. It was barely wide enough to crawl through, my sides brushing the muddy brick walls. My hands and pants were soaked with vile, black water. In the pitch dark behind Acturas, I was honestly debating whether or not I'd rather face off with the eastern armies than feel one more clump of wet fuzz in the stream.

"Acturas," I started, my voice echoing off the walls, "where are we going?"

"I'll explain once we're somewhere more secure. Just trust me."

That only made me more anxious. Nevertheless, I continued onward. After some time of crawling, I saw sunlight, and the clatter of Acturas wrestling off a cast iron grate resounded deep within the tunnel. Years of erosion without maintenance allowed it to be snapped off without too much effort. I slid out of the tunnel and fell onto a barren stretch of hillside which shed water into the Edden River. Acturas stretched a few feet ahead of me while I wiped myself off.

I looked around and froze. The city wall was behind us. "This tunnel goes all the way outside of the wall? I had no idea this was even here, how is that…"

"Safe? It's not. The castle guards noticed it a couple years ago, but I figured it wasn't worth fixing if nobody knew about it but us. Glad I did."

He walked over to me. I was about to ask him where the carriage was, but he pulled the cloak hood over my head and pointed to a wooden building on the road down the hill. "We're going to have to hire a ride at the public stables. Keep your head low, don't attract attention. Just let me do the talking until we're out of the city."

It was hard for me to accept that I ever had to stop talking, but sacrifices must be made. As we approached the stables, the smell of manure and wet farm animals hit me like a club. I would much rather wait outside for Acturas to get the cab, but he held the door for me, and I wasn't going to make a scene about it. Besides, I'd rather not be separated from my only bodyguard when the *working class* was mingling around me.

The clerk was a girl a bit younger than me. She greeted us with a narrow smile and slid the catalog across the counter to Acturas while I looked around. A small statuette of Genedene, the Elemental of horses, sat on the windowsill overlooking the pasture. Eh, the yard, I should say; "Pasture" implies more than an acre or two of brown weeds, and this close to the city, space was a luxury not many had. The interior was furnished with a chair for the clerk, a small couch for visitors, several randomly positioned tables covered with logs and legers, and a single unlit lamp. A throw rug was splayed on the floor, but whatever design it once had was now replaced by frays and muddy boot prints.

Acturas tapped my shoulder, receipt in hand. "They're bringing it around front."

I was ecstatic to step out into the fresher, albeit still horsey air. After a long while of waiting, a stablehand swung open the gate and wheeled out a small carriage. As he secured the horses' harnesses, Acturas and I piled into the back, a bench so narrow our arms touched.

The driver opened the partition and called inside, "Y'all're headin' out to Handen, right? Pretty long ways away — I'd say two days, but I heard the weather might turn. Better get a move on, then." He slid the slot closed, and moments later the carriage rumbled to life. I parted the curtains to let light in, but Acturas reached across and pulled them closed.

"We can't risk being spotted. Wait until we're further from the city, at least."

I didn't protest. Something told me Neiphorous would be itching to pursue just about any leads he could get to catch us, considering the threat the heir posed to his legitimacy. That was *if* he managed to take the city in the first place, though; I still had my doubts that he could. Excutatem wasn't *usually* an empire to be picked on, after all, but my father was right that these weren't usual times. Then, a thought occurred to me.

"Acturas… what about my dad?"

He didn't respond right away. He closed his eyes, took a deep breath, and avoided my gaze when he opened them. "If — *if* — the elves lay siege on the castle, the king will be the guard's responsibility. He needs to see through the war he started. He wouldn't have fit in the pipe, anyway."

I ignored that last remark despite how funny it was to imagine the king crawling through a muddy pipe. "But then why would he order the highest general in Excutatem to flee with the heir to the throne days before a major battle?"

"I'm just doing what he told me. He knows more than either of us, surely he has a plan."

That made sense, and I wasn't going to press any further. I was just glad he was leading me away from the war, and I didn't want to put any ideas in his head that maybe he was making the wrong choice.

The journey began smoothly as we traveled west along the Imperial Highway. As we passed the Wall of Obelevon and moved into the countryside, the ride grew bumpy, and my shoulder ached from bumping into Acturas. I would definitely come out of this with a few bruises.

Acturas and I rode in near darkness for miles before he determined it safe enough to crack open the curtains. I was happy to; the cabin was as claustrophobic as it was borning, and even watching the endless expanse of farms and wheat fields was better than nothing. We continued for the rest of the day like this, with only occasional breaks to stretch our legs or have some of the bread Acturas had lifted from the kitchen.

We came across an inn on the side of a forest as the sun dipped lower in the sky, and the driver decided to rest there for the night. It wasn't really a town, only consisting of one or two buildings conveniently placed almost exactly a day's journey from Exceres.

The driver informed us that he would be spending the night in the carriage, but made it clear that the offer didn't extend to us. Not that I would *want* to sleep in the cramped cabin of a carriage anyway, especially not when there was an inn. I had never stayed in an inn, but it was surely better by comparison.

The interior was *quaint,* to say the least. The lobby/dining room/kitchen wasn't nearly large enough to hold all of the furniture inside it, but that wasn't a problem because we had the whole space to ourselves — there wasn't even a receptionist at the counter. Only a small gavel lay on the table with a placard that read *"for asistants, hit hamer too tims"*. Acturas hammered twice, followed by a long silence. He was about to try again before a stout, irritated old woman hobbled in from a back room.

"What'll it be?" she asked from a mouth that had seen far too many smoking pipes.

"Two beds, one night," Acturas answered, "same room preferred."

The innkeep flipped through a ledger that looked curiously as though it had drawings instead of words. After much deliberation over whether we wanted a front-facing or interior room, she decided that we could just pick any room in the building except 1A. That was the only one currently occupied.

"That'll be fifty ply," she informed us. I was awestruck, and did something rash — I spoke out loud.

"*Fifty?!* Is that not excessive?" The question was half genuine; I really had no idea how much to expect, but I knew we only got away with four or five laed, minus the cost of the cab ride, and this would take a sizable chunk out of those funds. I wished we had picked up a couple stendar when we were at the palace, since it's not like the treasurers would even notice with the amount of money my father lifted for his war projects.

The old woman leaned forward with an exasperated sigh, as if she dealt with this on an hourly basis. "Business is rough these days, kid. Not many people out on the road. Plus, the Assembly just brought taxes up again, and I got a mouth to feed — mine."

Acturas gave me a *shut up* look. He dropped a laed on the counter. The old woman huffed contentedly and stuffed the coin in her pocket before opening a drawer in the desk and fishing out ten five-ply coins, sliding them across. "Here's ya' change," she said. "Go ahead and pick a room."

Acturas muttered a *thank you* and led me up the stairs. He opened the first door on the right, the number *2B* scratched into the oak paneling. Inside, the room was dark and cold, and there wasn't much inside besides the two small beds pushed against opposite walls of the room and a glassless window between them. Suddenly, the carriage didn't seem all that much worse. I tried to make myself believe it was just shadows making the beds look that stained.

"So… which one's mine?" I asked, hoping he would realize he made some mistake and relocate us to the *correct* room, with new bed sheets and real windows and a chandelier. Instead, he just shrugged.

"Whichever one you want. We're just staying a night, try not to let it bother you too much."

I guess that was that. I claimed the bed on the left and moved to go to sleep.

Chapter Three

I couldn't. Laying on that old, dusty bed, I failed to stop my thoughts from wandering to what had just happened — and what would happen now. We should reach Handen by tomorrow evening, but I still hadn't processed the fact that we had to flee in the first place. I could hardly believe that same morning I was in my soft, spacious bed in the castle. It was surreal. I wished I could drift off to sleep just so I could wake up and find myself back in my room, the nightmare faded by the time I sat down for breakfast.

"Acturas?" I whispered, but there was no response. He must've had a tougher day than me, since he did most of the heavy lifting for our escape. I almost felt bad for my complaining — Well, *most* of my complaining. I stood by some of it.

I sat up in darkness. The shutters were open, and I saw that it was starting to rain. The wind picked up and rattled trees in the woods across the street while stray raindrops flew through the open window and pattered on the floor. Lighting struck in the distance, briefly bringing light to the world. I stood and walked to the window. Leaning against the sill, I looked up to the black, starless sky. Storms and snow always calmed me down, and we had no shortage of them in Excutatem, but this one felt… aggressive. Almost too sudden, borderline violent. Thunder crashed.

"Ir Signel Elemantis, pleteskis forgis, Elet," I prayed quietly in the Divine Language I had been tutored in for my entire life. I didn't believe the storm could *actually* blow down even this shack of an inn, but with the groan of the walls as they were tested by the gale, I wasn't entirely sure.

My eyes fell to the street, the puddles forming in the gutters, the mud flowing like water along the road, the elven horse out front of the inn — why was there an elven horse outside? Though it was dark, the animal was unmistakably eastern, its armor detailed with silver in a typical elven fashion. And why was it *wearing* armor? It stood unbothered by the rain, and through a flash of lightning, I saw it wasn't even tied up. Why would it be here? *How* would it be here? It would be almost impossible to bring one through the South, and they could only have followed us from the North if…

I shook off the prospect. Neiphorous couldn't have taken the capital already, there was no way. It hadn't even been two days since they were first seen at the Pass, and a whole legion couldn't possibly move that quickly, much less besiege and conquer the entire capital. The horse was probably just someone's souvenir from a trip to the Minesran Coast. I swallowed my anxiety and felt silly for letting myself get so freaked out over nothing. I sat back on my bed, forcing the image of the horse from my mind as I tried to find sleep.

It was then that room lit up. I threw my arm over my eyes and peeked in the direction of the glow, only making out the source of the light once my eyes painfully adjusted: wings. Outstretched, golden, glowing wings, whose light drowned out the features of the person it was attached to. The wings folded in behind their back and dissipated into mist. Now, I could make out the intruder's details — he had ash-colored skin, almost gray. He was tall and thin, like a runner, and he looked about my age. His blond hair was streaked with gold, and he wore a leather satchel over his white tunic.

"Damion Excutari?" he asked me. He made no effort to lower his voice, as if this was his room and *I* had barged in in the middle of the night. Acturas showed no signs of stirring from his bed despite the abrupt chaos.

I could only stand in stunned silence, struggling to find words. He blinked. "So…?" he pressed.

"Um, yeah, that's me," I responded. My face flushed, somehow embarrassed by how long it took me to answer the… whatever he was.

He opened his satchel and pulled out a black wooden box, too long to have naturally fit inside the bag. "Right. I'm Exolirus, Elemental of Messengers, and this package is for you. Sign here."

He opened a scroll and brought out a tray of ink, but there was no quill or pen to sign.

"How do I–" I was interrupted when he held the ink tray out to me. Tentatively, I pushed my finger onto the tray, and then transferred it to the scroll, leaving an ink fingerprint to dry. He rolled up the paper and handed me the box. It was heavier than I expected.

"Be careful with that thing — it was made by Valkyries. Also, before I go, I was told to inform you that an enemy has tracked you here who you cannot defeat, and your only chance is to escape now before you're slain. Per cosmic laws, I can't say any more. Have a good night!" With that, his wings reappeared, stinging my eyes with their brightness, and he disappeared as soon as they flapped, a gust of warm wind hitting me. I was left in darkness. Was I dreaming? What just happened? It all went by so quickly I wouldn't have even believed he was here if it weren't for the box in my hands.

Inside was a sheath, and as I pulled it from the box, the room was bathed in soft, silver light. I was holding a knife of dark, unfamiliar metal, cold as if it had been left outside in the wintertime. It was thick-hilted with a sharp, jaded blade almost a foot in length, and its heft made it clear that this blade would be much worse for an opponent than the kitchen knife. I moved it around slowly, trying not to sever an artery. It sliced cleanly through the air. I understood why the Valkyries were so famous for their weapons.

Unsure what else to do with it, I re-sheathed it and dropped it in my bag, not eager to be in a situation where I'd need to use it any time soon. I realized I had been so caught up in the knife that I had forgotten about the last part of his message.

I stood and hurried across the room, nudging Acturas. "Wake up, we need to leave."

He opened his eyes and regarded me with concern and more than a trace of annoyance. "What do you mean? The sun isn't even up yet."

"This place isn't safe. There's an elven horse out front." I knew I should've told him about the visit from the Elemental, but I couldn't make the words come out. I had no time to explain, anyway, before Acturas leapt out of bed, slung his bag over his shoulder, and unsheathed one of his swords as he glanced out the window.

"How did they..." he muttered. He rushed back to the door, pushed it open just enough to see into the hallway, cringed at the loud creak it made, and opened it all the way. "Stay behind me — and get your knife ready, just in case." He didn't need to tell me twice. I thought of retrieving the Valkyrie knife, but opted for the basic cooking knife from the castle, not wanting to risk stabbing myself with a blade the length of my forearm. I snuck down the hallways behind him, listening for any movement. The whole building was silent. As we crept down the stairs, I saw that the innkeeper was sitting at her desk — strange, considering it was the dead of night in the midst of a raging storm.

She barely regarded us until we walked in front of her. "Oh, you two, checking out at this hour?" she said with a new politeness.

"Yes, you can keep the extra money for the remaining hours. Do you know how far it is to the next town?"

"Oh, there's no other towns for miles. A day's walk, at least. Storm doesn't help, anyhow."

As they went back and forth about the logistics of our abrupt departure, I began to take notice of my surroundings. Through the rain-smudged front windows — the only glass windows in the building, as far as I could tell — I could see the horse staring me down. I broke eye contact and looked down at the desk. There was a paper facing the other direction, but it was clearly written in a non-Humanic language. Next to it lay a pile of coins. Minesran Yil.

I interrupted Acturas's back-and-forth with the innkeeper in the middle of her explaining that the bridge would be flooded by the rain at least until morning. By now, I understood what was going on. "Acturas, *we should go.*"

He seemed to take the hint in my tone, because he just nodded and scooped up his bag. We turned to leave.

"Wait!" the innkeeper said, "I just remembered, a carriage service moved into town just this week and gave me a sale. I'll find it for you, give me just one 'sec…" She rummaged through her desk, fingers shaking as she searched for paper I didn't believe existed.

"That's alright, ma'am. Have a good night," Acturas said in a stony voice. We continued toward the door, and the old woman gasped. We froze and turned back toward her. Standing behind the desk, cloaked in shadow, was a soldier.

I could tell from the white armor that it was an elf. He was much taller than the innkeep, and at his side was a long sword curved outward, like a claw. Acturas noticed him just a second after I did, dashing in front of me with his sword raised. The elf brandished his own blade, longer than Acturas's, and waved for the innkeeper to leave. I glanced at the door, but the horse stood outside like a sentry, watching the scene from the rain.

When the elf attacked, it was almost too fast for me to react. Fortunately, Acturas was more prepared, and he parried the slash before it could reach him. The elf maneuvered the curve in his blade so that Acturas was forced to drop his own, a bleeding gash appearing where the blade struck his hand. He ducked back before the attacker could strike again and drew a knife which was sheathed above his knee.

While Acturas was out of the way, the soldier sprung at me — not with his sword, but with his hand. I was too slow, and he grabbed my arm with more than enough force to leave a bruise for a few days. I struggled in vain to pry myself free of his grasp, but he released me as his hand shot to his shoulder where the hilt of Acturas's knife now protruded through the joint in his armor.

Acturas was in front of me again, re-armed with his fallen sword, and he backed us toward the exit. He risked a glance back and locked eyes with the equine menace, ominously whinnying outside the doors like it was daring him to fight it. I heard him muttering something which I assumed to be a prayer. Was there really a chance Acturas could *lose* here? All of a sudden I had my answer: He spun around, grabbed my shoulder, and dragged me out into the rain.

Before we were even to the street, the horse was rearing and biting, and we only had a few seconds to get out of its way before it charged us like a bull. Acturas tried to slice at it with his sword, but the blade only scraped off its armor, and it reared up to kick him. He stumbled back just in time to avoid being decapitated. I could feel the force of the kick blow towards me, and knew that if it had landed, I would be fighting solo. The elf soldier stepped out of the inn. The knife was gone, and his armor was wet with fresh blood. It didn't seem like we could escape, until my prayer to Signel went through.

A clap of thunder shook the earth just as the rain picked up, cascading to the ground in a more violent torrent than I had ever been caught in. I heard the horse shriek as it kicked wildly into the rain, but Acturas had already dragged me by my arm into the woods. I was snagged by roots and branches, but I didn't dare slow down. I could do nothing but follow the glimpses of Acturas as lightning flashed through the trees and the horse's screams grew distant.

Chapter Four

The rain calmed to a drizzle as we crouched behind a tree to catch our breath. I was shaking from exhaustion and dripping wet, but we both stayed completely silent, listening for any signs of pursuit. It seemed that the rain had stopped them from tracking us. We were safe, for now, but the elves had definitely arrived in the West, and we were *definitely* being hunted.

Acturas interrupted my thoughts. "We can't stay here long. These woods get dangerous at night, and they'll figure out where we went eventually."

"I was about to say the same thing. I think we should go southwest. Maybe we can talk to the king of Nored or Hulland, or get a ferry to Eilym. The elves probably wouldn't think to go there, and I know the duchess–"

"We're going to Sitika."

That caught me off guard. I almost thought he was joking. "... Sitika? Why would we go *there?* Where would we even hide? It's the densest city in the world."

He rolled his eyes as if the answer would be obvious to anyone else. "Sitika is the holiest human territory, Damion. No one can get in except humans, not elves, not even Elementals. It can't be conquered without starting a holy war, and that's the last thing anyone needs right now. You of all people should know this. And even if the elves were willing to take the chance, the city is surrounded by mountains and walls, so it's borderline impossible to invade. They would need to push for diplomacy to get the Sitikan assembly to cooperate with them, and Elementalism is too strong there for the people to ever side with an aeverial regime like Minesra."

I still didn't like the idea of running directly into the most crowded city on the continent, but I had to admit it was better than stumbling blindly across the continent hoping we still had any allies left after a decade of war.

We trekked through the woods with no direction. Wet leaves stuck to my boots and my arms were cut by branches. Rain dripped from the fringes of my hood into my eyes, but I could barely see anything anyway with the cloud coverage blocking the moon. Neither of us said a single word beyond the occasional *'watch out for this ditch'*, or *'spider web here, go the other way around.'*

We continued southwest until sunlight spilt through the trees and I was on the verge of crumpling from exhaustion. I was about to recommend breaking for the week when I smelled smoke. Acturas shot me a knowing glance. We picked up speed, following the smell to the edge of the forest and into a small village which seemed to be setting up for a festival. A couple dozen people milled about, talking, eating, or taking part in the construction of three hay giants in the center of the town square. Two wore crowns, while the third held a disappointingly stubby wooden sword.

We integrated into the crowd, and nobody seemed to pay us much attention as we made our way to a bar. It was packed with people, so I kept my head down as Acturas led us to the counter where an old man served the many patrons who had stepped in from the festival. We took seats on the low stools set around the bar, and it didn't take long for him to make his way over to us.

"What'll it be, gentlemen? You look like you could use a whiskey," he said to me with a jovial air.

"That would be great, thank you." I replied. I figured this place wouldn't have champagne.

Acturas jumped in. "I'll have rum." He picked up his bag and began counting coins. "How much'll that be?"

"Five ply each, festival sale."

Acturas laid ten ply on the bar. "Out of curiosity, what exactly are you celebrating today? We're travelers from down south, just a bit out of the loop."

The man laughed. It seemed he was delighted to break the news. "Well, haven't you two heard? The imperials were overthrown! Well, see, I'm no fan of the elves taking over the capital, but any of them would be better than King Jourdan."

My heart dropped. They were celebrating the occupation? The hay statues… no, they wouldn't… that's grounds for life imprisonment, easily. But what king was there to enforce that?

Acturas was unfazed, like he really was just an uninformed traveler. "Is that *true?* We had heard rumors, of course, but I didn't think it could be possible…"

The man called back as he searched for the bottles, "Oh, it's true. I've heard the king's already gone, though nothing's confirmed. The former empress and some other nobles are set to be brought to justice after a trial, whenever that happens. But they say the heir and General Assix couldn't be caught. Probably drank too much and fell into a lake, I imagine. Either way," he poured the drinks and passed them to us, "I say good riddance."

I couldn't begin to process this information, it had all happened so fast. It felt like years ago that I had been safe, all cooped up in the castle. Was it really just yesterday? And I didn't need to be a genius to know what he meant by *brought to justice*. I couldn't let that happen. I tried to catch Acturas's eye, but he was still comfortably chatting with the barkeep.

The man continued, "So, you say you're coming from the South? How far's that, Retraun? Milltown?"

We were nearly caught in a lie before Acturas replied effortlessly, "Iterun, just a bit east of Retraun. I was on my way to check up on my grandparents." He gestured to me. "I figured I should bring him along for the trip. You know how the roads are at night, I wouldn't want to get caught traveling alone."

"Don't I know it. Got shivved by some miscreants a few months back on my way from the capital. Didn't expect somethin' like that to happen so close to the city. Got left penniless on the side of the road. Had to walk the rest of the way over night! Five miles!"

Acturas carried the conversation while I sat, convincingly appearing to care about the bartender's gratuitously embellished anecdotes while saying nothing and ignoring every word. I'd had a lot of practice with that type of stuff — a lot of Assemblies over the years.

Eventually, Acturas decided it was time for us to get out of this city before the villagers discovered who I was and burned real me on a stake next to hay me.

He set down his empty glass. "We should be hitting the road. Any stables in this town?"

The bartender nodded. "We got one by the inn, but it's closed for the festival. You might as well stay the night and hit the road in the morning — it'd be a shame to miss the festival, anyway."

He didn't show it, but I could tell Acturas was put off by this news. He waved goodbye to the barkeep as he led me back out to the street.

With nothing to do but wait, we went to the town inn. It was larger than the previous night's and better kept, with two or three people actually lingering in the lobby. Acturas handled the business of getting us a room for the night while I leaned against a wall to rest my eyes. I opened them only to accidentally lock eyes with a guy around my age walking in from a back door. He seemed to be just a little younger than me, with wavy blond hair and a dusty work tunic that still seemed much cleaner than what I had on. I looked down, suddenly extremely interested in the bare oak floor. Out of my peripheral vision, I could see him gradually turn away, as if something about me had caught his attention, but the flash of green in his eyes lingered in my mind.

Did I know him? He didn't seem at all familiar, and I doubted anybody in this town had gotten to the imperial court much. Did he somehow recognize me? I wasn't sure how that could've been possible, but I wasn't excited to find out. I stayed close to Acturas, who had bartered a one-bed room for twenty-five ply. I would rather have had five whiskeys, but the deal was done, and we went upstairs to the room.

We set down the bags on the floor and I sat on the bed. Acturas pulled out the small chair paired with the equally disappointing wooden desk. He didn't look particularly thrilled to be sleeping on it tonight, but as it was barely noon, he had more than enough time to mentally prepare himself. Once we were settled in, I mentioned the man in the lobby.

"We just ran through the woods for the whole night after getting four hours of sleep, he's probably just wondering why these dirty, exhausted travelers stumbled into his town."

I decided to accept his answer and write it off. Either way, it didn't matter whether or not he thought I *looked* like royalty; he'd have to have been insane to think I was *actually* the heir to the imperial throne. I lay down on the bed. I wasn't sure whether it was just my exhaustion, but it was surprisingly comfortable. I'd just rest my eyes for a couple minutes…

I woke from my nap as the sun was setting. Acturas apparently had the same idea, and was still asleep while I got up. Outside, the festival was going strong, and I could hear music thrumming through the walls. I knew it was a bad idea, but I quietly slipped out of the room and went down to the lobby. It was empty; not even the innkeeper was still inside. All the better for me, since I didn't want to run into anyone anyway.

Outside, people were gathering in the square while a man, who I assumed to be the mayor, gave a lively speech in front of the hay figures. I lingered in the background, where I wouldn't be noticed or bothered by passersby. Over the din of the crowd, I couldn't make out much, but I caught some keywords — "Imperial", "finished", "Excutari", "death".

I looked out into the gathering crowd celebrating the downfall of my empire. All types of people were present: the elderly who had spent their whole lives under the rule of my family, children who didn't yet grasp what a government was. Mostly, it was made up of the young adults who hadn't yet settled in their class and still thought the world could change — well, I knew it could change, but my father used to insist only *we* could change it.

The mayor raised a torch for the crowd to see. The cheers and hoots it spawned grated my ears, the most sinister sound I had ever heard. I watched as the torch fell into a pile of hay at the feet of the statue and began to spread like… well, fire. Flames seeped into the pile until it glowed, then broke free into the night in a flurry of sparks, licking up the legs and torso of the statues until they were completely engulfed. Black and burning flecks of hay dispersed in the evening wind. One wafted in front of me, and I caught it — it was hot, but cooled quickly, then crumpled to ash. I scattered the dust, and it disappeared before touching the ground. I looked up at the three smoking stumps where the hay statues once stood. Standing just beyond them, partially shrouded in the smoke, was the man from the lobby earlier today.

He hadn't noticed me yet, but I panicked when I saw him. I intended to stay out of his way, whether he suspected who I was or not. No good could come from him — he could be a robber or assassin for all I knew, or worse, an elf sympathizer. I ducked into an alley beside the hotel and watched as he walked off with a group of his friends. The idea of being friends with peasants was profoundly unsettling, but I did wish I had somebody I could hang out with while I was here. I mean, I wasn't in *immediate* danger, and there was no reason I couldn't get wasted on their cheap whiskey until the sun rose.

I reached into my bag and counted the money Acturas had left with me. Forty ply, easily enough to buy a round of shots. *Why shouldn't I have a little fun?* I thought as I made my way to the bar, *It's my money, I can spend it however I want.*

It was more crowded now, and my anxiety around the poor hit an all-time high. *Calm down, nobody will bother you if you don't bother them.* I walked over to the young lady working the bar, who I presumed to be the barkeep's daughter, and ordered a shot of scotch. She produced the drink quickly, and I thanked the elements that this backwoods town had access to liquor. I slid into an oak booth by a window and got to work on my drink, which, I realized, was not a good idea accompanied with an empty stomach. So, upon finishing my first glass, I bought a meat pie — another not-great idea — and partnered it with a round of rum. I didn't stop there. I should have.

I don't remember exactly when they showed up. I was four or five drinks in, not quite past my limit — I'd had a lot of practice — but definitely beyond my best senses. They came in a group — maybe four people walked in, ordered drinks, joked and pushed each other around. Each of them was probably drunker than me, and the green-eyed man I seemed to keep seeing chatted with the girl behind the bar. Maybe it was the alcohol, but I decided I was done hiding away from this stranger, and I swallowed my nerves along with my drink and walked over.

"Hey."

"What's up?" He had a really nice voice, smooth like whiskey. I should order more whiskey.

"Not much." I took another sip of my beer. "Do I, like, know you guys?"

He squinted as if trying to analyze me, then shrugged. "I don't think I've ever seen you before in my life. How about I buy you another drink?"

Who would I have been to turn down such an offer?

I woke up with a throbbing headache. It took a long while for my eyes to adjust to the morning light, and I realized I was alone inside the hotel room. I tried to stand, but my head spun, and I pulled the linen blanket over my eyes. Twenty minutes later, once my hangover had calmed to some degree, I pulled the blanket back down, just in time for Acturas to return. He stood in the doorway, his arms crossed, and sighed.

"Are you always gonna be like this?"

"Euhhhh," was all I could muster in my defense. I pushed myself up onto my elbows and kicked off the blanket. I rubbed my eyes, and Acturas set down the water he had gone out to retrieve.

I downed the whole cup. "Thanks," I said. "What happened last night?"

"That's what I should be asking you. This random guy showed up with you in the middle of the night, scared the shit out of me. He dropped you off and left with barely a word. You have no idea what you were up to?"

I really didn't remember much after I started our conversation the night before, but I had been down this road before. It wouldn't have been the first time I went out at night in an unfamiliar town, got hammered with a bunch of townsfolk, probably threw up on a horse, and this kind stranger brought me back to Acturas's loving embrace. I could name five cities off the top of my head where I would have been kidnapped and skinned by now, so I made a mental note to build a palace here when things were back to normal.

I decided it was time to change into another pair of clothes free of the mud and alcohol stains which marked my current shirt. Once I was in something more pleasant, I stood from the bed, my body raging at me in protest.

Acturas picked up his bag. "I think it's about time we head out. I was just at the stables, they can get us a carriage no farther than Semmerfall, but that's not a problem — the city will have tons of connections going south."

I nodded, but I was hardly paying attention. I trailed behind Acturas back into the lobby, where he informed the innkeeper of our departure. All things considered, this was a nice little town, but I wasn't sad to be leaving it behind, especially with the ashes of my burned effigy still scattered around the square. I followed Acturas outside into the cold afternoon. Townsfolk already bustled about, unbothered by the frigid weather, but a few more people had eyes on me than yesterday. Whatever I got up to last night, it definitely drew some attention. Good thing we were leaving.

We went to the stables. I pulled open the door, and as soon as I stepped inside, I stepped right back out

— my fight or flight must've kicked in. Standing behind the table which served as a front desk was the man from the bar last night. He hadn't seen me, and I wanted to keep it that way. I stepped out of the way so Acturas could handle this, and followed far behind so that I would be clearly out of the way of the interaction.

I wasn't sure why I wanted so badly to avoid this guy; he seemed nice enough the one time I could remember that we spoke. But what about all the times we spoke that I just didn't remember? Was I just cringing subconsciously at the things I said after midnight? Or was it something else…?

He started talking with Acturas, and his voice snapped a major piece back into the puzzle — almost. Something sat on the edge of my memory, but I couldn't figure out what. I knew we had talked at length. I felt like something important had happened, and it was driving me insane trying to dredge it up. The transaction took an uncomfortably long time, and I only felt my muscles relax when Acturas turned and began walking out of the building.

We stood outside and waited for the carriage to be wheeled around, and judging from Acturas's general demeanor, he didn't seem to recognize this as the same guy I presumed brought me back last night. Then again, he *did* receive special education from the castle on covert operations, so I imagine if he had wanted to hide something, he would have no problem doing it. Either way, I wouldn't dwell on this — the carriage was coming around the side, and I would thankfully never have to see that guy again

It felt like the Elementals were laughing at me when the carriage pulled up in front of us — driven by the same guy. Really not cool, Elementals.

Chapter Five

"Climb in back," the driver called to us. Begrudgingly, I followed Acturas into the back seat.

This cab was mustier and more compact, and no curtains lined the windows. No issue, really, since I probably couldn't be any more noticed than I had been the past two days. The carriage took off down the lane out of the village. I rummaged through my bag for a shirt to cushion my head, because I couldn't recline directly on the seat without the vibrations giving me a concussion. I regretted not asking the Assembly to fund smoother roads when I had the chance.

Acturas and I made occasional small talk, careful not to let the driver overhear us. Even still, neither of us touched on the obvious, heavier discussion relating to our escape. As dusk leached into the sky, I was relieved to gaze out the window and see the Semmerfall skyline at the base of the mountains. Finally, a *real* city, and one I actually knew.

The road smoothed and opened as we drove in, and the view from the window was quickly filled with stone buildings and impressively intricate architecture. Centuries ago, Semmerfall had been gifted as a peace offering by the dwarves to my family, who had been relentlessly gulping up more and more land nearby. It worked — at least, until Emperor Tirus caught wind that the dwarves had a furnace that could make diamonds out of coal, and he sent his son, Obelevon, to lead the empire southward. The dwarves didn't stand a chance — nor did they have the furnace. Those remaining disappeared under the mountains. I wished it would be as easy for *me* to escape underground.

We came to a stop in the public stables, which, like the rest of the city, were ordained with precious metals and meticulous carvings spanning yards. If *this* was the type of city the dwarves had no problem giving away, I would have loved to see their actual homelands — that is, if we could ever find them. Climbing out of the carriage, I rushed Acturas into the boarding house adjacent to the stable in an effort to avoid the driver, but it wasn't necessary: After securing the horses, he only turned and walked off into the city, not paying us a second glance. The Elementals knew how badly I wanted to do the same, but it was too dangerous. The elves were here.

They were everywhere, actually. I hadn't noticed when we first arrived, because their armor was astoundingly similar to the standard Semmerfallian issue, but there was no doubt they had claimed the city when we arrived at the stables. Besides the eastern horses present, there were elf soldiers patrolling the streets and Elvish translations printed under the posters on the walls, some with faces on them. Including mine. I couldn't see Acturas's picture anywhere, but they probably considered him too much of an inspiration to the people — their great general, fearless, strategic, victorious — so they would rather everybody assume him dead or captured. I pulled up my hood.

We entered the lodge. I'd never been inside before; I had always stayed at Semmerpalace, the aptly named castle overlooking the enormous volcanic lake in the city's heart. This boarding house, though, was still clearly more to my taste than any of the previous nights', packed with people, well-lit, and so gloriously spacious. I stayed behind Acturas as he made the arrangements, and followed him up to our room on the second-to-top floor, where nobody would bother or see us. Top floor was reserved for nobility. Ironic.

The bed sheets were cotton and the pillow was feather-filled, leagues better than the hay I hadn't yet become accustomed to over the past two days. I lay down and closed my eyes, almost able to pretend that this was my bed back home, and waited to fall asleep. And waited. And listened to Acturas's snores. And counted the beams in the ceiling. And waited. *I'm wasting my time,* I thought, and I sat up. Quietly, I re-dressed myself, grabbed my bag, and slipped out the door without a sound. I was getting good at sneaking around Acturas, and I just hoped his patience and understanding wouldn't wear too thin if he caught me.

Down on the street, I kept my hood over my head, but still absorbed every sight and sound. Maybe it was because I couldn't know the next time I would be here, or maybe it was because I had spent the last forty-eight hours trapped in a carriage cabin surrounded by nothing but the most repetitive, rural landscape on the continent. Whenever I crossed an elven patrol, I would shrink deeper into the crowd, keep my head low, and cut my stride down to a saunter without purpose or intention. The least important person you had ever seen, no reason to check him out. None looked twice at me.

The crowd dispersed as I came up to the lake. An island of moonlight floated on the waves as they washed serely on the shore. Steam lifted off its surface in thin, white tendrils; Thermal vents on the lakebed kept it warm all year, even during the frigid winter months, and I wished I could jump in right then.

Along the shore was my favorite place in the city, Troi's Bar. I would never miss an opportunity to stop in when I was in the city, and I absentmindedly cruised along the boardwalk to the door. I grabbed the handle, but froze. I had known Troi for as long as I had been visiting Semmerfall. Even if I could cover my face, he would know my voice instantly. I let my hand drop and stepped back, but bumped into someone standing behind me.

"Oh, sorry, I…" I stammered, but faltered when I saw who it was.

The driver laughed and put up his hands. "No, that's on me. Just didn't expect you to turn around. You okay?"

I was suddenly painfully aware of how stupid I must have looked. "Yeah, I'm fine. Thanks. I just remembered that I… owe the owner. Money. Probably shouldn't go in there."

He smirked, but seemed to buy it. "I've been in that spot my fair share of times." Thinking that was the end of it, I stepped aside so he could enter, but he added, "How about I cover it for you? If you pay me back, of course. What do you want?"

I was taken aback by the offer. I had never expected anyone to do me any favors if they didn't need to, or if they weren't just trying to get on the good side of the crown prince. "If you're really offering, their champagne is top tier."

He raised an eyebrow. "Champagne? Didn't think you'd have that kinda taste, but I guess I can get it for you if you've got the cash."

I nodded and fumbled around in my bag for coins. I knew they were in here somewhere, but couldn't feel the cold silver. I shook it for good measure, and to my horror, there was no clank of coins.

My face burned. "Sorry, I don't know where they went. I really thought–" It suddenly occurred to me where the coins were. Acturas was going to have a problem when I got back — but, as I remembered I was standing outside a bar offering to hand money to a complete stranger, he probably took them for expressly this reason.

He seemed unfazed, almost amused. "No worries. I guess it's only fair that I pay you back for the drinks you bought me last night."

I didn't remember buying him any drinks, but if I had been left alone with a bag full of ply while blackout drunk the night… I hated to admit it, but I saw where Acturas was coming from. He disappeared inside the bar, leaving me awkwardly waiting outside the door for him to return. Five minutes later, he did, two glasses in hand.

My savior and I went out onto the beach, and I hopped up onto the pier, hoping he wouldn't follow. He jumped onto the platform, too. Damn. Once I determined I was far enough from the beach, I pulled down my hood, the cold breeze immediately wafting through my hair as he set the drink down on the wooden rail.

"Thanks for that," I said as I started on my champagne.

"Don't mention it." He leaned over the railing to look into the water.

I felt like I should say more, at least *try* to be friendly after he put himself down twenty ply for essentially no reason. "Uh, sorry, I don't think I caught your name?" I asked him.

He cracked a smile. "Cedric," he said, and I felt like I should've already known that.

"Alright, nice," I continued. "I'm–"

"Damion, right?" he interrupted. I panicked before remembering all of the things I didn't remember from the night before — it's pretty safe to assume I at least gave him my name.

"Yeah, that's me." I took another sip. "So, Cedric, I don't really remember much from last night. I don't know what I said, so if it was a little… *bizarre,* don't worry about it." If I had actually revealed something about my situation, I doubted he would be hanging around me, much less buying me drinks and chatting me up on a pier. Still, damage control couldn't hurt.

There was a brief, tense pause. Even in the steady moonlight, I couldn't discern anything from his expression. I had no idea what he was going to say as he looked me in the eyes. Then, he shrugged.

"I have no idea what you're talking about."

I managed to stop myself from doubling over in relief. Cedric looked back at the water, then climbed up onto the railing. I got worried he was about to jump into the lake, but he just sat down on the wooden rail.

"Was there something you were worried about telling me?" he said with a grin. Despite myself, I felt blood run to my cheeks, so I diverted his attention by climbing up onto the railing myself.

From up there, the waves looked like a coiling, writhing mass. The persistent anxiety that had set in me since I left the capital led me to imagine horrifying monsters hidden under the surface — things with tentacles and giant, ship-eating maws that can swallow whales. The alcohol, on the other hand, made me not care.

"Nope, nothing," I said, trying to change the subject before I made a fool — or criminal — of myself. I nodded toward the water. "Looks pretty cool. I haven't been here in ages."

"Yeah, me neither. I used to stop by here every few weeks with my mom, but I've been stuck in that village for ages 'cause of the war." He glanced up at the star-filled sky. The moon was full and vibrant, while a gargantuan cloud was rolling in to swallow it up. "Guess that'll change now."

I felt guilty for my place in the war, even though I couldn't have changed much if I tried. I turned toward Cedric, and saw that he was already looking at me. There was a moment of comfortable silence. I could see his breath billowing in the cold air, and just for a moment, I thought he was about to say something. He glanced quickly at the water before looking back at me with a half-drunk smile.

"Ditch the cloak."

With that, he pushed off from the railing and plunged into the lake below.

I was too stunned to even process what had just happened. Ripples broke across the surface. After a second, he resurfaced, wiping water from his face as he laughed and looked up at me.

Acturas is gonna kill me, I thought as I dropped the cloak onto the pier before sliding off. The fall was thrilling as I hurtled toward the lake. The warm water washed over me like a blanket as I broke through the still sheet of the surface. I came up fast, but as I looked around, Cedric was nowhere in sight. Confusion, then panic, hit me. I just about jumped out of the water entirely when I felt a hand grab my leg.

He resurfaced, laughing, as I tried to calm my heart beat. *"Fuck you!"* I said half-joking, but I had started laughing too. I treaded water for a moment, savoring the feeling of the heat in the otherwise cold night.

He started to say something, but only shook his head. I couldn't tell if it was the heat or the liquor, but he seemed flushed. He ducked back under the water. I felt around to make sure he couldn't get under me again, but he was nowhere to be seen. Finally, he resurfaced ten feet away, facing me and treading backwards.

"If you can catch me, I'll buy you a whole bottle of gin," he said, and he set off toward the beach. Oh, it was on. I pushed off one of the posts of the pier to get a boost and went after him as fast I could. He had a head start, but he didn't seem to be a great swimmer, and I grabbed him in no time.

He sighed overdramatically. "Fair is fair, I guess."

"Just consider our debts settled," I said, though the prospect of more liquor didn't put me off.

"Nice," he responded, "because I was just about t– *wow.*"

I followed his gaze up toward the sky. It took me a second to notice without much light: It was snowing. Columns of steam rose from the points where the snowflakes met the water, and I laughed at how out of place it was. Here we were, swimming in a bathwater-warm lake, and people on the beach were probably cold as hell.

"Never seen that before," he muttered.

"What, snow?" I joked.

He chuckled. "You know what I mean. Pretty cool."

He was right. It was pretty cool.

Chapter Six

We climbed out of the water and onto the snowy beach, cursing at how cold the air was. I took off my wet boots and planted my foot onto the sand, but lifted it reflexively when something hard dug into my foot. I looked down to find a shiny, white pebble lodged in the sand.

"Oh, neat," Cedric said as he picked it up and dropped it into his pocket. I wasn't sure why; it was just a rock on the beach.

We walked through the thinly snow-coated sand up to the boardwalk, the pedestrians on the street pulling their coats around them as they passed under dwarven oil street lamps. Children ran out of houses, despite the late hour, to play in the snow. I was terrifyingly exposed without my cloak, but I didn't want to give Cedric any cause for suspicion, so I just prayed to no one in particular and pretended it was just the cold that made me pick up the pace.

Cedric and I got back to the stables and split up, since he was staying in a smaller inn a few blocks away. I snuck back to my room exhausted, but, by the grace of the elements, didn't wake Acturas. After changing out of my water-logged clothes, I settled into bed and looked out the window at the city — the lights from the street, the snow drifting across the rooftops, the extinguished outline of Semmerpalace on the lake. I considered whether I could just stay under cover here, keep a low profile for a few months and work on getting back to the capital once things settled.

But I wasn't stupid. I couldn't make it a week without some random, scorned shopkeep recognizing me and turning me in. I had to get as far from Excutatem as possible before I could start to plan my return to grace.

I had my best sleep in about two days, and when Acturas woke me up, the sun was well into the sky.

"Figured I'd let you sleep in. We have a long day ahead of us," he said while fastening his shirt. "Where's your cloak and bag?"

"No idea," I lied while rolling out of bed. I got dressed and tied my boots. "I thought I left it by the door."

"Damnit Damion, you had important shit in there," he grumbled.

"No money, though. Thanks for that."

"Like you were gonna spend it on anything other than liquor."

I feigned indignation and stretched my arms. Acturas gave me his coat and pulled the hood over my head as we left to find a ride west. The stables were buzzing with late-morning activity as merchants and travelers came and went. Coincidentally, Cedric was there, preparing his carriage for the trip back. Acturas paid him no mind, but when Cedric noticed us, he pulled something from his carriage and jogged over.

"Lucky I caught you two. I think you left your stuff in the back." He passed me the things I had left on the pier.

"Thanks, I appreciate it," I said, suppressing a smile.

Acturas took the bag and glanced into it, making sure everything was still there. He tossed Cedric a ten ply coin. "Thanks for not selling it off," he said with no hint of humor. He patted me on the shoulder. "Anyway, we gotta get going. C'mon."

"I think I'll hang out here," I said. I hoped I didn't need to elaborate that going into the packed stables would put me at risk of being recognized. Luckily, Acturas got the message, and nodded before heading inside. I led Cedric behind his carriage where it would be more secluded.

Once out of the way of the horses and in a quieter spot, I spoke first. "Thanks for that. And for last night, too. You did me a huge favor at the bar, and the lake was… fun."

"The bar was nothing, we're just equal now. Where are you guys heading?"

I knew I shouldn't tell anyone our plans, but if he suspected who I was, he'd have already turned me in by now. "Sitika. We weren't really planning on it, something just… came up."

"You ever been before?"

"Not yet. It's pretty far, and I don't have any— uh, family there." I came dangerously close to saying '*houses*', but remembered that most people didn't have summer palaces sprinkled around the continent. The idea of having any family outside Excutatem was foreign to me, but it was a good enough excuse. "How about you?"

"Yeah, actually. Mostly when I was a kid — my mom knew some people down in Ramethus and was kind of obligated to see them every few months. I'd go with some friends to Sitika for most of the time. I haven't been in a few years — you know, the war."

"That… sucks," I said. Obviously it sucked, but it was the most I could say about the topic without asking who his mom had been an indentured to. Of course there could be other reasons, but that seems like the type of thing that sort of contract would bring, especially that deep in the South.

There was no sign of Acturas finishing up. I wondered what was taking him so long. Sitika was a long journey away, though, and they might not have many available coaches–

Acturas stormed out of the building, just calm enough not to draw the attention of the police or passerby, but with urgency clear on his face.

He pulled me aside. I heard him muttering curses under his breath until we got out of earshot of other people. "They got us, Damion. I held them off for a few minutes, but we have to get out of this city *now.*"

"What happened?!" I demanded, but he shook his head.

"No time right now. We need horses, or a carriage, or to start running while we still have the chance."

The solution came to me easily, but it approached us before I could even suggest it. "I can get y'all out," Cedric said as he came up behind Acturas.

I could see the gears working in Acturas's mind, but he seemed to put his natural cynicism aside just this once. "Alright. Just to get us out of the city. We can work out payment later."

Acturas and I loaded into the back of the carriage while Cedric climbed into the driver's seat, and just as the carriage shook into motion, elven soldiers came rushing out of the stables as if they were charging into battle. Acturas and I ducked down immediately below the window rim.

We were almost onto the street when the carriage lurched to a stop. I pressed my hand over my mouth to keep myself quiet. On the street in front of us, I heard an elf soldier demand something in Elvish, and to my surprise, Cedric responded in Elvish as well. Neither Acturas nor I spoke much of the language, so we could only pray he wasn't turning us in for our sizable bounty. Only when the carriage rolled onward did I let myself exhale. We stayed low as we rumbled onto the main road, toward the city gates.

Once Cedric called back to us that it was all clear, I sat up, my face sweaty despite the cold weather. We were well beyond the city at this point, no other travelers on the road in sight.

"You have no idea how much we appreciate this," I said, "it would've been bad if they caught onto us back there."

"I figured. Pretty cool my Elvish came in handy for once, though the circumstances weren't exactly great."

"How'd you learn it? Your town doesn't seem like the type to have many elves."

"Yeah, no," he shot back with a light laugh. "My mom taught me while we were on the road. I guess it just stuck with me."

"How'd *she* learn it?"

He was silent for a few seconds. "I don't actually know, come to think of it. She was real good, though, and I wasn't what you'd call a prodigy."

"You'll have to teach me sometime." I meant it as a joke, but he seemed to take it to heart.

"Once you're not running from elven police, I'll hand off everything I know."

I couldn't see his face, but I knew he said it with a smile.

We pulled over a few miles outside Summerfall.

Cedric turned to face us from the driver's bench. "So, what now? I don't figure you guys just want to get out and walk to… uh, wherever you're going." He shot me a subtle glance, and I was thankful that he didn't let Acturas know just how much I had shared about our plans.

Acturas took a second to think, but it didn't seem to be too hard a decision. "If you're willing, we *do* need a ride. What's your price to get us to the next town over?"

"I usually don't go this far out for jobs, but I guess I could do it for… I don't know, fifty ply? That seems fair."

Acturas seemed almost dumbfounded by the low offer. There was no shortage of drivers who would charge double that for half the distance if they knew we had no alternatives. We exchanged a glance, but we both knew our answer.

"Sounds good," I said.

Cedric nodded, then turned back to the driver's seat and took up the reins.

"Let's get going, then."

Chapter Seven

We rode south into an expanse of wild plains and meadows. Huge, fluffy clouds swallowed chunks of the sky, and a herd of wild horses grazed far in the distance. The winter sun beating down warmed the air just a bit.

We stopped at a crossroads. The road sign told us that we could turn right and travel southwest, past the Great Wall and toward the plains in the middle of the continent, while the road branching left would circumvent the wall and lead us east, toward the coast.

"We're heading south, so take the road on the right," Acturas told Cedric. But before he could start up the carriage again, I interjected.

"Wait. If we go that way, it'll take way longer to get there — like, months. I don't know if we have that kind of time." I let the idea settle before continuing. "I think we should go east, find a harbor, and get on a boat. We can go anywhere in the world, and twice as fast."

Acturas rebutted, "I seriously doubt we have the money to get on a ship, and even then, it opens up a whole new array of problems. We should just play it safe."

I saw his point, but I couldn't concede. If we took a ship, it would slice weeks off our journey, and that's not even considering the amount of money we would save buying a one-time ticket as opposed to so many carriage fairs and inns.

"Fine — since we can't agree on this, Cedric should be the tiebreaker. Do we keep going south, or be rational, intelligent people, and go east?" I said.

Acturas scoffed at the idea of bringing this peasant coach driver into a conversation between nobility, but he didn't interrupt. Cedric quietly weighed the options.

"I think… east. It's worth the risk, and even if you can't get a ship, it's not the end of the world. Once you're out in the plains, there's no way for you to change your mind without turning around completely."

Acturas shot him side-eye full of loathing, but begrudgingly allowed us to begin our journey east. According to the sign, it would take two days or so to get to the nearest port of Senim. From Ramethus, it would just be a matter of chartering a cab to Sitika, and we would be all set. Honestly, it was almost laughable how easy it would be to pull this off — if we didn't eat up the rest of our money before reaching the coast.

We continued through the fields until we reached a village. It was easily the smallest town we had visited so far, consisting of at most twelve huts around a town square lined with a sparse market. The air was dusty from the dirt road and the fields of grain surrounding it, but the few people perusing the produce stands seemed used to the grime.

"How much bread do we have left?" Acturas asked. I looked into the bag and grimaced.

"Not too much. Enough for today, but after that..."

Through gritted teeth, he directed Cedric to pull over. The market featured a handsome variety of produce: bread, bread, wheat, apples (all green), and then another table stacked with bread. Acturas sectioned fifteen ply to spend, and he was very clear that he'd rather kill himself right in the street than spend a single ply more. He ordered me to stay in the carriage while he went off bartering, but he should've known by now that I wasn't one to take orders.

As soon as Acturas had his back turned, Cedric and I left the cab to explore, even if there was nothing but dust to see. A bit up the street from the town center was a stout church decorated with carved wooden statues and offerings. I offered to go in and take a look, but Cedric seemed vehemently against the idea. I let it go — I mean, churches weren't usually tourist spots, and I wasn't some puritan zealot. Well, I wasn't *that* much of a puritan zealot, but being an aristocrat in the largest Elementalist empire in the world definitely left me a bit radicalized.

We were coming around the side of the church when I suddenly found a knife poised at my throat. Cedric stumbled back in surprise, and I tried to turn around before an adolescent voice behind me spoke.

"Don't move. I want to see your hands."

I held my breath. I didn't have any cash or valuables on me, but what if he didn't believe that? Or just didn't want to leave any witnesses... I had to find some way out of this. I looked to Cedric for backup, but he was nowhere to be seen. *Did he seriously just ditch me like that?*

The robber dragged me out of the street and into a nearby alley. "Your friend left, man. Sucks. Now, give me your cash, slowly."

"I don't have anything on me, I swear to Aethrus. Really, I'm not worth the trouble," I said, though the nervousness in my voice may have misconstrued my plea for stalling.

"There won't be any trouble if I slit your throat right now and loot your corpse. I want cash, *now.*"

I had learned how to handle situations like this, though they all relied on holding attackers up until fifteen knights came running to my rescue. I didn't know how long I could delay this guy — he seemed awfully intent on getting something out of me.

The knife pressed harder into my throat, and I panicked as I realized I had no way out of this myself. Then, my attacker lost half his ear. He didn't notice at first, but he definitely felt something, because he whirled around and thrusted his knife toward Acturas, who stood just out of range with his sword in hand. I saw my attacker was nothing but a teenager wielding a carving knife. He stepped back, preparing to flee, but stepped on something squishy on the dirt ground. He looked down at it, then felt at the side of his head, and released a blood curdling scream that must've rang out across the plains. I almost felt bad for him, but I was too busy sprinting down the street toward the carriage.

The town was alive at once. This was probably the most excitement they'd had in decades, if not ever: three foreigners arriving by carriage, splitting up, mutilating one of their rapscallion teens, and running to escape. Some men tried to stand in our way, but

Acturas's sword did not discriminate, and they luckily had enough sense to get out of his way before more townspeople lost extremities. Cedric had already taken the driver's seat as Acturas and I climbed in the back.

I watched out the window as villagers rushed to the square, the ill-prepared and unequipped town guards flocking to the scene, but they obviously couldn't catch up to the horses. We flew down the street, heading east, only slowing after the last signs pointing to the town passed us by. Acturas had managed to secure some apples (but no bread) before Cedric found him, and he had only gone through half of his budget. I hoped this would improve his mood, but that was nothing but wishful thinking.

"I can't believe you would be stupid enough to go out on your own this far from the capital. Do you know how dangerous these towns are?"

"Well, I do *now*. And I wasn't 'on my own', I had—"

"Cedric? Yeah, and good thing you did, because if he hadn't gotten me, you would be dead. From now on, you stay in the carriage."

I still wasn't used to being commanded by anyone but my father, and I didn't like that Acturas was sounding more and more like the king. I was about to stand up for myself, but Cedric beat me to it.

"I think Damion's old enough to walk around a town at midday." Acturas and I went quiet, neither of us expecting him to interject in our argument. "Besides, it's not like small towns are any more dangerous than the capital, but I guess you don't get out enough to know that."

Acturas sat with his mouth hanging open as if he couldn't believe this peasant would talk back to him.

"I– who do you– stay out of our business. This doesn't concern you."

"Really? Because it feels like a lot of your business concerns me, or else I wouldn't be helping you flee south a hundred miles further than we agreed to. If you want me to shut up and drive, maybe I could just charge you an extra two laed and drop you off at the next town."

"Maybe you–"

"Acturas, *stop*," I jumped in. I would rather he argue with Cedric than me, but not if it meant we'd have to find a new driver for an extra hundred ply. He didn't seem ready to let it go, but I gave him a glance that reminded him that I was technically his boss, and he reluctantly closed his mouth.

We arrived at another town just before sunset. This town was busier than the last — even at this hour, passerby walked along the streets and entered shops — but equally dusty. It was bordered on the other side by a river, but the ferry was closed, forcing us to finally stop and give the horses, and ourselves, a break. We checked into the inn, a musty building of only two floors under a sparsely-shingled roof. We were greeted mirthlessly by a clerk who seemed like he would rather be anywhere else in the world.

"Three beds, one night," Acturas said.

The man chuckled to himself. "Not in this hotel. Largest room comes with two beds, going for forty ply."

Acturas heaved an exaggerated sigh and looked at Cedric. "Guess you're crashing in the carriage tonight."

Cedric snapped back. "No way I'm doing that. Don't forget I'm *driving* — if anybody stays in the cab, it's you."

"I'm the one who's paying for both the room *and* your service!"

"With my money," I added. Acturas glared at me, and the innkeeper jumped in.

"Look, if y'all don't want the room, find another inn. I ain't listening to this all night."

Seeing as Acturas and Cedric would be going at it for days at this rate, I declared, "We'll take the two beds, thanks. Acturas, get the money."

He sighed and dropped forty ply onto the table. The shopkeeper meticulously counted them, savoring the touch of every bronze coin. Satisfied, he handed us a flimsy key attached to a board hastily labeled *Room 5*.

We climbed the rickety stairs to the second floor and found the room. The key fit poorly, and it took two tries before the door flung inward, revealing a compact space stuffed with two beds and practically nothing else. The only light came from the large, messily-cut hole in the wall which I assumed was intended to serve as a window.

"Well, now what?" Acturas said as he laid his bag down on the bed he apparently claimed as his. Cedric sat on the opposite bed, leaving me standing awkwardly in the middle as they stared each other down.

"Either you two are sharing a bed, or one of us is sleeping on the floor," I said.

"I'd rather sleep in the lobby than with him," Cedric said, and I didn't doubt for a second that he meant that. We all knew *I* wasn't sleeping on the floor,

and neither of them would concede, so I was left with
no other option.

"For fucks' sake, fine. Cedric, move over," I told
him. Acturas began to protest that I would rather share
a bed with a near-stranger than with him, but I was tired
— both literally, and of his attitude these past few days.

Cedric pushed himself up against the wall
to make space for me. I lay down on the other side,
forcing myself to ignore the awkwardness of the
situation, and eventually managed to get to sleep.

In the morning, I was the first one awake.
Sunlight filtered in through the window, casting a subtle
glow over the frigid room. I climbed carefully out of the
bed, not waking Cedric, and pulled on my jacket and
boots. It was too early to wake the others, so I decided
to take a look outside in the meantime, since *nothing*
bad had ever come from exploring unfamiliar towns.

The air outside was colder than inside the
inn, sharpened by the breeze flowing from the river.
I pulled my coat tighter around me and took a deep
breath. Despite the frost in the air and the general
circumstances I found myself in, it really was a
beautiful morning. I thought it would be nice to hang
around out here for a while — until I heard the pound
of galloping horses from down the road. I slipped
behind the corner of the inn and watched. There were
four riders all together, each with a sword. One had a
bandage around the side of his head, and he looked like
he had a rough night.

While they were tying up their horses, I snuck
back inside the inn as fast as I could and ran up to
the room. I threw open the door and shook Acturas
awake, then Cedric. The second I began to explain the
situation, Acturas bolted up and grabbed his sword.

Peeking over the rim of the window, I watched as they filed into the inn through the only door. We had to find another way out. The last option was the window, but I wasn't sure I was built for a two-story fall. I heard the thump of footsteps on the stairs at the end of the hall. Acturas readied his sword and positioned himself beside the door, none of us making a sound as the footsteps approached, falling silent just outside. Then came a knock, soft but threatening.

"Come on out," a familiar voice said from the other side, "let's talk. Settle our differences." I recognized his voice as the mugger from the last town, and his tone suggested that he did not, in fact, just want to talk.

Another knock, this time louder. Acturas might have been able to take them, but I didn't want to be walking away from four dead bodies — or worse, laying with two others. The knocking became banging, and judging by the creaking of the hinges, I knew the door wouldn't hold up much longer.

It was a split-second decision, something I never would have done if I thought about it for even a second longer. I leaned over the sill, looked down toward the ground — *it really can't be that far, can it?* — and jumped.

I crumbled to the ground, but with some long-overdue luck, managed to climb to my feet unharmed. I looked up and saw Cedric looking out the window. I was about to call for him to get down here too, but didn't get the chance.

"Behind you!" he yelped.

I spun around, and in a second, another attacker was swinging at me with a sword. I ducked back as he stabbed forward. I pulled my kitchen knife out from my belt, the blade tragically short and dull compared to that of my opponent. He came at me again, and I was forced to fall back against the wall. As he stabbed straight at my chest, I actually used some of my self-defense training in real life, using my forearm to parry the sword. It left a shallow, red gash in my sleeve, but the sword planted deep into the wooden wall. I took the chance to lunge forward, tackling my attacker to the ground. He didn't fight back. I sat up and saw my knife lodged over his heart, and he wasn't moving.

The whole ordeal had happened in ten, maybe fifteen seconds, and Cedric was just now jumping from the windowsill. My flight response made me move before I could process what I had done. Acturas followed quickly as I heard wood splinter and the stomping of boots from up inside the room, and he picked up the man's fallen wallet from the ground before leading us back to the carriage.

Cedric grabbed the reins and guided the horses toward the ferry. The ferryman was confused about our rush, but didn't ask any questions after Acturas just about threw coins in his face.

The attackers didn't pursue us to the river. I took a deep breath and sat back as the ferry cruised across the water, glad to have distance between us and the events that just unfolded.

With nothing but plains for miles around, we continued riding east, toward the coast. Acturas counted the money in the dead guy's wallet — two laed. A steal, literally. As the sun drooped over the horizon, I tried not to think about the image of him laying on the street below me, but I pictured it every time I closed my eyes. I hoped that it wouldn't follow me in my dreams, at least, as I took a long-overdue nap before we even stopped to make camp.

Chapter Eight

We arrived at the port of Senim three days later. Senim was about as large as Semmerfall, but without any of the luster — its economy was based on trade, and most people in the city were only merchants stopping over. We pulled into the stables and immediately began searching for an inn, even though it was barely noon. Having spent several days crammed into a carriage with only some apples and whatever stale bread was left over from the castle, all of us could have used a day off. Besides, we had a long journey ahead, and a lot of hard conversations to have.

We stumbled into the hotel room and each of us collapsed on our respective bed. It wasn't a *huge* room, just big enough to fit three beds and a side table for each, but it was a solid upgrade from the last inn. It even had glass windows. We all lay there for a while before I suggested we find something to eat.

"With what money?" Acturas said somewhat pointedly.

"We have almost six laed after yesterday, and we should still have enough left to cover the ship if we bargain," I said, my stomach overruling his financial concerns.

"Yeah, right," he scoffed, "we'd be lucky to get to Sitika with a stendar."

"Well, it's what we have, unless you want to organize a fundraiser."

He just rolled his eyes. A minute later, we filed back out to the street, and Acturas isolated one single laed for spending. In this area, I wasn't sure if even *that* would cover the three of us, but I didn't try to get us to spend any more than we had to. For the first time in my life, I had to be frugal with cash. It was my lowest point.

Crashing waves thundered from the docks in the distance, and I could see masts of ships jutting out from the harbor. It hit me for the first time that I was *leaving* — not just the capital, not just the country, but everything I knew. Though I didn't know any of these people I passed on the street, they all knew of me. I was their prince, I was supposed to be their leader. And I was abandoning them.

We ate at a bar, but not even the whiskey could repair my mood. I suspected Cedric took notice that something was amiss, but he was too busy with his meat pie to pry. Acturas, on the other hand, seemed to be on the verge of tears upon seeing the prices.

After, Acturas and I went out to the dock so he could try to find a ship to Ramethus while I wandered to the pier. Cedric was back at the hotel, getting his stuff in order for the ride back. I felt stupid for being disappointed — this was *our* problem, not his, and it wouldn't make sense for him to go all that way with us without even knowing who we really were.

I sat at the edge of the pier overlooking the waves. No ships were leaving this late in the day, so not many people were around. I stared into the water. Sickly green, muddy — not at all like the crystalline lake at Semmerfall. I stayed there for a while, until somebody came up from behind and sat down next to me.

"What's the matter?" Cedric asked.

I sighed. I wanted to talk with him, but I couldn't explain. "Nothing," I lied. I knew he didn't believe it, but there was nothing else I could say.

Silence stretched between us. Then, quietly, he said, "So, y'all are heading out to sea tomorrow?"

"If Acturas can get us tickets, yeah," I said. "We probably have the money to get a spot on some cargo ship, but I don't know if we'll be able to take it all the way to Ramethus. Might have to break down the trip, which'll take us way longer."

Cedric looked to the horizon, where the sun was melting impatiently into the waves. "I've never been on a ship before — well, not that I can remember. I guess my mom had to have taken me on one when I was really small, but obviously that was… a while ago. We always went over land when we went south."

"That sounds rough. It's a long trip," I said, as if he didn't already know that. "You know, you've mentioned your mom a couple of times, but… you never said where she is. Or if she's… still around."

He stared at the horizon. "… she died a while ago," he replied after a subtle pause. Though he was covering it, I detected a years-old melancholy behind his voice. "I was sixteen, so about three years ago. Normal stuff — fever going around, she got sick, doctors checked her out but didn't know what to do.

She left to stay with some family in the East, and I never heard from her again, so I assume she didn't make it very long."

"Damn. I'm… really sorry to hear that," I said. "My mom died, too. When I was eleven. Really messed me up back then. I'm pretty over it now, but I get it."

"What happened? If you don't mind me asking."

I did mind, but not because the subject upset me. Actually, I just didn't know how to explain that my father ordered her execution for conspiracy against the throne after a spy intercepted a letter from her to the Mol Stihirn of the Minesran Silver Council.

"It's… complicated, I guess. It would take a while for me to get into it, it's a story for another time." It wasn't a real answer, but Cedric took the hint, and didn't push for any more answers from me.

We sat in silence for a bit before he spoke again. "You know, I could go with you two. If I sold the horses, I'd easily get enough money to pay for all our tickets, and probably on something nicer than some cargo ship."

He let the idea linger in the air, and though I desperately wanted to accept his offer, I knew that it was something I just couldn't accept. "Cedric, you can't do that. You have a life here — a pretty good one, too, all things considered. And not even *I* know what happens after Sitika. Honestly, I'm not a hundred percent sure we'll ever be able to come back."

He scoffed slightly. "Yeah, I wouldn't say shuttling people around in a carriage once a week for twenty ply has always been a dream of mine. I wouldn't be leaving as much behind as you think — really, it would be an improvement. And–"

"No, Cedric," I forced, cutting him off before he could convince me. "This is for me and Acturas. It's for your own good to stay away from us."

"Why do *you* get to decide what's for my own good?!" Frustration dripped from his voice. "Oh yeah, that 'stuff that came up', right? That's so urgent you're running to a holy city-state five thousand miles south of here? You ever try to, I don't know, *ask other people for help?!*"

I didn't expect the vitriol, and now *I* was mad. "You seriously think the only thing stopping us from bringing you along is my *ego*? Don't you think if we could use your help, then we would've already asked you for it?" It came out harsher than I wanted, but it was too late to backtrack.

"This coming from the guy who I had to smuggle out of Semmerfall, ten feet from being arrested by elven soldiers? Or the one who got mugged immediately after setting foot in the *second village* he visited? And then jumped out a window directly into an ambush? Oh, yeah, you're *real* competent, Damion."

He abruptly stood up and turned to march off. I called back to him, "Don't bother selling your carriage. You probably get along better with the horses anyway!" Even as a last word, it wasn't satisfying. My face was flushed and my hands were shaking, but not just because of the cold ocean winds.

I looked back at the line of the horizon. A last-minute ship was gliding into the bay as the sun dipped out of sight, and I blinked tears out of my eyes. I wasn't sure why we were so mad, but I knew he didn't deserve to be called, essentially, a worthless chauffeur. I cursed myself for saying all that to someone who had done nothing but help me.

I knew I had to apologize, but when I went back to the hotel, he wasn't there, and neither was any of his stuff. Acturas was sitting on his bed, getting ready to go to sleep.

"Hey, where's Cedric?" I asked him, hoping it wasn't already too late, but he rolled his eyes.

"He came back all pissed about something, didn't say what. Then he grabbed his stuff and left." This was the opposite of what I wanted to hear, but Acturas seemed relieved. "Better for us, anyway. We don't need to involve more people in this than us — plus, it's just fewer tickets on our way to Ramethus. Speaking of," he reached into his bag and retrieved two slips of paper, "it took just about the last of our savings, but I got us spots on a ship leaving tomorrow morning. There were only four tickets left on the last ship leaving for the next two weeks, so it actually worked out perfectly."

Quite frankly, I couldn't have cared less about the tickets. All I cared about was finding Cedric and making things right, but I knew he had probably found a dingy alehouse somewhere and would be long gone by morning. I sat down on my bed, wanting to be left in silence, but Acturas didn't seem to catch that.

"Yep, I better get some rest too. Long day tomorrow — commercial sea transit isn't much like the stuff the castle arranged for us. Probably best to enjoy solid beds while we have them, because we won't for a few weeks."

Chapter Nine

The second I saw it, I knew the ship would
be a nightmare. The hull was warped and sunken, the
sail was yellowed with fraying edges, and the sailors
all seemed to linger just off the gangway, reluctant to
go back on deck. I loathed sea travel in general, but
this took it to a whole new extreme. I stood on deck
as they loaded cargo of lumber, ore, and weapons,
debating whether it would be more pleasant to swim to
Ramethus, until Acturas called me down to the sleeping
area to pick a hammock.

I chose one close to the wall, but far enough
not to put me at risk of hitting a wave and being slung
into the hull in the middle of the night. Acturas claimed
the hammock next to mine, one of the few left over
that hadn't been claimed by resident sailors. Other than
them, most passengers below deck were merchants or
businessmen.

I sat on the bunk and took in my surroundings.
The walls weren't any cleaner on the inside, but the
smell of mold and rotting wood was unbearable in the
confined space. I never wanted to be on an imperial
navy ship so badly. I had a sinking feeling in my

stomach as I remembered all the times I took their mildew-free hulls for granted.

I went up to the deck to get some fresh air while sailors prepared to set sail. The rocking of the ship calmed my nerves — the one redeeming quality of being at sea. I walked around the deck, though there wasn't much to explore. I examined a stack of boxes labeled 'linen' sitting by the mast which I could only assume would be used to repair the sales when we were attacked by the kraken in the middle of the Median Sea.

I was leaning on the railing when they pulled up the ramp and threw off the ropes. The receding tide pulled the ship out of port and, slowly, into the wider bay. Fishing boats dotted the surf by the beach, but we were soon too far for them, and our only company were the other cargo ships cruising in from the open ocean.

I stayed by the railing and watched the sea, but couldn't make out anything below the surface. I wished I saw something beneath the sea foam, anything to prove that it wasn't just a bottomless abyss beneath me, but waves were what I was stuck with, and so waves I watched until my forearms hurt from resting against the wooden rail. A splinter had become lodged in my elbow, and I pulled it out with growing disdain for the vessel and the Elementals for putting me in this situation. I looked to the sky, seagulls circling overhead until we were too far from shore for them to reach us.

I turned around and noted the other people on the deck. An expensively-dressed woman walked across the deck while a short man in a ratty tunic scurried after her with heavy bags. Directly across from me was a sailor sweeping the deck, though it didn't look any cleaner because of it. I noticed a hooded figure emerging from the lower levels, but they turned away and went around to the other end of the ship before I could see their face. I didn't think much of it — there were always some strange people heading south. I once again wished I had something to pass the time. I decided to go below deck and try to find something to do, even if it was just hallucinating in my hammock from scurvy.

Few people were down there — nobody would rather be *inside* the ship than on deck. I went over to Acturas, who was polishing his blade absentmindedly. I laid on my hammock and stared at the ceiling, listening to the creaking of the hanging lanterns and the groaning of the ship as it crashed over the waves. I thought of Cedric again. Damn, I really screwed that up. When I returned in however many months… or years… I would have to go back to that town and apologize to him in person. If I made it that far.

I sat up and looked around. The only other people under deck seemed to be having a rough time with sea sickness, and I didn't want to be around if their breakfast made a return appearance.

"Come on, let's go up top. They're distributing dinner rations soon," I said to Acturas, who reluctantly put down his sword and rag. The sun blinded me as we stepped out of the lamplit darkness of the lower deck. As the sails caught wind, Senim gradually dwindled into a nondescript dot on the shore.

I got my stale bread and rum, which wasn't all that bad this early in the voyage, and I went to eat by the rail. As I pushed through the small crowd of passengers, the ship plunged over a steep wave, and I was knocked into someone standing nearby. It was the hooded figure I'd seen a few times before, but now their hood had come off, and I could do nothing but stare.

"*No way,*" I muttered. I was hit by so many questions, unsure whether to be overjoyed or horrified. "What– how– what– *how are you here?!*"

Cedric laughed awkwardly as he rushed back to his feet. "I sold the horses. I just figured you guys wouldn't be able to make it two days without my help, so I decided to be all generous and come along."

What a dumb thing to say. I decided to settle on feeling relieved — I mean, since he was already here, there was no use fretting over it. And I wasn't going to pretend that I wasn't at least a *little* glad he had ignored what I said on the pier. He took his own rations and we found a more secluded spot away from the rest of the ship.

"So, you'd really rather spend the next month on a ship to Ramethus? With no money or sailing experience?" My brain hurt as I tried to understand his motive. I mean, I had known him for less than five days, and he was already on his way across the world with me?

"I'd honestly rather do anything than spend another five years driving people around in that cheap cab. I'd say it got old, but I never liked it that much to begin with."

"That's… fair enough, I guess," I said. Even with all of my privilege and luxury, I'd had my fair share of tedious work, and I was glad *one of us* was happy to be there.

We talked at the rail until the sun again began to dip beneath the horizon. Watching the sea turn indigo as the first stars began to appear in the sky ahead of us, I almost felt like the coming weeks might not be that bad.

Acturas, on the other hand, was less pleased to learn that Cedric would be joining us. When we came down to the bunk area together, I swore I saw him grip the handle of his sword just a little bit tighter. He would just have to get used to it, though — it looked like Cedric was in this for the long run.

Chapter Ten

A week later, I was back to being miserable. I'd done practically nothing but play cards with Cedric since I got on the ship; he'd taught me every game he knew, and I was getting tired of losing at all of them. The shore long out of sight, and still with hundreds of miles to go, I was struggling to settle into the rhythm of ship life, and I couldn't have been more excited to get back to dry land, and actual food, and air that didn't reek of fish.

In the afternoon, Acturas, Cedric, and I were playing our fifteenth round of blackjack to pass the time. I was winning, for the first time since we'd departed, and had collected sixteen ply, though the majority of it was my money to begin with. I decided to cash out, putting my 'winnings' back in my bag and slinging it over my shoulder.

"So, what now?" Cedric asked, clearly as bored as I was.

"Not sure. We could try to swim to Sitika — I mean, it would probably be faster." I was joking, but it seemed to resonate among us. We all sighed in unison, and I stood with some difficulty as the deck swayed.

The water was growing restless. In the distance, I could see deep black clouds blocking the horizon. Great. Knowing my luck these past few weeks, the storm would land right on top of us and follow us all the way to the Minor Channel. I walked to the railing and watched the sea churn below, and for the first time, my stomach began to turn with it.

An hour later, the first raindrops fell in a drizzle. I was standing on deck and pulled my hood over my head, despite my desperate need for any sort of shower at that point.

I stood in the rain, fighting to hold my coat around me as the wind lapped at the ship. I would have enjoyed the rush as the ship came over the waves if the hull hadn't groaned like a dying beast each time.

A gust of wind pulled down my hood, and I ran to get back inside before I was fully drenched. My hair soaked, I descended the stairs to join the rest of the passengers in the main cabin. Lit only by a handful of oil lamps hanging from the rafters, everyone who wasn't essential to keeping the ship afloat sank into their bunks. Some conversed in dark whispers drowned out by the raging weather, but most kept quietly to themselves. The rich lady I had seen on the first day, who I now knew as the niece of the Baron of Wrest traveling to Ramethus to secure her family's assets in the South after the economic upturn of the invasion, wrote in a journal on her cushioned bunk as her servant dried rain from her hat.

I weaved around the rows of bunks until I reached mine. Acturas was sewing his shirt after it had been torn by a plank of wood which did not survive one particular impact — we were lucky his arm wasn't taken off, but it did leave a nasty bruise. Cedric was taking a nap after another exhausting day of sitting on deck doing nothing. I figured sleeping through the storm wouldn't hurt, but I couldn't let myself relax under the incessant pounding of sailors' boots on the deck.

"Acturas?" I whispered once I was sufficiently bored of staring at the ceiling.

"Mhm?" he shot back absently, not stopping with his shirt. I sat up.

"How long do you think we'll have to stay in Sitika? The more I think about it, the harder it is to believe we'll be able to finish this… soon." I came dangerously close to saying 'ever'. I needed to be careful about that. That mindset wouldn't help anything.

"No one ever said this would be easy. It could be years before it's all sorted out — all we can do is take it one day at a time and trust the plan."

"But what even *is* the plan? What happens after we get there?"

He put down his shirt. "Damion, you have to trust me. When your father told me to leave with you, he made it clear that Sitika is our best option. Actually, he made it clear that it's our *only* option. I know what we need to do, and once we get settled in the South, we can start to work on getting back. Okay?"

I decided to let his assuredness satiate my concerns, even if he didn't really answer my question. This was one of the times when I just had to trust that he knew better, and it's not like he had ever failed me before.

"Okay."

I wanted to say more, but Acturas had refocused on mending the gash in his shirt, and I didn't want to risk accidentally oversharing to our captive audience of bored passengers. I reclined back on my hammock and closed my eyes, hoping the rocking of the ship and the drone of the storm would send me to sleep.

I lurched up in my bunk. Cold sweat coated my forehead; I wiped it away and squinted through the darkness. The cabin was cold, the lamps having all gone out, and eerily silent, though any noise inside would have been completely smothered by the tempest which now seemed to be fighting to tear the ship apart — and winning.

"Acturas?" I called out. Nothing. The ship hit a wave, sending my hammock rocking nauseatingly back and forth. I kicked my legs out and staggered to stand.

"Damion…?" Cedric said groggily, "why are you yelling? It's, like, midnight."

"I don't know, something just feels off. Where is everyone?"

"Probably sleeping?"

"It's too quiet. And Acturas is gone, too." I felt for his hammock and found the fabric hanging empty.

I heard Cedric sit up with an exaggerated groan. "Fine, let's take a look around. Can you find a– *ow, fuck.*"

I had to stifle a laugh as the lamp clanked and swung through the air, Cedric cursing quietly and rubbing his forehead. It squeaked from years of humidity and neglect as he fiddled with it. A small flame appeared in its center, lighting just enough for me to make out the lines of Cedric's face and the silhouettes of the hammocks around us.

Cedric unhooked the lamp and held it out, guiding us around bunks toward the stairs. As we neared the hatch, I thought I heard some commotion coming from the deck, but it was too muffled by the thrum of rain for me to discern what was happening. Cedric and I exchanged an equally curious and anxious glance, neither of us wanting to open the hatch and face the storm. Finally, he relented.

"Let's just get this over with," he said as he handed me the lamp and started up the stairs toward the hatch. Just before he reached it, though, he froze. His brow furrowed. "Do you hear that?" I listened, but couldn't make out anything beyond the rain.

"What is it?" I asked hesitantly.

He didn't look back. He answered distantly, as if deep in thought, "I don't know… it sounds like–"

We both jumped when the hatch was thrown open, its squealing hinges startling Cedric back down the stairs. Rain fell through the gap, and for a split second, I heard a sound masked by the rain, but it didn't last long enough to make out what it was. I held the lamp and peered up the stairs, while the intruder frantically slammed the hatch shut behind him.

"Acturas, what are you…?" I started, but he ignored me, pushing past us and racing to his hammock. I followed him, my nervousness mounting. "Acturas, what– why are you getting your sword?!"

His weapon in hand, he slung his bag over his shoulder and faced me. I just stared at him expectantly, still waiting for an answer. He blinked.

"Oh, sorry," he said, pulling his hood down with his free hand. There was thick fabric wrapped around his head; he pulled it back, letting it fall around his neck.

"We need to get ready. Here…" He took the shirt he had been sewing and tore it into strips. "Wrap these around your ears. I don't know how much time we have."

I took a strip, but didn't wrap it. "No. You have to tell me what's going on first."

He collected my bag and tossed it to me as he spoke. "The storm knocked us off course. We went too far out to sea. We're passing Sirisyris."

A dizzying chill crept up my spine at the mention of the mythical island. "You mean… *there are Sirens out there?!*"

"That's what I said. Now quick, we might still have time–"

The ship jolted and we were thrown to the ground. An ear-splitting crash reverberated as the ship grinded against a rock and the hull caved in. Crests of waves lapped into the room, wind tore at hammocks, and I pressed my hands to my ears so hard I thought my skull would crack before the Sirens' song could get to me.

As the boat listed, everything that wasn't tied down began rolling out of the cabin to be swallowed by the churning sea, and I held myself in place with my feet to stop myself from joining them. A flash of movement to my side made me turn.

Acturas was fastening his ear cover back over his head, but Cedric sat motionless, his hands at his side and no fabric over his ears. He stared blankly ahead, clearly trying to process whatever he was hearing. I saw a flicker of horror cross his face — then, he moved.

As if pulled by gravity along with the rest of the things in the cabin, he sprung to his feet and bolted for the water. I staggered to my feet and took off after him, but Acturas was up too, grabbing to pull me back. He mouthed something to me: *It's too late*. Fuck that.

With my hands still against my ears, I elbowed him in the face and pushed him off. Cedric was almost to the edge, but another collision made the ship shudder and sent him sprawling into a hammock. He thrashed to free himself from the entangling fabric, desperate to reach the source of the Sirens' song. I nearly caught up to him before he broke free, and I fought to maintain my balance against the tilting floor as I pushed myself to catch up.

We neared the jagged edge that remained of the hull. Sea spray burned my eyes. Before he could climb over into the water, I kicked his legs out from under him and pinned him down with my knee. He immediately fought back, grabbing my leg and pulling me down beside him. I hit the ground hard. The impact stunned me, and my grip over my ears let up for just long enough to catch a note of the song. It was like the first time I ever had sugar imported from the Isles of Penelopene — insatiably delicious. It took everything in me to force my hands over my ears again.

Cedric was back on his feet, and I could do nothing but watch as he stepped onto the ledge. I winced as he prepared to jump, but he didn't — instead, he staggered backwards, gasping as Acturas pressed over his ears. I could see he still wanted the song, but without hearing it, he could at least gather enough sense to step back from the sea.

I was relieved, before I remembered that I was still stuck on a sinking ship off the coast of the Sirens' shipwreck island. I pushed myself back to standing. Cedric had now taken over the responsibility of covering his own ears, neither he nor Acturas wanting to touch the other any more than strictly necessary.

Catching Acturas's attention, I mouthed, *"What do we do?!"*

It was obvious he didn't have a good answer. Dread filled me like the black water that was filling the cabin, freezing cold and hungry for three more souls to add to the ocean's vast repertoire. We filed away from the water line, but the ship was listing so steeply we could only make it a few feet back. My boots hit a board slick with water, and I slipped with no free hands to catch myself.

Acturas grabbed my arm. His other hand grounded himself with a hammock. I knew it was no use — I couldn't even get back to my feet before the ship struck its third death knell.

The entire vessel split apart, sending beams collapsing above us and chunks of the hull falling in. With no other option besides being crushed to death or impaled by stray debris, Acturas let go of the hammock, plunging us both into the storm-swept sea.

Chapter Eleven

I awoke face-down on a rocky beach, bruised all over and soaked down to my bones. The rain had weakened to a drizzle, but clouds smothered the sky and breaking waves spat bitter water over me. I coughed and sat up. Every part of me ached, but I managed to stagger to my feet after a few minutes.

I looked down the length of the beach. Slouching among the imposing rocks which jutted from the sand were rows of desolate, gray ruins of stone and marble. Three standing columns supported a slanted, shingleless rooftop, and a marble platform, cracked and weathered, rose out of the sea like a pavilion. I knew the legends of Sirisyris, how it was swallowed by the waves as punishment for the Sirens' neutrality during the Elemental War, but actually being among the ruins was another thing altogether. They felt hostile. Vengeful. With no sign of Acturas or Cedric, I decided to start walking — anywhere was better than there.

I stumbled up the beach and onto what appeared to be a weathered path through the mountainside, the stone slick with rain. I leaned against the mountain face, the percussive clash of waves against the cliff far below daring me to venture closer to the ledge.

My legs were killing me when I reached a peak overlooking the sea, though I couldn't see the water as a mist rolled in. The crash of the waves below echoed through the fog like thunder from a deadly lightning storm. I found a cave in the face of the mountain that I used for shelter from the rain. I couldn't see much of anything in the darkness, but as I sat back against the rock wall, I grazed a tight gap, just wide enough for me to squeeze through.

I knew nothing good could come from it if I went in. I was about to ignore it, but something seeped out from the crack that wrapped around my mind stronger than any sugar: humming. Sweet, rhythmic humming, and even from out there, I was entranced. Logically, I knew the danger it posed to me — I had just experienced the effects of the Sirens' song firsthand — but I still found myself pushing through the opening, needing to hear it clearer, needing to hear *more*.

I broke through to the other side of the crevice, which abruptly widened into what I could tell was a much larger cavern, with reverberant echoes and a cold emptiness like I was the first to visit in thousands of years. The floor sloped steeply downward in a spiral, leading into the heart of the mountain. The path wound around an empty void, and I could make out a soft, flickering glow at the bottom. Whatever was down there must have been the source of the humming, which was amplified by the echo inside the cavern, and now it was just too much to bear. I set off down the slope as fast as my legs could carry me, no longer caring that they ached.

I almost tripped several times, but I couldn't slow myself. Anything that created such a lovely sound must have been equally as beautiful, and I had never wanted to see any creature as much as in that moment. Nothing mattered more than being in the presence of its song.

When I reached the bottom, I had my wish. Warm light emanated from a lava pool in the center of the smaller chamber, and kneeling on the other side of it was… some thing. I stopped dead. It looked like some sort of fish, or maybe a seal, up to the waist, after which it harshly transitioned into the torso and head of an emaciated old woman with a spiny fin lining her back. With the talons of her fingers, she picked at a silver harp.

I felt nauseous. I couldn't bear to believe my eyes, but I had no doubt that she was the one humming. I choked on my revulsion. It was impossibly hideous, yet it lured me down here with that song. How dare this awful *thing* manipulate *me* like this? Had I not suffered enough? Why did it hate me this much? I couldn't let her get away with this sick betrayal. My eyes landed on a cast iron fire poker hanging near the pool.

The Siren was too preoccupied with her humming and playing to notice as I crept to the stand holding the poker. It lay propped beside an elegant silver oar and a cracked shield bearing an ancient emblem I didn't recognize. When I wasn't looking at her, the music was more beautiful than ever, which only fueled my wrath. Its form practically mocked the music, the most beautiful music I had ever heard. I would rather see it dead than let it continue on. I lifted the poker from its stand without a creak and positioned myself behind the creature. When I raised the poker, though, I misstepped, and the lava behind me cast my shadow across the ceiling. She noticed the silhouette and spun around in a panic. Her humming stopped.

I was startled. My rage compelled me, urged me to bring down the poker while I had the chance, before she had the opportunity to start singing, luring me to step back into the molten rock. But with the humming gone, I found myself dazed, like I had just been returned to my body after sleep walking. Why was I here? Why was I doing this? I looked down at the Siren, her large blue eyes remarkably beautiful despite the horror of the rest of her body. Beautiful, and scared, and sad. I dropped the poker. I ran.

I sprinted as fast as I could, never looking back, not stopping even after I fled the cave and chose the first path I saw. I continued along the stone trail, away from the beach and the Siren's cave, the crashing waves against the sheer cliffside drowning out my gasps for air.

I finally slowed to a jog, then to a walk. Tears stung my eyes. I stopped walking as I was nearing the end of the path. Ahead, the mountain dwindled into the rocky beach, but what was the use of carrying on? What would I find there? Another Siren, this one more depressed than the last? I looked over the cliff's edge toward the black waves undulating behind the mist.

I didn't want it to end like this, but I wanted this to be over. I wanted to go back to before. Before I got on the ship, before I killed the man in that town, before I had to flee my country. I wanted to go back to the castle, to my old life, before the war, before I stood in the Imperial Square at eleven years old while they brought out my mother in shackles.

My mother. If she were here, none of this would have happened. She could have ended this war, could have replaced my father on the throne. I was the heir, but she would've ruled better than me, my father, or Obelevon. She would have been as revered as Queen Jennira herself. I wished I could see her, but was too scared of what she would say. Would she be proud of how far I made it? Disappointed in my ever-mounting failures? I wished I could ask her what to do, where to go, who to pray to for salvation.

Then, the mist was driven away, and I found myself back in the castle.

I crouched in the dungeon, lit only by a dwindling candle placed by the bars of her cell. In a voice I hadn't heard in years, marred by tears and childish confusion, I asked, "What are we going to do?"

"There's nothing we *can* do, Damion. Sometimes the Elementals give us challenges we can't overcome. Sometimes faith just isn't enough." My mother spoke softly through the bars, careful not to alert the guards upstairs that I had snuck down to see her.

"So he's really going to do it?"

"His mind is made up. But let's not think about that right now — we may not be seeing each other again for a long while, so we shouldn't dwell on tomorrow."

I shook my head; at this point, I hadn't yet learned to maintain my composure. "No," I whispered, "it doesn't have to happen. I can make him stop. Or else I'll go to the elves, like Aeres did — I'll never stay here with him if he does it, I'll never forgive him–"

"Damion, stop," she commanded. I fell silent. She took a quiet breath. "I know how you're feeling, but you cannot go on like this. This may be my end, but I will not let it be yours. The only thing for you to do is abide your father however long you must, and ensure that one day, when you come into your own power, these dark days are left behind. Do you understand me?"

I nodded.

Softer, she added, "You have the greatest opportunity I could have ever hoped for you. Use it for good."

My younger self within the memory spoke in unison with my current self on the cliffside.

"I will."

Chapter Twelve

At the other peak of the mountain, I finally found a good view of the entire island. Moonlight filtered through cracks in the clouds, giving the rock a pale yellow hue. I scanned the ruins on the beach, not daring to lose hope. They had to be there. I gasped in relief when I made out two tiny figures laying by the tide, waves washing over them. I knew it was them. It had to be.

I set off down the narrow ledge along the mountain while avoiding falling to my untimely demise via plummet from eight hundred feet. Within minutes, I was kicking sand up behind me as I ran across the beach. I scanned the shore for any sign of them, but the mist was too thick on the ground. They must have been around here somewhere–

I froze. A sound crept through the mist, like a man dragging a seal carcass behind him. I crouched down behind an abandoned column from the ruins of the city and stayed quiet under cover of the fog, peaking around the side. My breath caught as I saw the Sirens.

The four which crawled through the mist were even more hideous than the last: They dragged their inflated bodies along the beach with fat, wrinkled hands adorned with jagged talons. Their fishlike tales were stained gray and brown from millennia of dirt and blood. Warped jawlines exposed rows of chipped teeth, and their eyes were sunken and blackened, like the depths of the ocean. They were crawling away from me, onto the beach — toward Cedric and Acturas.

I had to do something, but without any sort of weapons, I couldn't take them on my own — especially when they just needed to hum a tune to make me turn around and walk into the ocean. I just needed to make them turn their attention away long enough to sneak my friends away. On the ground at my feet were piles of bricks, long since fallen off the ruins after centuries of constant storming. I picked one up and chucked it into the distance, but the clatter was drowned out by the crashing waves. The Sirens continued undisturbed.

An idea occurred to me, one that would no doubt lead to my death. I picked up a brick — the biggest, heaviest one within reach — and I launched it as hard as I could directly at the nearest Siren. I broke into a sprint away before it landed. The waves covered up the sound of my steps, but not the shriek of the Siren as the brick made contact. The sound wasn't as pretty as their singing. The Sirens changed course and converged on the column, seeming more confused than threatened for the time being.

I ran through the mist so fast I almost kicked Cedric in the head when I reached them. He was so still, I panicked that he might have already drowned, but his labored breathing reassured me. I could make out the form of Acturas maybe twenty feet down the beach, and he was even beginning to move, though it appeared to be little more than restless, unconscious stirring. I shook Cedric, trying to wake him, but he was too out of it to respond.

Behind me, the Sirens were starting back to their prey. I didn't know what to do, but there was no way I would leave my friends in the Sirens' grasp. I searched Cedric's belt for a knife, and found a steel dagger sheathed at his hip. Its blade was barely the length of my hand, narrowing into a triangular edge. Its patterning was more ornate than I would have expected from him; I didn't recognize the design. Maybe elven? It could even have been custom-made, though there was no way he could afford that.

The Sirens approached, intent on securing their kills. Fighting them directly would be suicidal. Hoping the centuries had made them complacent, I lay down on the beach, pretending to be unconscious as well. Listening to them squirm towards me, knowing any second they could drive their claws into my throat, was a kind of terror nothing had ever compared to. I held my breath, and thankfully, the Sirens appeared convinced that I was just another sailor washed ashore, ready to be devoured.

One came close to me. My heart raced. I didn't dare look for fear of blowing my cover, but just when I could hear it drag itself within striking distance, I leapt up. My knife found the Siren's throat, and it didn't even have a chance to scream before it collapsed, limp, in the sand.

It took the other Sirens a moment to realize what was happening, and I tried to benefit from their surprise. As I rose and charged the next Siren, though, all three opened their mouths in synchrony. I immediately collapsed to my knees. I had gotten a taste of their song on the ship, felt its effects in the cave, but unprotected, this close, more just humming… I didn't stand a chance. It would be impossible to describe it as anything other than a dark euphoria — a pure, wretched bliss so potent and compelling nothing but an Elemental could resist it.

As I knelt, entranced, watching the Sirens converge on me, a sudden new voice echoed from the mountains — another song. This one, though, was different. The melody wasn't black like the rest; it was golden, overpowering the others. The Sirens in front of me swiveled toward the mountain in shock, their singing wavering from fear. This new song, though, did not falter. I honed in on it, let it drown out everything else. Instead of forcing me down, it drove me to stand. I raised my knife.

A Siren in front of me rose up like a snake and bared its claws. I charged it first. It slashed at me, but I swiped at its wrist, severing its hand and leaving a smoking stump. I hesitated for just a moment. *What kind of knife is this?* I drove it into the Siren's heart, and it fell like the last one. I turned to the next.

I closed the space between me and the Siren, hearing nothing but the song from the mountains as it belted with all of its force. I ducked under its talons as it slashed at me, and I brought the knife up through its chin. It fell backward, spilling blue blood onto the sand. The two remaining gave up on their song and turned to retreat. I couldn't let them get away — not for vengeance, but justice: If I let them escape, there would be more like me in the future to fall victim to them.

I chased one down quickly, leaving a smoking wound in its back where I drove Cedric's knife. It collapsed like the others. The last Siren stared me down with fear and hatred, but I had no remorse for it like

I'd had for the first one I encountered. The one in the mountain hadn't been all innocent — none of the Sirens were — but she had remorse. *This* one knew nothing but cruelty and revenge. I stepped up to it, parrying its claws with the blade as I made one final slash. It landed heavy on the beach. With it, the song from the mountains faded, all of the Sirens dead but one.

I was watching the waves crash on the beach as the sun rose over the horizon, and with it, Acturas. He sat up dazed, and took a minute to even process the scene of Sirens around him. He leapt to his feet in surprise, stumbling away from them and grasping for his absent blades.

"Sleep well?" I asked. He rushed over when he saw me.

"Are you... did you *kill* them? *Yourself?*" he asked me in stunned disbelief, gesturing to the Sirens. I struggled to respond — I could hardly believe it myself.

"It's a long story. I'll explain it some other time."

He looked around, at the mountain, the Sirens, Cedric, the ocean. "Damion... *how* did you even do that? They're divine, they can't be killed by mortal weapons."

I realized I didn't have an answer for him. What about Cedric's knife let it kill near-immortals? I showed him the blade and explained the effect it had on them.

He almost laughed. "Ah, I see then. Guess I should've seen that coming."

"Why would Cedric have a knife that can kill Sirens?"

"I guess I never told you, did I? Cedric is–"

The Cedric in question loudly groaned a curse word and sat up. He rubbed sand from his eyes as they tried to adjust to the morning sunlight which cast an out of place pleasant glow over the otherwise dead island.

"What happe– *WHAT IS THAT?!*" he yelled as his eyes landed on the Siren corpses splayed next to him. He scurried away as Acturas broke into a laugh.

"Don't worry, it's pretty dead," I assured him. I quickly added, "Oh, compliments to your knife, by the way."

His hand went to his belt where he found his knife was not, and I realized I left it on the ground. I reached down to get it, but he beat me to it, snatching it from the rocks and sliding it in its holster covered by his shirt.

"Um, cool, okay," he stammered, "so they're all dead? How are we supposed to get off of this island?"

I looked at Acturas, who looked at me. Neither of us had an answer.

"We could try to find some sort of raft. I'm sure there's a boat around that's still sort of in sailing condition." I wasn't actually sure, but we didn't have many options at our disposal. As Cedric scanned the black rocks that surrounded the island, rough and deadly sharp, I began to doubt my theory.

"We can make our own raft, then," Cedric suggested.

"There are no trees on this island. I saw the whole thing last night from on top of that mountain — it's just a lot of rock."

I looked to Acturas, who had been apparently deep in thought for the whole conversation. "Anything to suggest?"

"Yeah, sort of," he responded, not sounding totally sure of himself. "So, in the second lore book, where it talks about the Sirens, it says that they crashed a ship that had found a divine artifact of Selene — y'know, as revenge for her sinking their city. Supposedly, it's an oar that can take you anywhere in the world. If we got that, we could use literally anything to get back to the mainland. It might still be here somewhere."

It wasn't a good idea — I mean, it wasn't a sin to admit that the lore books were more full of elaborate metaphors than authentic historical accounts. I thought back to when I had been in the mountain cave, the beautiful silver paddle propped up next to a fire poker. I hated the idea of going back there, but it seemed to be our only shot.

I led them up the mountain path, now dry as a bone under the noon sun beating down. We reached the crevice at the top, but halted.

"I'll be back in a few minutes. Don't follow me," I said, stepping up to the crack.

"Why not?" Acturas asked, "what's down there?"

I hadn't told them about the Siren who saved me, but I couldn't bring myself to explain it. It wasn't any of their business anyway. I had to do it alone.

"Just trust me," was the last thing I said before I squeezed through once again. I waited a moment to make sure neither of them would follow me, and I began slowly down the spiral. As I descended, I noticed that there was no more humming, and the glow at the bottom was reduced to nothing but a dull shimmer on the stone. Reaching the bottom, I saw only dying embers in the lava pool, the rock cooled and dried up.

The Siren still lay beside it. But she wasn't strumming. Or moving.

I rushed to her, but there was nothing I could do. She lay dead on the stone floor of the cavern, but no blood or visible wounds marred her wrinkled flesh. Her eyes, once vibrant and soulful, now stared glassy into the ceiling. I knelt beside her and touched her cheek, cold as ice. I squeezed my eyes shut. I couldn't help but feel as though I'd had some hand in this.

I wiped my cheek and rose to my feet. I was here for a reason. Next to the fire poker's empty stand on the wall hung the oar. I walked over hesitantly, as if I might scare it off with any sudden movements. It was cast in a bluish-green metal that shimmered under the embers' subtle glow. I lifted it up. It was weighted, but not heavy. It had to be the one. I took it with me and started back up the stairs, not risking a glance back to the Siren.

We returned to the beach immediately to search for anything we could use as a raft. Some wood beams had washed up on shore, but they were too rotted to support our weight. Lodged between two boulders was a ship that might still have been in sailing condition, but there was no way we could have dislodged it from the rocks. I planted the oar in the surf and closed my eyes. My fatigue from the past night was just now catching up with me.

Cedric tapped my shoulder, drawing my attention to something floating in on the tide, maneuvering around rocks and ruins: a raft. Not a fragment of ship wreckage, or a scrap of cargo that tumbled off into the sea miles away, but a full-fledged raft, with sturdy beams and rope binding. The oar sparkled aquamarine as the waves washed over its base.

We all gathered around as the raft beached. I noticed three bags of dripping wet linen on its center. I climbed on with the oar, and I recognized one as mine. Inside, it was just as I had left it — if I had left all of its contents soaked and reeking of fish. Cedric and Acturas followed, pushing the raft back out onto the waves before climbing in themselves. I didn't pay a glance back to the island as I dipped the oar in the water.

Chapter Thirteen

The oar seemed to flow naturally with the waves, and each stroke propelled us impossibly faster. The waves parted for us as we glided over the water, faster than imperial triremes, faster than the wind. I began to see ships in the distance, and we soon soared under seagulls as the thin line of the coast came into view.

We arrived in Ramethus before my arms had even begun to hurt from rowing. I wasn't sure which port the oar had taken us to, but it was no backwoods town: Low brick buildings sprawled the length of the coast, the tallest being three or four stories tall. The beach was full of people fishing, swimming, or laying on the sand. Miles inland, a sandstorm raged against the pale blue sky.

The oar grew heavy as we neared, and once we came close to the shore, it slipped from my hands and disappeared into the waves without a ripple. Acturas cursed me out for dropping it, but I got the sense that the oar wasn't going to let itself end up locked away on another land mass any time this century.

Carried by the tide, the raft landed on the beach with a jolt. We collapsed off the wooden beams onto the hot sand. None of us spoke for ten minutes, and none of the beachgoers seemed to want to bother with three northerners who washed in from the open ocean.

"So, what now?" I finally asked.

"We might be able to find a hotel that accepts ply, but we don't have much," Acturas said, sifting through the few damp coins in his bag. "I say let's use the rest to get a carriage northeast to Sitika, or at least anywhere out of here. We're probably better off walking than hanging around in the city."

I knew what he meant. Being stranded in the Deep South, the elves weren't our only enemies. Getting as far from the Ghânt Desert as possible was a matter of life or death.

Cedric sat up, his brow furrowed in thought. "Actually, I might know someone around here who can do us a favor. I don't know if he's in the city, but we can hope for the best."

Acturas groaned. "Great. I love *hoping for the best* until a desert witch cult catches and sacrifices us." Although I shared a similar sentiment, I would rather face the witches than deal with their childish feuds.

"We might as well check it out," I said. "No use trying to bargain with some driver over a currency he doesn't use, and it's better than wandering aimlessly while those witch cults hunt us." I gestured for Cedric to lead the way.

We wound through packed city streets, flanked on both sides by low apartments and shops. I would often see idols — banners, sigils, bronze chimes — of Kha'zat, the Ghânt's predominant religion. Kha'zat and Elementalism had a *very* long history, and rarely a friendly one. The faster we could leave, the better.

Weaving in between carts and merchants, I noticed Cedric was keeping his head low and fidgeting with his hands. I leaned in and whispered, "You okay?"

He didn't seem like he was in the mood to chat, but he managed a smile. "Yeah, it's just a lot to be back here. I hope…" He seemed to lose himself in thought, then shrugged. "Never mind, it's probably fine. We're almost there, anyway."

I looked around. We were at an intersection lined with vendors and bustling with people. The desert sun baked the crowd, but most of the locals wore scarves or coverings to counter it, and I wished I had brought a hat when I was fleeing the castle. The crowd was so dense, I noticed it must've been next to impossible to get around on horseback, much less in a carriage. Was Cedric not going to find a stable? He hadn't said where he was going, but I had assumed it was to get us a ride.

"You two wait here, I'll be back in a bit," he said. "See if you can get anything at some vendors. I haven't had a fruit in a week."

"Wait, you're going alone? Why can't we come with you? And why won't you even tell us where you're–" I protested, but Cedric put a hand up to tell us to stay, and he slipped into the crowd before I could finish. Acturas's expression told me that he wasn't any more of a fan of it.

"What's his deal?" I asked.

Acturas only shrugged and led me to the vendor stands. We found a vendor selling some sort of spiced cheese, and we figured it couldn't hurt to make up for all the days we subsisted on bread and watered-down rum.

"Do you speak Humanic?" I asked the clerk, self-conscious for asking. She looked up at me and squinted.

"Yes, my father came from the Isle of Wenn. Do you want any huerma?" she said, gesturing to the cheese.

"I do, but… you don't happen to accept ply, do you?" I asked, daring to get my hopes up.

She chuckled at the question. "Ply? *Excutatian* ply? Why would I accept ply? This is Ramethus."

"I know, ma'am, but we don't have any Renglets," I said before quickly adding, "after the elves arrived, we had to get away from the fighting, and we got on a ship here." It wasn't really even a lie, and there was no harm playing the sympathy card.

She sighed with pity. "I'm sorry to hear that, young man. How about we do each other a favor — I have a shipment to make to the Minesran embassy, but my back has been paining me terribly. If you take this satchel to the office of the ambassador, you can have your pick of goods. No need for Renglets."

"Where's the embassy?" I asked. I was prepared for it to be ten miles uphill, probably through the desert, so when she told us it was just around the corner, I thought the offer was too good to be true.

"We'll do it, thank you," Acturas said, taking the bag without even paying me a glance to confirm.

As we set out toward the embassy, I was pissed. "What the fuck was that? We're just gonna walk into an elven embassy? Chat with the ambassador? You think he won't recognize us?!"

"Well, no, I don't think so. Even if he recognizes us, which isn't likely, he'd have to be crazy enough to believe it's *actually* us. Besides, I'm hungry."

I just had to hope his logic was sound.

We came around the corner onto an empty street with only four buildings — or, more accurately, palaces. I saw the Perheath and Epona flags flying over two. The Excutatian flag flew over the largest, but the gates were chained shut and no guards stood at attention. The embassy across from it, on the other hand, waved its banner high above the domed roof: the Minesran flag and seal. It felt wrong to be going *toward* the elven authorities, but I didn't turn around.

"Undé hegesté! Melila emin?" one of the guards asked me as we approached the gate, his voice echoing menacingly from inside the helmet.

Acturas answered, and I was glad. The lump in my throat would've made me incomprehensible to even the best Humanic speaker.

"We have a package to deliver to the ambassador," he declared.

The guard examined the satchel in silence, then pulled open the gate. It slammed closed behind us as the sentries resumed normal positions.

We stepped into the embassy's vast lobby, all adorned with silver and natural light. An elven woman walked over to us from behind the desk. She was taller than either of us and wore her blonde hair in a braid over a Minesran gown which glimmered red and yellow in the light.

I assume she noticed we were human, because she first spoke in perfect Humanic. "Hídé to the Minesran embassy in Port Hameth! You can call me Veina. How may I help you gentlemen?"

"We have a delivery for the ambassador," I answered.

"Then I will take you to him right away. Please, follow closely. A human would not fare well becoming lost here." She smiled professionally, but there was a subtle coldness to the way she acted that I found typical of elves. Although, it's not like I could say humans were much warmer to *them*.

We walked through the wide halls for what felt like miles. We climbed staircases, went through doors, and passed through interior gardens. It was like the embassy went out of its way to show off to visitors at the expense of sensible floor planning, and my legs ached by the time we reached the ambassador's office. Our guide didn't seem the slightest bit winded, and I wondered why she couldn't have simply taken the satchel to him herself. Regardless, we were already there, and I just wanted to get this over with.

She opened the ambassador's office door, revealing a spacious room lined with elven armor stands and shelves of books and trophies. An elf stood behind a desk with his back turned to us, gazing out the floor-to-ceiling window at the far end of the room. My gaze flickered to Acturas, but he seemed fixed on something — or some*body* — else.

Sitting at the desk from him was another guy, also facing away from us. I could tell he had wavy blond hair, and his skin was suntanned to a light bronze, kind of like–

"Cedric?" I gasped louder than I meant to. The ambassador whipped around to face us, but Cedric only dropped his head. I looked again at Acturas, his face contorted with hatred. Something had gone *very* wrong, and I suspected we wouldn't be delivering any packages.

Acturas stepped into the room. I thought he was crazy, giving up his only chance to run, until I noticed that the hallway was quickly being blocked off by elven soldiers. I followed close behind him.

With unexpected confidence, Acturas spoke first. "Ambassador Menindeon, it *has* been a long time. How have you enjoyed your relocation? Ramethus winters are quite nice." The words were friendly, but there wasn't an ounce of kindness in Acturas's voice, and as he said the name, I understood why. An early memory flashed of sitting beside my father while he argued with some elven officer. This was before the war, and the elf had been sent to prevent a conflict once it became clear that the situation was beginning to spiral. If he had been stationed here as punishment for his failure to handle things in the North, and if he already knew who we were, we were in *much* deeper trouble than I feared.

The ambassador spoke, his stoney voice the same as I remembered. "It is wise not to speak unless spoken to, General Assix. In any case, you are not the one I care about. I want the Excutari."

My eyes flitted to Cedric, who had his hands at his head like he was covering his ears. A sickening thought occurred to me. Had Cedric… lured us here? I hated to admit it would explain all the favors he did us, and his insistence of coming along, which only raised an even heavier question: *How far back did this go?* And the hardest one of them all, *why?*

Acturas fired back, "I don't care for the wants of *elves*. I lost respect for your people — *you* in particular — when you all thought you could defend the Elven Highlands with *dragons*. As if you thought you could control them." I bit my lip, wishing he would try to be a bit more appeasing. "Oh, and that pawn you sent to bring us here. I always suspected him, but he was just so foolish and useless that even *I* was deceived into thinking it would be safe to trust an elf. I suppose, for the first time, your incompetence served you."

My head shot up. Did he call Cedric an *elf*? That couldn't be true, there was just no way… but I couldn't deny that it filled in the last piece of the puzzle. How had I not realized it when he spoke fluent Elvish in Semmerfall? Or when he mentioned his family came from the East? Or when he was *secretly carrying an elven blade?* I couldn't believe I had been this blind.

The ambassador stepped forward. Why this elf was an ambassador and not a military brute, I didn't understand — he towered above me and looked as though he could crush my skull between his finger and his thumb. What I did understand, and quite clearly, was that he intended to do just that, right now.

"I was directed to turn you over to the Silver Council for trial. In that case, however, I would be forced to miss the spectacle, and I simply can't have that. You *will* face retribution for your crimes against me and my people. It just won't happen in the East."

He waved his hand. The armor stands began to stir, stepping off of their racks and drawing their weapons. "Do you have any last words before you face the consequences of your actions? Please make them desperate and pleading, I would hate to have to forge them."

I was too stunned to speak. We had just gotten here, and I already found myself in *another* life-threatening situation. I could barely process his words, and only muttered the first thing that came to mind: "Cedric, what have you done?"

Not allowing for a response, the ambassador flicked his hand. In synchrony, his armor soldiers began to march toward us, weapons ready to strike. Knowing there was no escape through the door, in a panic, I scanned the room for any way out.

My attackers only walked, but they were quickly closing in. Before I had time to think, I channeled my hurt and betrayal and rage into my legs as I broke into a run, and Acturas followed. I raced to the desk, jumped on it, and used it to propel myself into the air as I lunged at the ambassador. It happened quickly, but he was fast to react, grabbing my knee before it collided with his high-set nose. Though he was bigger than me, he couldn't control my momentum and was sent tumbling back straight through the second-story window. Realizing my mistake, I grabbed for the curtain, but his grip on my leg dragged me down with him. I found us both barreling toward a stone embassy patio.

I braced myself for the landing. With my eyes closed, the fall didn't last as long as I expected, and my shoulder made a hard impact with something not rocky and tough, but firm and… fleshy? I opened my eyes to see the ambassador under me, blood gushing from where his head hit the ground. I rolled off of him in a daze, hyperventilating, and couldn't take my eyes off his lifeless face as Acturas dropped down from the ledge. He ran over to me and tried to pull me up, but I couldn't stop myself from screaming from the sudden pain that hit me. I looked at my right arm, and… oh. I was no doctor, but I didn't think my shoulder was usually at that angle.

Acturas cursed and pulled me up by my other arm. An alarm bell rang from somewhere else in the complex, and we booked it to the gate. It was too tall, and spiked at the top, and with my arm…

"I'll hoist you up, use your other arm to pull yourself over," Acturas ordered. He took off his coat and thrust it into my good hand. "Use this to cover the spikes."

He squatted down and I climbed on his shoulders. When he stood, I could reach the top, and I laid the jacket down over the spikes, hoping it would be enough to dull their razor edges. I strained every muscle in my one arm to drag myself up to a point where I could get my foot on top of the fence, using the leverage to push myself over. I fell over the fence and rolled down a hill through tall grass. When I opened my eyes, I saw Acturas leap down much more gracefully than I had. I was laying in a forest, tree tops devouring the sky above me. Acturas found me and pulled me up.

He led me away from the embassy, through the woods and toward the city. Whether it was the pain, or the fear, or the stress, or the betrayal, or likely all at once, I wasn't sure, but tears tore down my cheeks, and I didn't have a working arm to wipe them away.

Chapter Fourteen

We used the coat, freshly torn from the spikes, to cover my injury as we weaved through the crowd. Acturas looked into the bag the merchant had given us and turned it upside down — only flour spilled out onto the road. So she tricked us. She probably knew who we were as soon as we offered to pay in ply.

We had no money for a carriage, but we couldn't stay here. The elves had too much influence; there would be a hundred soldiers scouring this area within minutes. Sitika wasn't too far, maybe two days of travel with infrequent breaks, but that could turn into weeks on foot.

Acturas knocked me in the arm by force of habit, and I stifled a sob as my shoulder throbbed. He gestured toward a shop. I didn't understand what he was getting at until he pointed out a horse tied to a wagon out front. It was the first horse I had seen in Ramethus, and I immediately knew what he was suggesting. After all I had just been through, I had no objection.

We walked over inconspicuously, and in the crowded street, nobody thought anything of it when we used a knife to cut the rope, nor of the nervous whinnies of the horse as two strange men led it down the street. They probably hadn't seen horses often enough to know when one was upset, and it stopped resisting by the time we were riding northeast from the city.

I rode in the back of the wagon, which had been left empty after I assumed the owner took its cargo into the shop. Maybe if I got back to Excutatem, I could send him a new one as an apology, though I doubted I would have any chance of finding him.

The outer-city roads were bumpy and paved with sandstone. We passed a single sign post which read "SETICKA - 2,500 BERLARDES". I didn't know how to convert berlardes to miles, but I prayed they weren't a one-to-one ratio.

I kept low in the wagon, struggling to keep my mind off what had just happened. I had barely processed the Sirens, even my first escape from Exceres was fresh in my mind, and now *this?* Cedric was an elf? And he had been conspiring with Minesra this whole time?

"You knew all along, didn't you?" I asked Acturas quietly.

He inhaled deeply, then let it out before responding. "Not *all along*, but ever since Semmerfall, I suspected. I knew for sure when you found the elven knife — if I was smart, I would've left him on that island."

"Why'd you let him come with us, then? Knowing how dangerous he was?"

"Because I knew you wouldn't let him go."

I didn't say anything to that. I lay down in the wagon, the sun in my eyes, but I didn't care. Somehow, I fell asleep.

When I woke, we were pulling over to the side of the 'road', though at this point it was hardly more than a traveled stretch of grass. The moon was already in the sky, but apparently Acturas had wanted to cover as much distance as possible before he had to sleep.

He came around back and lay down on his coat. I stayed awake, watching the stars, the different constellations present in this section of the world. I figured I might as well stretch my legs, but when I tried to stand, my arm — which Acturas had properly set and bandaged once we were far enough from the city — screamed in protest. I got up anyway, spiting the pain. I didn't dare go near the tree line, remembering stories of creatures which lurked in southern forests, so I circled the perimeter of the carriage, the same questions floating in my head:

Will I get to Sitika?

What will await me there?

Will I ever reclaim my empire?

Will I see Cedric again? I mean, without him trying to lure me into the hands of the elves?

But why do I still want to?

In the morning, Acturas was startled to find me still awake. He usually used the morning while I was sleeping to get a break from me and prepare for the day's journey, so I kept my distance and waited to set off.

The sun was just beginning to rise when we continued on the road. We left the forest and entered boundless hills of wheat and hernasede, Ramethus's chief grain. The road snaked through the amber expanse and disappeared over a ridge, no sign of the city in sight. I wiped a thin line of sweat from my forehead.

"Are you finally going to tell me what the plan is?" I asked.

"You know what the plan is. We're just going to hide away from the elves and prepare our return to Exceres."

"I know that, but you've never told me what *exactly* we're doing."

"You'll see when we get there," he shot back dismissively. I sat up.

"No. I just crossed the entire continent to get here with no idea what's waiting for me, I think I deserve to know."

He glanced back at me. I held his gaze, not willing to back down on this. He rolled his eyes.

"There's a safehouse in the city where our forces are supposed to regroup. We're a little late, but they should still be there, if Jourdan didn't–" He cut himself off. My brow furrowed.

"If my father didn't what?"

He cleared his throat. "Nothing, I–"

"What were you going to say? I'm ordering you to tell me."

He paused, clearly not expecting me to exercise any sort of power. I was tired of the secrets, though, and if that's what it took for him to tell the truth, he would have to get used to it.

"Fine," he said, his eyes fixed ahead. "They should be there if Jourdan didn't *stop them*."

My head hurt. "Why would he stop them? Wasn't this his plan?!"

"No– well, yes, his plan was for *us* to escape, not for the *rest*."

"I don't believe that. He wouldn't send us alone with no backup — at the very least he'd have sent someone to meet us here. What aren't you telling me?"

He was silent. I was about to demand he tell me, but he answered first, resigned. "... you wouldn't have left."

"I... what?"

"If I told you the truth, you wouldn't have left. Jourdan would have had us both die in Exceres, but I wasn't going to let that happen. You're too valuable to Excutatem."

I felt sick as I pieced together what he was saying. "You mean he never told us to escape? You– you mean you tricked me into abandoning my country?!" The fields were spinning in my vision. If I wasn't too dizzy to stand, I would have climbed right off the carriage.

"Damion, *please* listen to me. There was no way we could have beat Neiphorous. I tried my best to convince him to escape with all of us, but he wouldn't allow it, so I did what I had to do to save the bloodline — what was best for *Excutatem*."

"We're *traitors*, Acturas!" I shouted, my voice cracking, though the fleeting echo was quickly absorbed into the plains. "We betrayed our people! How could you do this?!"

"Because if we stayed, *then* what would have happened to them?! The real treason was Jourdan's selfish last stand, endangering the bloodline and everyone in Excutatem who would suffer under another Neiphorous reign."

I didn't know what to think. I knew he was right — staying in Exceres would have been suicide — but the fact he would lie to me over something as serious as this… I couldn't wrap my head around it. It was so far from the Acturas I had always known, but I guess I had changed a lot, too. The one thing that seemed to have stayed the same between us was that we both cared about Excutatem more than anything. I decided I couldn't blame him for that.

I sat back in the cart and watched the fields pass us, trying not to think about what this meant for me. As we crested over a hill, my breath caught in my throat. In the distance, massive stone blocks towered gloriously over the plains and cut across the horizon. The Elanastis Wall.

It cast an ominous shadow across the road. It was hard to look directly at it with the sun rising behind, but I could make out statues lining its top, busts of the Elementals and heroes. Among them marched silhouettes of the Elementalist Guard on patrol. The front gate hung open, and even from a distance, I could tell why it was known as the largest city on either continent. The sounds of the city echoed through the gate and over the walls.

Before we even approached the wall, the road crowded with traffic, mostly wagons of supplies or offerings. We joined the line, a hundred wagons and carriages trying to fit through a single gate. I noticed a man in light armor ahead of us walking from carriage to carriage.

"What are they saying?" I asked Acturas.

"That's an apprentice inquisitor. They just need to make sure we're really believers. Heretics aren't allowed in the city for– well, obvious reasons."

"How are they proving it? Do you have to pay a tribute?"

"Not that I know of. Mostly you just have to show that you're devout and they'll take your word for it. It should be fine for you, speaking the Divine Language and all that. I'll let you handle it," he finished. Acturas could barely speak the language, since he hadn't grown up in a particularly high rank of nobility.

The inquisitor-in-training approached, clearly exhausted and bored out of his mind. He'd probably done this all day, most days of the week, on the off chance he'd be promoted to full Inquisitor. Every person in this city dreamed of becoming Elanastis Inquisitorius, and every person in this city was delusional.

He asked, completely devoid of interest, "Hera boll siddharthes uyuna Milla Elementus?". *Why do you wish to enter the Elemental City?*

"Crethsus harlume eraldé, prochlis g'horn," I replied. It came easier to me than ever. "Henemeck valdour Markus Grevel writomis'dor" *I invoke my right to entry by the writ of Markus Grevel.* Markus Grevel, the third Elanastis, declared that any follower of the Elementals bore the right to enter the city under any circumstances that they deemed important enough to invoke the writ. I figured this was sufficiently important.

The inquisitor's expression seemed to perk up. A well-spoken traveler invoking an ancient right of passage? After two dozen wheat farmers and countless more pilgrims, it had to have added some intrigue to his day.

"Re luis? Ibin?" he asked me, gesturing to Acturas. I nodded in affirmation, and the inquisitor waved us along. Then he turned and continued onto the next carriage, the 'day ruined before it began' expression returned plainly to his face.

After an hour longer in the line, we passed through the gate. Everywhere I turned was religious paraphernalia — statues, banners, church bells ringing every five minutes. Pedestrians flooded the road, making it impossible to move faster than a snail's pace, and even harder to hear anything over the roar of merchants advertising their wares and preachers feverishly warning that the divinely foretold Trench War was imminent.

Sitika was the holiest city in the entire religion of Elementalism. It was the cradle of humanic civilization, the largest city in the world. And, more than anything, it was awful.

Chapter Fifteen

Acturas seemed on edge the moment we passed through the gate, but also newly determined. I wished I could let myself relax now that we were safe within the city's limits, but I couldn't shake the feeling that we had only just finished the first step.

Over the din of the crowd, Acturas yelled back, "Our spot is on the other side of the city, by the north wall. It's going to take a while."

We made our way painstakingly slowly through the winding, crowded streets. The walls turned the city into an oven that broiled even when we were shaded by the towers that lined the road. I held Acturas's coat above my head in a futile attempt to keep myself from burning up, but he didn't seem to mind as sweat dripped from his forehead.

It took us nearly two hours to reach the north side of the city, and I was just about to die from boredom and heat exhaustion. This area was quieter because it bordered southern Perheath, which had less business to do in Sitika as the lingering effect of its strict wartime policies.

"Are we almost there?" I asked Acturas for the fifteenth time. He seemed to be scouring the road ahead for something, but didn't answer. I rolled my eyes and continued fidgeting with my fingers.

He pulled over to check a street sign. It was written in the Divine Language, which made perfect sense to me, but I realized Acturas couldn't read it. No wonder we were lost.

"You know, if you told me where we're going, I could probably help out. This is like riding in a cart drawn by a blind lady," I said.

He snapped his head back at me, and I saw a flicker of anger that I hadn't ever seen from him — at least not toward me.

"How about I drop you off here and you can find your own way to the safe house? If you're so much better at navigating," he snapped.

I was about to call him out for acting so hostile all of a sudden, but he snapped the reins of the horse, and I was knocked back. We galloped down the street for several hundred feet, nearly crushing a fair number of pedestrians, until he turned a corner. Immediately, I knew our destination: An Excutatian flag flew over the front door of a small, unassuming townhouse. I felt a flush of relief in the knowledge that I was about to be back with my own people, but it drained away as I noticed a mix of problems — the gate was chained shut, there was no activity inside or out, and there were elves. A *lot* of elves, armed on chariots, blocking our path.

One rode forward on a terrifying black horse, a commander. He called, "Did you think Sitika would protect you, Acturas? After all that Excutatem has wrought here? It was easy to arrange a treaty — the inquisitors open the gates to us, and we root out the threat for them. The threat, of course, being you two."

Acturas gripped the reins, his hands white. The horse whinnied nervously and backed up, and the soldiers began to close in. Acturas seemed more nervous than I had seen him since the first night, and as the commander came nearer, I realized why: It was the same elf that had attacked us in the inn outside Exceres. And I presumed it was the same awful horse. His armor was no longer bloodstained, but I could tell the grudge was still festering in the wound in his shoulder.

Acturas took a moment to consider, then yanked on the reins and spun the horse around, toward the northern gate. The wagon nearly flipped, and I gripped the sides with my heart pounding as the elves gave chase. I heard the rumbling of chariots behind us, but I stayed low, not daring to peek out as a volley of arrows thudded against the cart.

Their chariots were designed for speed, and they were easily gaining on us. We would've been caught in seconds if Acturas hadn't maneuvered the wagon down an exit just before they reached us, forcing them to swerve out of the way or continue past the street. We lost only four or five with that trick, but it bought us some time.

We neared the wall, and I doubted Acturas could pull off another flank. We barreled down the street as fast as the horse allowed, the open gate directly ahead of us. It seemed like we were going to make it, but the elves were coordinated, and the gate began to grind closed faster than I thought possible for one that size.

Acturas didn't stop. He continued to whip the reins faster and harder, the horse picking up speed, and I could have reached up and touched the gate as we slipped under it. Once they saw we had escaped, they tried to reverse the gate from shutting, but it cost them valuable time, and by the time they were outside, we were gone.

We pulled off onto the side of the road, the sounds of the city long behind us and thick woods on all sides. We took a moment of silence to catch our breath before Acturas directed me to get out. I did. He took his bag and sword from the wagon and led me deeper into the trees, where it would be harder to be spotted.

He looked exhausted. I was too, but he had done the brunt of the work. It was no wonder he snapped at me before — I'd snap too if I had to deal with me all the time.

"Hey, thanks for that back there. It was… a lot, and I don't think anybody could've done it except you," I said. I had never felt so lucky to have him on my side.

He was quiet for a second. "You know," he finally muttered, "you almost seem sincere."

I was taken aback. "I– what do you mean by that? I was only thanking you for saving our lives, what's the matter with you–"

"With *me?* What's the matter with *me?!* You're the one who's being hunted to the edges of the continent by an enemy your fool of a father practically *invited* to come conquer us. You would be dead twenty times over if it weren't for me, and you're asking what *my* problem is?!"

"Why are you acting like this all of a sudden? I just told you that I appreciate your help! *I'm* supposed to be in charge, but I let you call all the shots, use *my* money, I even let you win at poker on the ship! What else do you expect me to do?" I demanded. I had never expected that kind of contempt from Acturas.

"You Excutari are all the same. Doesn't matter if it's Frema, Jourdan, or you, every one of you is just as disgraced," he hissed with a hatred that made it very clear he meant it. "And you think that saying 'hey, thanks' *one time* after we barely escape with our lives is good enough to make it worth it? You live in a bubble, Damion. You're completely disconnected from the real world. You on the throne would be the death of Excutatem."

He drew his sword.

"I won't let that happen."

It took me embarrassingly long to understand what he was getting at. Once it hit me, I couldn't help but laugh at the absurdity of it.

Between laughs, I managed to squeeze out, "*You– you mean–* to what, *kill me?* You really think you can do that?"

"THIS IS NO TIME TO BE LAUGHING!" he screamed as he slashed at me with the sword, leaving a fresh, deep cut across my forearm. It wasn't as funny anymore.

He reached down and tore the sheath off my belt, tossing my knife to the side. I tried to back away, but he grabbed me by the shoulder and pushed me to the ground.

He breathed in sharply. "You know, Damion, you've always been a little slow, but this has to be a new low for you. '*You really think you can do that?*'" he mocked in an exaggerated, high-pitched voice, "I do. Because you have no real power, in Excutatem or anywhere else. Who's going to stop me?"

I tried to steady my voice. "Are you stupid? You made an oath to the Elementals, you can't let any harm come to me. Did you forget about that? You'd go to Trench for this."

His eyes shifted to the cut across my arm. "Well, if I'm already damned, I might as well see it through. I just wish I had let you die earlier, if it was going to end like this anyway."

My heart sank as I realized the full weight of what he meant. "So… you've been planning this all along? Why take me all this way, then? Why not just kill me in the beginning, or leave me to die in the castle? I–" My voice cracked, but I couldn't calm myself. "I don't understand."

He sighed. "I've been planning this far longer than you can imagine. I had to escape with you if I ever wanted to return — if I went alone, I was a coward, but if I went with you, then I was the noble warrior *defending* the coward. I could smuggle you out of the empire, all the way to Sitika, which happened to be the only place in the world I could finish you off without the Elementals seeing." He wiped a smudge of blood from his sword. "It's a little late for that, but I'm sure they'll forgive me if it means saving the empire." He seemed almost giddy with the brilliance of his plan, and I hated to think how long he had been waiting for this.

"Now, Excutari, I am going to do just that. I am going to return with an army, push out the elves and that old clown Neiphorous. The people will celebrate my victory, and I doubt anyone will even ask what happened to you. You're nothing but an afterthought, an obstacle between me and the strongest human empire to ever exist."

"Now," he said, "die."

He raised his sword above his head, ready to strike at me. I would've been killed instantly if he did; Acturas knew what he was doing. Instinctively, I drove my hand into my bag, desperate to find anything that could save me. My knuckle knocked into it, and it came rushing back to me in a blur: the first night on the run, in the inn, the gift the Elementals had given me. I unclasped the sheath blindly as Acturas's sword swooped down. It never landed. Swinging wildly, I slashed the Valkyrie knife into his sword, deflecting it just before it landed.

Acturas was too stunned to react. He hadn't expected me to have any more weapons, since I had never told him about the Valkyrie blade, which was now clutched heavy in my hand. He reacted quickly, but I moved faster. His sword caught my upper arm, but the adrenaline carried me off the ground. In a flash, before I even understood what I was doing, my knife was driven into Acturas's chest.

He stumbled backwards, mouth agape in disbelief, and I withdrew my knife with both hands to stop them from shaking. I took a step back. Acturas's shirt quickly darkened as he fell, and I did too, letting the dagger drop to my side as I was paralyzed by shock.

I was about to turn and run off when I heard a distant snap. I whipped around just in time for an arrow to whiz past my head. I heard shouts through the trees as the elves closed in on us, and it was clear that there was no use running. Still, not willing to give up, I scrambled to my feet.

I hadn't even stood up before another thud knocked me back into the dirt. I felt blood flowing from my shoulder. There was no pain, just intense pressure, and I could see the arrow shaft in my peripheral vision above my arm. I pulled myself to sit up and looked at the elves — nine archers along the street, their bows all nocked. So these would be my killers: faceless, nameless soldiers who would get a medal for their bravery and tell the story in bars for the next fifty years. That wasn't fair. But none of this was, was it?

Another snap, another arrow, this one in my chest, knocking me flat against the ground. It felt like a prick, nothing more. More blood. I was suddenly dizzy with vertigo, and it grew hard to breathe as my vision began to fade.

My ears were ringing, but I could feel the vibrations through the earth of the commander's footsteps as he walked to me. He was wearing no helmet, clearly showing off his smug satisfaction as he finally won his revenge. He savored the moment as he raised his lance above me. I couldn't bring myself to move.

Time slowed as he drove it down directly over my heart. There was no way he could miss. This was it. I stared past him, toward the treetops, blackness edging into my periphery. But I stayed alive.

Why?

I refocused on my executioner to see he was no longer above me, but crumbling to the ground, an arrow in his throat. I could barely process what was happening, especially when an exhausted Cedric ran up beside me, bow in hand, firing toward the elves. Was I hallucinating? More arrows flew from unknown sources behind us. After a minute of exchange between the elves on the street and whoever had arrived to my rescue, the air stilled.

Cedric glanced at Acturas, slain, and then at me. He shouted frantically to someone deeper in the woods, but I couldn't hear what he said, and I had no time to see who it was before the world faded to black.

Chapter Sixteen

When I awoke, I was laying on a cot in a large
tent. The arrows were gone, and my wounds were
bandaged, though too sore to move. I took a handful
of minutes off staring at the linen ceiling of the tent,
but when I turned my head, a banner hanging by the
opening caught my eye. The black trim and silver
detailing was unmistakable: the Excutatian flag. I was
skeptical of it. After all I had been through, I struggled
to believe that the flag signified anything more than
some farmer stumbled across it on the ground and
figured it would make for a nice tent door.

I tried to sit up, but the adrenaline had long
since worn off, and every scrape and bruise on my body
flared at once. I groaned and collapsed back down. I
didn't like being incapacitated — it was dangerous. I
heard sudden movement outside, and I shut my mouth
immediately, but I knew whoever was out there had
already heard me. Footsteps approached through the
grass, and I gritted my teeth as I propped myself up
on my elbows to see my visitor. When she entered, I
couldn't help but smile.

"Commander Mauria?" I choked out, startled at how raspy my voice was. "I had– I mean, I didn't expect… I thought you had, uh, *gone down with the ship* in Exceres."

Meghan Mauria, commander of the castle guard, stood by the door of the tent. She wore the same navy blue uniform she'd worn in Exceres, albeit marked with dirt and scratches, with her hair tied back in a definitively not-uniform fashion. She smiled back, but I could tell there was a long and hard-fought journey behind it. "Well, many did. I was one of the lucky ones."

My face quickly dropped. Sensing my incoming question, she somberly informed me, "We have four hundred accounted for. It's less than ideal… much less… but I'm sure this isn't all that's left. There must be thousands more of our soldiers scattered across the continent, and more are arriving every day." Before I had a chance to follow up, she changed the subject. "But that's for later. How are you feeling?"

I rolled my shoulder as if to check, even though I was already familiar with the searing pain radiating from beneath my bandage. "Bad. Although, for what it's worth, it could definitely be worse. I honestly didn't think I'd make it."

With complete earnesty, she said, "That makes two of us. You wouldn't be here if we didn't get a healing powder from one of our contacts in the desert. I can't count the number of times I thought you were gone before they got it to you — no one can come back from that naturally. It's good you're feeling better than dead, though, even if not by much."

I nodded. I decided to shift the conversation off of me, needing a distraction from the pain. "So, you've all just been hiding out in the South? Regrouping? All this time?"

"I'd prefer *laying low* over 'hiding out', but yes, we've been amassing our forces here since the attack. I actually only arrived here recently, since we ran into our share of obstacles in the plains up north. The elves are all across the continent, now — though, with a fair bit of luck, we made it past them. How did *you* get this far? Is it true that General Assix fled with you?"

The mention of Acturas brought back violent flashbacks of cutting him open. The room began to spin. "Yes, that's true," I mumbled. I had to tell her about what happened, but the question of who she was really loyal toward tugged at me. I was the prince, but he had been her direct superior. I could just lie, say the elves took him, or that he died at sea, or that…

No. No more lying. There was a good chance that by next week I would be the sole living Excutari, and I was going to act like it whether it was easy or not. Besides, Mauria might have been the only one in the world I could trust.

I collected my words. "I'm sorry to say he had ulterior motives. He put me in a situation which forced me to relieve him of duty."

She took a moment to digest the news, but she clearly understood. "I… I can't believe that General Assix could commit treachery against *you*. What unforgiving times we live in." She fixed a button on her coat. "Well then, I only wanted to see what state you are in. I will leave you to rest now, my lord." Before she turned to leave, however, a realization struck her.

"Oh," she said, "I nearly forgot. There's a boy who wants to see you — Cedric? What shall we do with him? If I may speak freely, I don't trust him —

the tales he told of your journey together were wildly embellished. He even claims you slayed the Sirens of Pleay."

"Well, four of them. Long story, for another time. Is Cedric here?" I was suddenly presented with a more important issue than Sirens or Acturas: I had to talk to Cedric.

"He is. We've kept him detained in a holding tent until you awoke to pass judgment. Shall we bring him?"

"Yes, I would appreciate that. Thank you," I said almost too quickly.

Before she turned and left, she glanced at me with a sly expression, one I couldn't quite decipher until a moment later. The last time she'd seen me, I wouldn't have said 'thank you' to just about anybody. She left to fetch Cedric, and I held my breath waiting for their return.

It took only a handful of minutes before another hand parted the flag, and Cedric entered with Meghan at his heels. He looked pretty messed up — every part of him was smattered with mud, and he had cuts across his face and arms that I couldn't begin to place. They had given him fresh clothes, though they fit too loosely, and he was wearing sandals for some reason. Though, after weeks of running around in boots, I couldn't blame him, and I made a note to ask Meghan if they had any extra pairs.

Now for the hard part. Cedric was standing in front of me. The same Cedric who had potentially lured us to the elves, conspired with the elves, *was* an elf. Why was he here? Why did he save me from who I assumed were his allies? I didn't know his motives, I didn't know his side, I didn't know his past. Did I even know *him?*

"Hey, Damion," he said weakly. There was a melancholy quietness in his voice unlike anything I'd heard from him.

I closed my eyes, already unsure of how to proceed. It was clear, at least, that whatever happened had to be between us alone.

"Commander, would you mind stepping out?" I asked, but it was clearly an order. Hesitantly, she complied.

Once we were alone, I started. "So. Is it true? What Acturas said?" I wouldn't believe it until I heard it from him.

"Acturas said a lot of things, Damion, you have to be more–"

"Are you an elf?"

He fell silent. I couldn't read the expression on his face. Shame? Frustration? Anger? I held my breath.

At last, he simply replied, "Yeah."

To be honest, I expected more. I expected my heart to break and for tears to cascade down my cheeks and for me to banish him from my sight, but after all the ways my world flipped on itself the past few days, this suddenly seemed so unimportant. I couldn't muster much more than an "oh, okay".

He blinked, surprised. Nervously, he continued, "Well, see, I'm not a 'full' elf. My mom was from Aural. She came to Excutatem after she met my dad. He was a human sailor, but he died when I was really young, and she got caught up with some people from Ramethus… and then there was the war…"

I thought about what he was saying, and I couldn't help but chuckle. He looked bewildered, and I rushed to backtrack.

"No," I said, failing to control my laughter, "I'm not laughing at *that*, I promise. It's just, Acturas made such a big deal about this, but… I expected it to be more climactic, that's all. I honestly don't really mind."

He exhaled deeply. I could just about hear his heartbeat calm.

"By the way," I continued, "what were you *actually* doing in the embassy? I mean, I'm assuming you weren't turning us over to the elves."

"The former ambassador was this old guy named Lucciun. He and I go way back — he helped my mom get out of her debt. Anyway, I figured he could get us a carriage if I asked, but I didn't know he'd been recalled to Minesra after the war, and that new ambassador was… worse. Apparently, the elves knew we were traveling together and sent birds ahead with warnings, so they arrested me as soon as I showed up."

"How'd you get away? They just let you go?"

He laughed hard, then pointed out the scratches on his arms that appeared suspiciously more like blade cuts than branch scrapes. "No way, they tried to take me out like twelve times. After you went down with the ambassador, the guards were breaking down the door, but I couldn't jump down right after y'all because I knew Acturas would gut me. After you two got up on the fence, I hugged the windowsill and climbed onto the roof, then jumped over the fence and into a tree. It sounds cooler than it was — I totally thought I was gonna die."

I grinned at the idea of Cedric doing parkour over the Minesran embassy. My wound ached from laughing, but I didn't care. After everything, Cedric had been on my side all along. I would be content sitting in silence as long as I was beside him, but something occurred to me. My face dropped.

"So," I began slowly, "I guess you know who I am now — I mean, who I *really* am. Are you just okay with that?" I couldn't expect him to just ignore that I was probably the last rightful heir to the Excutatian throne.

A smirk crept up on his face. "Yeah, about that," he started, and I had a feeling he wanted to get this off his chest for a long while. "I knew this whole time. You told me that night you got drunk in my town."

No words came to me besides "oh". I couldn't believe Acturas and I had put so much effort into keeping our identities secret when I had told him upfront the day I met him. That settled it for me: Cedric was on my side, and I was a complete idiot.

We talked until he had to leave so an army medic could tend to my bandages. Meghan came in with three men trailing her whom I recognized as high ranking leaders in the imperial court. They bowed their heads when they saw me.

"Lord Excutari," she started, "as the highest noble present, you assume military command of the encampment. We have a plan, but only with your direction can we carry through with it. Please, consider carefully."

She laid down parchment on a table they had brought in, and I saw it was a map of Exceres. "We've been working for weeks to formulate the best retaliation strategy. We all believe it's capable of taking back the city."

She began to explain. It started promising, but as it went on, it seemed more and more outlandish.

"So, you're saying that we should attack at my *family's execution?* You really think that would work?" I asked.

"Well, like I said, it would be easiest to sneak in, there will be leagues of elven military leaders present, and it's the closest they'll allow a crowd to get to the castle for the foreseeable future. We have the soldiers and the plan. With your support, we can do this."

I thought about it. Really, it was *insane.* But one question would not leave me alone, and I could no longer ignore it. *What would a king do?*

PART II

Chapter Seventeen

Two weeks later, I stood in the crowd, which made me uneasy. I had a role to play, but not right now. Now, I was just waiting. Waiting, and watching for the signal.

I looked around for faces I recognized, but I couldn't see much with my hood pulled up. If there was anywhere I would be recognized, it would be here, and this was *not* the time to take that chance. The Valkyrie knife hung heavy from my belt. I shifted my weight from side to side. Even if everything went according to plan, there was a fair chance we would lose anyway, definitively and ingloriously.

There was a rumble through the crowd. I looked up as far as I dared and felt a chill roll down my spine. On the stage a hundred feet away from me, high enough to be seen over the heads of the hundreds of spectators, they were bringing out ten prisoners. Each wore plain garbs, stained, with their hands chained in front of them and a sack over their heads. I knew my sister and grandmother would be among them, but everyone in the procession was too pale and thin to distinguish.

A man stepped up to a podium. Not an elf, but a human. My mouth went dry; he was a terror to behold for any human nobleman. Acturas's mentor and predecessor, Remius Neiphorous. *With Remius as a role model, no wonder he turned into such a snake,* I thought. He radiated power as he stepped up to the podium with leisurely confidence, the way a lion would approach a wounded deer, intensified by the shadow of the castle looming in the backdrop.

"Excutatians!" Remius began heartily, his voice powerful enough to reach even the furthest fringes of the crowd, "the time has come at last. For too long, we have been battered by the horrors of this dark era — an era of war, an era of division, an era of famine. For too long, we have been crushed under the oppressive weight of the imperial family and its wrongdoings. I stand before you all to declare that we have reached the end! The end of that era, and the end of the Excutari reign!"

The crowd burst into cheers. Remius paused, letting the clamor build, harnessing the crowd's energy to carry his point. As the applause naturally settled, he continued.

"For ten years now, our people have anguished under the tyranny of a king who saw ships stacked with blood-stained shields dock in the bay and ordered a thousand more be sent out. Well, that king is nothing but a memory now! And his heir, who fled in silence as his city was under siege, is nowhere to be seen. A Hall of Elements molded by the personal whims of an emperor who had no true loyalty to the Elementals. And he called *me* the heretic, yet I had Elementalists of my own — Aeres of Felfort, who had been driven from his homeland for daring to stand up against the regime, now returned as a hero!"

More applause followed, my stomach turning at the mention of that name. If he was still in the city, that would complicate our plan — Elementalists are the most powerful mages left in the West, and we were woefully unprepared to fight one.

I was relieved when Remius added, "Though he wished to be here today, he had been called to root out imperial strongholds elsewhere. Thankfully, *I* am here to stay. As we cast out the Excutari line, the Neiphorous name will take its place, as it was always destined to do. My ancestors were the first emperors of this land, and at last, we are returned to our rightful place on the throne. Excutatem will never again suffer illegitimate kings — I, as emperor, will undo their damage and rebuild our empire greater than ever before!"

Finally, to the primal satisfaction of the crowd, he turned to the executioners at the side of each prisoner and waved for them to remove the bags. I saw, at last, each of their faces: I recognized each of them from the court, military leaders or noblemen, but I didn't know six of them by name. I knew one to be a baron, one was an admiral who led the conquest of the Isles of Penelopene, and of course, I recognized my sister and grandmother. I had never before seen them so fraught. I couldn't imagine the torments they had unjustly suffered — well, maybe not so unjustly in the former queen's case, considering her reign wasn't what you'd call *beloved*. Her abdication was a festival, and now it seemed her execution was, too.

It was clear Remius didn't intend to make the crowd wait long. I could feel the rabid urgency in the air — he had masterfully worked them up, as he always did. He raised his hand, and the executioners raised their axes at attention. Then, loud enough it echoed down the whole length of the street, he shouted, "Our new age begins here!" and dropped his hand.

The axes never landed, because the arrows did first. I had never felt such relief as the moment I saw the executioners crumple to the ground. The archers had been positioned inside nearby windows, out of view of elven sentries but still close enough to avoid any chance of missing. Remius, though, did not fall. He seemed to notice the arrow before it had even covered half the distance between them, and he ducked out of its path a moment before it would have embedded itself in his eye. He drew his sword as screams erupted and spectators scattered from the scene.

From within the crowd, hundreds of people surged forward instead of back. Not civilians, but soldiers whose armor had been concealed by coats and the density of the crowd. They drew knives, swords, and axes, charging the stage where elf soldiers rushed to meet them. I ducked out of the way and into a back alley, as the strategy directed, and I rushed to get to the back of the stage before the entirety of the audience had fled.

I paid no mind to the sounds of battle which had sprung up around me. I knew more of my soldiers had arrived at strategic points around the city and were fighting to the death to reclaim control, at least for a time. I had my own role to play, and no time to waste.

I arrived at the stage. Despite my cautiousness, I kept my knife sheathed to create a facade of calmness, and I climbed the steps. I froze at the top. It was empty, save for the corpses of the executioners which lay motionless on the ground. The hostages were gone, somehow — but, even worse, *Remius* was gone. It didn't seem possible they could have escaped so quickly. I looked out to the crowd, but saw no sign of them anywhere. How…?

I cursed under my breath. They knew we'd come. I needed to find Mauria as soon as possible and improvise a new plan. I spun around, but stumbled backwards at once, drawing my knife and backing into center stage. A huge soldier in human armor climbed the steps, casually spinning a flail at his side. Behind him, four elves blocked the stairway, trapping us together.

"Damion Excutari!" he shouted over the cacophony of the fleeing crowd. A few people turned back to see what was happening, but were quickly ushered away by elven soldiers trying to control the situation. The new challenger took off his helmet with his free hand, and I would have groaned in annoyance if we weren't about to fight to the death.

"Arrat Neiphorous," I returned, since it seemed we were exchanging names.

"Aw, you remember me?" he called back with feigned flattery. He was a complete meathead, absolutely nothing like his father, but he was freakishly good at two things: One, beating me in jousts when we were growing up together in the court; and two, killing people.

"How could I forget? Not many people throw up on the crown prince at his ninth birthday ceremony. It leaves an impression."

"You're still mad about that? It *barely* got on you. But there's no time for that — my dad really wanted to kill you himself, but he said that if any of us got the chance, it was fine to go ahead and do it. You really made him mad by running, you know. Not a good idea," he said with a flick of his flail to accentuate the point.

I raised my knife and tried to mask my panic. His flail looked pretty heavy, and the ball at the end of the chain was splintered into violent spikes. I remembered sparring with him as a kid, and if this would be anything like that, I was painfully unequipped for it.

Arrat stepped forward and to the side, beginning an obvious circling maneuver he'd love to pull off whenever we practiced. I countered by backing up, moving opposite to him so that he would always stay in front of me.

"You were never good at sparring," he said as more of an observation than a jab.

"Who knows? Maybe I learned," I replied, suddenly wishing I had trained more with Acturas when I had the chance.

Without warning, as if to test whether I really *had* improved, he lunged forward, swinging out with his flail directly toward my head. I ducked out of the way just in time, though I could've sworn I felt the wind from the weapon graze me.

"I don't know," he said, completely deadpan, "you're still kinda slow. Maybe it would be easier if you just stood still and let me kill you."

I was going to think up some clever and quotable retort before I realized he was completely serious, and I lost any capacity to respond. It cemented for me what I already knew: A fight between me and Arrat would only end one way. I needed to get off this stage, but the only exit was blocked by guards, and there was an eight-foot drop on both sides.

My attention was drawn back to Arrat by the rattling of the chain as he spun the ball around in a figure 8 in front of him. Jumping off the platform seemed preferable to being on the receiving end of a twenty-pound spiked ball to the face. I backed up to the ledge as he charged me again, but my nerves won out, and I dodged to the side just in time. No matter how life-threatening it was to be *on* the platform, I couldn't beat the part of my brain that was designed to make me *not* fall to my death.

I brandished my knife again. He would never let me get close enough to land a hit. I thought about how much I wished I had a–

Arrat cried out and stumbled back, hands grasping at his shoulder. An arrow had lodged itself in the crack between his breastplate and sleeve, and I rushed to the side of the platform to see who had fired it.

"Come on!" Cedric yelled at me, bow in hand, as he nocked another arrow. I looked behind me; the soldiers, having realized what had happened, now flooded onto the stage to help Arrat and stop me from escaping. I had no time to waste. Clenching my teeth, I scooted to the very edge of the platform, and right before a soldier reached me, pushed off.

The fall felt like it lasted an eternity, though it was probably no more than two seconds. What was very real was the flare of pain that shot up through my leg the second I made contact with the ground. I groaned, but found myself being pulled away from the stage as Arrat shouted orders to his troops behind us.

We dashed down the street, past fighting soldiers and civilians still caught in the commotion. We needed to strategize and regroup, but neither of us knew where to find Commander Mauria or any semblance of an organized authority. Through the din of battle, I heard rapidly approaching clopping behind us. I pushed Cedric out of the way just in time to avoid him being bludgeoned by Arrat's flail.

His horse overshot us, and he had to make a wide turn to reverse direction. I spun around, looking for anywhere to go. In front of us, Arrat blocked the road. We could run the other way, but I didn't like our prospect of outrunning a horse. Surrounding us was nothing but fighting between my soldiers and elves, and I didn't want to get caught up in that any more than I wanted to deal with Arrat. That left…

As Arrat charged back at us, I grabbed Cedric's hand and pulled him to the right. There was a long walkway up towards the front gate, but Arrat would have to ditch the horse if he wanted to follow us, and that would buy us enough time to get inside — probably. We neared the top of the path, and I saw the doors were… open? I figured they just didn't expect an attack, but it still felt like an oversight.

I had no choice but to continue on, though, since Arrat had already leapt to the ground and was gaining on us, clearly bloodthirsty and itching to put his bludgeon to use. Together, with me leading the way despite the flaring pain in my leg, Cedric and I slipped past the gate and into the castle.

Chapter Eighteen

We tore up the steps, my shin burning like fire with each stride. The pounding of Arrat's armored footsteps on the hardwood was steadily gaining on us, and I could barely push myself any faster down the gilded corridors.

The one clear advantage I had in this moment was that this wasn't just my home territory, it *was* my home. Pulling Cedric along, I did my best to slip down side hallways at every opportunity, hoping that it would put me ahead enough to lose him for just a moment, enough to sneak out and somehow regroup with my forces.

Coming up on a T-intersection in the hallway, I turned right, and then immediately turned down a shallow corridor branching off. At the end was a door to the servants' passages — easily ignorable, perfect for escape. I slid open the small iron lock, pulled the door open, and silently ushered Cedric in. Glancing behind me only for a second, I squeezed through, clicking it closed as quietly as I could.

Not wasting any time to see if he would follow, we squeezed down the narrow hallway, my shoulders scraping against the rough walls and my hair occasionally brushing the low ceiling. I had never been back here before, but I knew that the kitchens were in this *general* direction, and I happened to have had prior experience sneaking out from there.

After shuffling down the passage, dodging hanging beams that were never a priority to fix, I stopped Cedric hard and gestured toward a door. Painted in white on the splintering wood was the word "Kitchen". Desperate not to waste any more time, I twisted the handle. It wouldn't turn. I tried again with both hands, twisted so hard my hand burned, but it was locked. Beginning to panic, I continued down the passage to the next door, labeled "Dining Hall". It was locked from the other side too.

Deciding that there was no sense in trying to break down solid oak, we moved on. We tried every door we passed, and each one was locked tight. The hall was cut off by staircases, and we had no choice but to climb to the upper levels, not willing to accept we would have to turn back the way we came.

After testing every door we came across, with my back aching from crouching, I couldn't keep going. I sat back against the stone exterior wall and put my head in my hands.

Everything had gone wrong. We were *so* close to winning, we were *right there*, yet now I was trapped in a dusty servants' corridor while my last remaining soldiers fought in vain just on the other side of this wall, the castle that was my home now my prison. I was no emperor; I was hardly a survivor. A fugitive. A conspirator. There was no end to the list of titles the elves would put after my name once Neiphorous inevitably caught up to me, brought me out onto the stage with my sister... and Cedric...

A shuffling just outside the nearest door made me shoot to my feet. I tentatively snuck closer, my heart racing, and Cedric readied his knife as he positioned himself on the other side of the door. It was a muffled conversation, clearly not in any Humanic language. Elvish, surely.

Cedric positioned his ear until it hovered just next to the door, careful not to betray our hiding spot. He listened in on the conversation, his brow furrowed — whether in confusion or concern, I couldn't tell.

After an eternal minute had passed, he leaned over and whispered in my ear, "They've put two soldiers at every door to the maintenance halls and are planning to send a squad through soon to catch us. We need to get out now."

I didn't need to be told that. Waiting around in these tunnels only gave Neiphorous more time to pin us down. If we were going to survive this, we had to act now. I leaned over to Cedric's ear and whispered my plan; he returned an anxious glance, but nodded and readied himself behind the door.

I took a series of deep breaths. I felt for my knife sheathed on my belt. Content that I was definitely about to die, I cleared my throat and knocked on the door.

The conversation froze. I knocked again. There was a pause, then the door swung open, and I found a sword to my chest in an instant. My heart was ready to break out of my rib cage and escape on its own, and it took all of my self-control not to show it. I saw two elven soldiers standing in the doorway — they glanced at each other, unsure of what to do.

"I surrender," I said, "you caught me. Take me to Neiphorous."

The elf with the sword to my chest made no move; the other shifted on his feet, barely blinking so as not to take his eyes off of me for a second. Then, they both spoke at once, looked at each other again, and silently agreed that the one with the sword would do the talking for now. He glanced briefly around the hallway. Cedric had positioned himself so that when the door opened, he was concealed from view. It seemed to work on the soldier.

He spoke in a cripplingly thick accent. "There are two of you. Where is the disgraced half-elf?"

"We were separated. I can't defeat you alone, so I'm surrendering. Please, take me to Neiphorous," I repeated, never thinking that those words would ever leave my mouth.

The elves glanced at each other again, skeptical of my surrender, but it seemed it was simply too good to let go. As the other elf stepped forward to grab me, Cedric whirled around the door with his knife, plunging it into the heart of the one with his sword against my chest. I pushed back against the second soldier, stunning him, but he didn't fall back against the wall like I expected him to. Instead, he drew a long, concealed blade from his arm guard. I lurched away, but with my back already against the wall, there was nowhere to go. The elf lunged at me with the knife.

Before it reached me, Cedric threw himself in front of the elven blade. It cut through his side, reappearing bloody from the slice it made in his shirt. Cedric seemed unfazed, jamming his knife into the elf's collar bone just below his helmet, killing him just as quickly as the first. He watched the elf collapse to the floor, then turned towards me, his breathing harsh.

I tried to ask him if he was okay, but he cut me off. "Don't worry about me, I can take care of that later. Let's go."

He didn't wait for a response, turning and stepping through the door. I followed, trying to push away my concern. I was probably just imagining that he was leaning more on the door frame than usual. He would be fine.

In the hallway outside the door, I immediately recognized our surroundings. "There's a staircase nearby that should be able to take us down to the kitchen. If we can get through–"

I was cut off by the echo of several pairs of metal boots marching from around a corner at the end of the hallway. A group was coming, and I thought our chances of them being a band of survivor Elementalists here to save the day were pretty slim.

Wasting no time, I grabbed Cedric's forearm and broke into a sprint in the other direction, skipping past the maintenance door and turning onto another hall. If they hadn't seen us, they surely heard our pounding footsteps, because they picked up to a run after us. Searching for any way to hide or escape, I remembered that my room was on this hall, my room with my sword, my imperial armor, and a door reinforced with steel hinges. I picked up the pace, flying as fast as I could with Cedric just behind me. I heard our pursuers not far behind, shouting out to us in Elvish, but it only made me push harder. Just to the end of this hall. Just a little bit longer — we'd make it. We'd make it.

I practically collided with the door, twisting the handle and throwing it open. I slipped in, pulling Cedric in after me and slamming the door closed as soon as he was through. The locks on all of the bedrooms in the castle were virtually unbreakable. I took a shuddering breath and leaned back against the door. Cedric collapsed.

He fell back against the wall, his breathing strained and exhausted. I saw that blood ran down the entire length of his left leg. I dropped down to my knees next to him, grabbed his shoulders, but his eyes were focused on the space behind my head. Then, they flickered just a bit, and he whispered, "Damion, behind you".

I rolled to the side and scrambled to my feet. My blood burned when I saw Remius standing beside the door. He must have been waiting for us, hiding the same way Cedric did from the soldiers. My hand went to my knife, but he lifted his rapier to my chest, and I backed away.

"Damion Excutari, it's been so long — or, should I say, *Emperor* Damion." He clicked his tongue and sighed. "Doesn't roll off the tongue very well, unfortunately. Luckily for us both, you won't be needing the title much longer."

I shot a glance around, but my armor stand was empty. He had planned that we'd come here — knowing Neiphorous, he probably planned every step of this precisely, from the escape into the maintenance halls to the killing of the soldiers and the chase through the corridor. There was no way I was ever getting away from him alive. Maybe if I had just surrendered, then Cedric wouldn't be bleeding to death on the floor.

"Remius," I started. At the very least, I could try to negotiate so that one of us would survive. "It's over. You win. You always would. I'll go with you, but–"

"If you're going to beg me not to kill your boyfriend, don't bother. I won't even have to; things are looking pretty grim for him way down on the floor there."

My face burned. Desperation began to gnaw at me.

"If you let us live, I'll abdicate. To you, publicly. You'll get everything you ever wanted, we'll disappear forever. You don't gain anything from killing me, and Cedric doesn't pose a threat to you at all. This is the wrong move."

"For the one with a blade at his chest, you *do* seem to be an authority on 'wrong moves'. If I were you, I'd be directing my last breaths in the mortal realm toward the Elementals, though none of them can save you now."

He didn't give me any chance to respond. "Damion, since my masterful operation that claimed this city for the Neiphorous manor, to whom it has always rightfully belonged, *you* have been the only deviation from my plan. *You* have been the only threat to my dominion. The elves want me to bring you to the chopping block in Mésura, but I can assure you, you will not leave this room ever again." His gaze flickered to the window, then back at me, a grin slowly etching itself onto his face. "At least, not through the door."

He closed in, and I backed up until I hit the wall, not wanting to be anywhere near that window. He thrust his sword straight into where I was standing, forcing me to move, practically herding me. Why didn't he just stab me? Why was he prolonging this? His rapier came straight for my nose; I ducked out of the way, incidentally inching nearer and nearer to the outer wall of the room where I would presumably make my final fall. He swiped at my legs, forcing me to jump back, then stabbed again, making me stumble out of the way.

I could feel sunlight from the window warming my arms through the glass. The glare from behind me morphed Neiphorous into a sinister silhouette lurking closer, his sword a horrible extension of his form. I couldn't do anything but shake my head softly, unable to conceive that *this*, after everything, was how I would end. Remius raised his rapier to jab straight at me one last time, knowing that I had nowhere to go but out. Then, there was a second shape through the glare, and I ducked out of the way as Neiphorous was sent stumbling into the window.

It shattered instantly, and he fell back against the sill, but was caught by his rapier as it buried into the wooden frame. Cedric stumbled away, clutching his side, and for the first time I hesitated. My fear overpowered my will to fight, and no matter how much I wanted to, I couldn't force myself to bring my knife down over Remius. In the split second I stood frozen, he pulled himself back in from the window and reclaimed his weapon.

Staring down Cedric, he hissed, "You stupid *elf*." Disdain dripped from his voice. Cedric was in no position to defend himself as Neiphorous raised his rapier over his shoulder. I could only watch as he brought it down, spraying blood across the broken window fragments. I don't know if I screamed; all I remember is breaking out of my stupor and launching myself into him. He pivoted, but not quickly enough to stop me from grabbing his armor and plunging my knife into his side. He reared away, but my hand caught on his breastplate, sending me tumbling into him. My momentum carried us both past Cedric and toward the window.

Shards of glass scraped my side, and my head collided with the frame hard enough to leave my ears ringing. A fragment of wood splintered in my forehead, but I didn't feel it. I was overtaken by an intense dizziness, my entire body numb and cold as I plummeted fifty feet from the broken window into the moat below. Looking up at the bloodstained, cracked windowsill, I couldn't think of anything except that *this* must finally have been the worst failure of my life.

Chapter Nineteen

When I came back to life, I wished that I hadn't.

Soaking wet and freezing, I lay on my back on a riverbank downstream from the castle moat. Blood had dried down the length of my face and scattered across the sand, but the real pain raged inside my head. I stayed motionless for a long time, watching the stars only in my peripheral vision because I feared the exertion of turning my head would make me throw up. Once I finally found the strength to push myself up onto my elbows, I threw up anyway. Even propping myself up an inch off the ground was the most exhausting effort of my life. Maybe I really had died from the fall.

Once I caught my breath, I rolled over and sat up, quickly swallowing the nausea that accompanied the motion. I looked up at the sky. I could just barely make out the rumbling of ocean waves far downriver. I might have appreciated how quiet the city was if it didn't carry the coldest, cruelest revelation I'd had yet: the battle was over. I was alone. My remaining soldiers would never follow me again after the failure that day. I prayed Cedric wasn't dead, but if the alternative was being captured, I wasn't sure which was worse for him.

I almost began to miss Acturas — at least, the Acturas I used to know. Even the moon hid behind the tree line, embarrassed to look at me. I guess I was never able to do this after all. I was never meant to be king.

One star in particular caught my eye. Not any bigger than the others, but somehow brighter. And moving. At first I thought that it was a shooting star, but it was too slow, and it gradually grew brighter as I realized it was getting closer. Astounded, I watched it until it was too bright to look at. I covered my eyes with my arm, the light burning red on the back of my hand.

I heard a sound like large wings folding in, and the light dispersed in wisps of luminous fog. I put my arm down and saw a figure who, to my surprise, I recognized. He wore the same basic white shirt over his ashen gray skin as he had when I first encountered him that night in the inn.

"Damion Excutari?" he said.

"Exolirus?" I returned, my voice hoarser than I expected.

"That's *lord* Exolirus to you. I might just be the messenger, but I'm still an Elemental. Speaking of, I have another message for you."

My face burned. Now I could add 'insulting a god' to my long, ongoing list of blunders in the past twenty-four hours.

Exolirus continued, "The Elementals were *really* betting on you taking back the city yesterday, but now it looks like you're in a worse position than before, so they've decided it's time for a little more intervention. Be warned, though: This is the last time we'll be meddling in your affairs. You have no idea how embarrassing it is for us."

I waited for him to continue, but he seemed to be waiting for me to ask him for dramatic effect. I conceded. "So you're going to help me defeat Neiphorous?"

He rolled his eyes. "No, I think we've seen that something like that would be *way* too impressive for someone like you. There's vomit on your sleeve, by the way." I hid my arm behind my back and looked at the ground as he continued. "Instead, we've decided you should take it up behind-the-scenes with some of the bigger players over in the East. Your official quest is to journey to Minesra, find an audience with the Silver Council, and settle this *civilly*. It's the only way you can possibly fix the mess you made yesterday, what with Neiphorous still on the loose."

My stomach dropped. I hadn't even thought of him, but I guess I had hoped he didn't survive the fall. Stupid assumption; people like him could survive the realms collapsing on top of each other and still find an angle to take advantage of it.

"You know, no offense — I mean, I appreciate that you all planned this for me — but I am *not* going to Minesra, especially not with Neiphorous still alive. Actually, I think I might just take my chances with the witches in the Ghânt desert."

I expected fury at my insubordination, but Exolirus only sighed and rubbed his eyes. "We did expect for you to say something like that, so there's one more thing we think you should be aware of. You remember that elf you've been travelling with for some reason?"

"Cedric?" I muttered quietly. Saying his name sent a fresh pang of misery through my whole body, but the Elemental continued without missing a beat.

"Right, yeah. Him. Sort of good news! He hasn't reached Death yet, but he's lost so much blood I can't say he's still in this realm."

My heart dropped. If he wasn't dead, but also wasn't alive, that only left one place he could be.

"You mean he's in Coma?" I choked out. Coma was the land between life and death, and almost no one came back from it.

Exolirus nodded. "You dipped into Coma, too, after the fall, but we pulled you out in the nick of time. Once you're dead, Polyoktraphin won't let you go no matter what I do, and I'm afraid that applies to your elf friend as well — *but…*" He drew the syllable out, building suspense. "I *might* be inclined to go down to Coma and bring him back before it's too late, if it would be worth my time."

He didn't need to explain further. Nausea once again swelled in me as I realized what I had to do, but I forced it down. I got Cedric into this situation, and I would get him out, no matter the cost.

"I'll do it."

Exolirus nodded. "Great. Now that that's all done, I have another delivery for you." He reached into his bottomless satchel and presented a glass bracelet. It shimmered subtly gold, bending the moonlight along its gilded ridges. "Since you're heading into the East, you'll be dealing with greater magical forces than you're used to. This bracelet will absorb magic used against you and help quell the effects of the change in Vibrancy in the lands you'll visit. It's indestructible to your mortal means, but remember: It can only hold so much, and once it's full, it'll shatter. And if I were you, I wouldn't want to be wearing it when all the magic breaks out. At least not if I want to keep the arm." He spun it around on his index finger, then unclipped the latch so that it fell open.

Tentatively, I reached out my palm under the bracelet. He dropped it into my hand, making me wince in apprehension — after all, it was a divine artifact — but it felt no different than any ordinary piece of jewelry. I weighed it in my palm. The glass was strong and cold. I clasped it around my wrist.

"It's a little loose," I commented without much thought.

The messenger scoffed. "Oh, sorry, does it not fit the king's wrist to his liking? Upset it wasn't fitted to your specific dimensions? Do you wish me to send it back to the divine smiths?"

"No! No, no, I'm sorry, I just assumed it would've been, like, enchanted. I appreciate it, seriously," I said, trying to backtrack before I got smote by a falling hammer to the cranium. That would probably help my headache, though.

"That's what I thought. No need to sign — I don't really want you touching my ink until you wash your hands. That's all I have for you," he said, and the intense golden light of his wings began to form — but faded away. "Oh, no, there's one more thing. Since it seems like every time we meet, you're unwittingly in mortal peril, I should probably let you know that the elves are sending boats to dredge the river. They think you're dead, but you can imagine what they'll do once they find out they're wrong. Best of luck!" With that, his resplendent wings returned, showering the river bank with divine light, and with one flap he was gone.

I gritted my teeth and pulled myself to my feet, staggering from the vertigo it brought. Heeding his warning, I climbed up the sandy hill of the river bank and raced down onto the city streets.

Having grown up in the city, I knew this area like the back of my hand. Stepping out into the open would be risky for me — this wasn't some backwoods farming town, or a port on the other half of the continent. *Everyone* in this city knew what I looked like, sounded like, how tall I was, my birthday. And with the elven patrols that would be coming any minute, I wasn't sure if my usual trick of head-down-hood-up would cut it. Besides, I didn't even *have* a hood, or a coat, and the last time I saw my knife it was buried in Neiphorous as he fell out a window.

It was obvious I would need some help. I knew somebody in the city who would — or, at least, who *could* — get me on a ship to Minesra, if she was willing. It was stupid, *really* stupid, but it was either that or a promenade through the midnight streets of the most active and dangerous region in the capital, just hoping to stumble across a ticket to the elven homeland. I knew that seeing her would be a risk, but being caught by elves would be a death sentence.

I kept to the alleys of the port district, weaving in between buildings, taking care never to step too close to the street lamps. As I passed through a narrow lane between shops, a figure stepped out to block off the other end of the alley; turning around, two others had appeared behind me. I reached instinctively for my Valkyrie knife, but it was gone, probably at the bottom of the river. Of all the things to lose, that must have been a new low for me.

The man in front of me stepped forward and held up his arm. I saw he was holding something in his hand — presumably a weapon, but in the darkness I couldn't see. "You ain't from around here, are ya'? 'eryone here knows not to get caught alone after the sun's down — 'cept you, apparently."

"Look," I said, trying to deepen my voice on the off chance these criminals had heard enough of my public addresses to remember it, "let me save us some trouble. I don't have any money — I'm only in the area for work. That's all, I mean it."

I heard the two behind me snicker, and the one I was talking to — presumably the leader — took several steps toward me. I stood firm and completely terrified as he approached.

"Oh, you 'mean it'? Patrick! Haven't we heard someone say that before?"

One of the voices behind me spoke up, but I didn't turn to see who. "Uh, I don't remember exactly what people've said — I mean, proba–" He was cut off by the frontman again, his voice sharpened to a growl.

"Patrick, shut up. Mr. 'just looking for work' here thinks that we *actually* believe he's out of cash." He raised his knife to me. "I know what brokes sound like, *smell* like, and you are *not* one of them brokes. And besides, even *they* pay one way or another." This time, I stepped away, and really wished I still had that knife.

"I– uh, I was…" I racked my brain for an excuse before I realized that maybe the truth was more compelling than any lie I could conjure up. The hardest part would be saying the words out loud. I took a deep breath. "I was going to see Meca Khumalo. She owes me a favor — I need a ship, she can get me on one. You know what she can do." I decided to leave it there, not wanting to overshare and reveal who I really was.

My potential assailant stood in silence for a couple seconds, his knife still raised but wavering. I could practically hear him weighing all of the options. He knew the danger if I were telling the truth and he laid me out anyway; was it worth the loss of letting me go, only to find out I was lying? I held my breath, not daring to make a sound.

"You know," he started, "you're bold. Bolder than most. Most would be smart enough not to speak *her* name on the street — especially not for a lazy, fake excuse. I think we should put some respect on Meca's name and find out what kinda cash you're *really* carrying. What do y'all say, boys?"

Two grunts of affirmation sounded behind me, accompanied by the scrape of knives being unsheathed. I pressed my back against the alley wall to keep my attackers in front of me. They all closed the distance scarily fast. My first attacker neared from my left, almost within range of me. With no weapons, no backup, nothing for protection, I struck out my hand in a futile attempt to hold him back — and felt a weight fall into it from the sky. I looked down, awestruck, as my assailants froze in unison.

"Where'd he get that knife?" one of them said.

"How is it *glowing?*" another added. I recognized the voice as Patrick's.

"It sure as hell wasn't there before," the leader said. I could hear he was just as confused, but trying to maintain his aggressive edge. "Must've been carrying it in his sleeve. Let's see if he knows how to use it."

I raised the Valkyrie knife, its silver sheen revealing my attackers to me. As the leader's dagger came for my throat, I ducked to the side and slashed out. He shouted in pain as my knife grazed his side, and I used the moment of weakness to push past him and break into a sprint down the alley, leaving them in chase, but they didn't seem as eager to pursue me once I was armed.

I ran until they had all given up long behind me, then ducked back into another alleyway to gather my bearings. I walked to the far end, sealed off by a brick wall, and crouched down so I couldn't be seen. I held up the knife, its edge sticky with blood, to examine it in whatever moonlight I could get. It was definitely the same knife — I doubted there were many like it in the world. Its hilt was still damp with river water. But how was that possible? I could only stare at it in stunned disbelief until I heard the falling of boots approaching from the street. I was quick to slide the knife into the sheath that still hung from my belt; it was illegal to be caught with an exposed weapon in the capital, though that never helped the crime rate.

I stayed perfectly still as the police patrol marched by the alleyway entrance. Though I couldn't see perfectly in the darkness, they appeared to be human. This surprised me for a moment — *why would a human be working under an elven invader regime?* — until I remembered that police, too, had to make money. Although it was hard for me to accept, the empire-scale politics in disarray probably didn't impact his daily routine as much as I would expect. I wondered how long it would have taken for them to notice that the imperial family had fallen if they weren't in the heart of the country; were there any remote villages out on the far border, so far from any regular contact that they had no idea any of this had even happened? I found myself slightly envious of the idea that someone could be living completely oblivious to the biggest crisis of my life.

After his footsteps had moved onto another street, I peaked out of the alley. I scurried to make my way down the empty street, occasionally checking the street signs to make sure I was still on the right track. I passed the occasional suspicious merchant, but the people out at this hour minded their own business, for the most part, and I figured that if I kept to myself, they would never notice that they were passing within ten feet of their exiled king.

Chapter Twenty

It took me longer than I hoped to get to Tricknet Street, but it was better to take it slow than to rush into another patrol. I stepped off the main road and onto the narrow, lonely alley, my shoulders almost brushing the walls of the buildings on either side of me. The passage sloped down toward a cellar door beneath the hotel which operated above Meca's palace. I shuffled down the slanted path to the door.

I remembered the passcode: one hard knock with my right hand, two hard knocks with my left, another fast knock with my right, then one final knock with both at once. I stepped back as the visor slid open, and an unseen hand held up a lantern to it. I suppressed a wince at being seen, but I knew that I could trust anybody here to help me — as long as I could pay. The visor slid closed, and a second later, I heard the many locks being unlatched. The door was pulled open hard, and a large-built guard seized me and pulled me inside. I stumbled as he released me and flung the door shut, making the ceiling shake from the impact.

The guard paid me no further mind as he returned to his seat on a stool next to the door, etching on a foreign drawing pad from the South. I turned away from the light of the lamp and ventured down the dark maze of tunnels. I held my hands out to feel for walls as I traced the correct path — it was easy to remember, since it was the same as the knocking pattern.

I gingerly made my way around the first right turn, then the following two left turns, followed by one last right turn. I squinted against the light at the end of the hall, enough to fully illuminate the large room directly ahead of me. I could make out the expensive furnishings and elaborate decor adorning the chamber. Meca had a taste for style and class: She was the queen of the capital underground, an empire in and of itself, and she made sure her visitors knew it.

As I stepped out of the tunnel, the first thing to catch my eye was, as always, the fountain of gold in the center. I had always been enamored with it, but Meca firmly refused to sell her Kha'zat method of melting gold without heat, even after I offered her an *actual* palace in exchange. It seemed to entice me to reach out my hand, let the gold spill out onto me, but Meca warned me the first time I ever set foot there that the gold never left the fountain, even if she had to cut off my hand to get it back. I never came within an arm's reach since, but that didn't stop my eyes from wandering.

Behind the fountain, on an elevated pedestal, sat Meca Khumalo's empty throne. I was confused. Every time I had visited in the past, she had been seated, waiting, but I guess even Ghânt witches slept, and it *was* the middle of the night. The room was still staffed with attendants, though, all keeping their heads low as they waited along the periphery of the room; one of them ran off down a hallway as I entered, and minutes of awkward waiting later, Meca Khumalo stepped into the room.

She was a little shorter than me, but carried herself with the same stature that I had seen so many times in the nobility. She wore a red robe that I had seen often on the street in Ramethus, the shade perfectly complementing her dark skin. Her long hair swung behind her in a tight braid as she strode into the center of the chamber, climbed the stairs to her chair, and reclined back on the throne.

"Damion," she started, her voice echoing off the walls, "I never expected to be seeing you again — off the chopping block, at least." Her voice carried the weight of a stormfront before the first thunder crash. Peaceful, imposing, and threatening to turn into wrath at any moment.

I started, "Meca, I–"

"I know why you're here. You're hanging over a boiling pot and want me to work up a sweat bailing you down. Last I heard, you were up in the castle trying to kill Neiphorous. Guess that didn't work out." She had an almost comedic edge to her tone. "Just cut to the chase so I can get back to my night."

My face burned red, and I hoped that I was lucky enough that it would blend into the lantern light. "I… I need to get to Minesra. I don't have the cash right now, but if you could get me on a ship, I can pay you back tenfold later."

Meca's brow furrowed as she peered down at me. "I'm not about to ask you what your business is in the East with the *elvinestes*, but this is no small ask. Now, I *could* get you on a boat, but it would cost more than I think you can afford."

"Meca, please, I just need a favor. Consider it a loan — when I'm back in my means, I'll arrange a palace for you, a fleet of yachts, anything," I bargained. "Oh," I added, "and remember, you owe me for that time I–"

"*I don't owe you one single thing, Excutari,*" she snapped. "I owe a favor to a little prince who's gonna inherit an empire, not to some backcountry fugitive running blind around the continent, offering 'loans' on the *chance* he gets back his footing. I'm usually in the business of offering a hand to people when they're at their lowest, but you're looking a little too low for even *me* to start handing out 'favors'. You want my help, you *earn* my help."

My face burned again, but this time with anger. I was stupid to expect that she wouldn't jump at the chance to capitalize off my desperation. Then again, I had no real alternative — either I did whatever she asked, or I would find myself crossing Jennira's Pass on foot, or worse, in a prison cart. She had forced my hand, as she tended to do.

I took a deep breath. "Fine, alright. What do you want me to do for you?"

She took a second of silence, as if considering options. "At last we're being sensible. I have a proposition. It should be trivial, even for you. Tomorrow at noon, there will be a shipment coming in from the Elven Highlands I've found an… invested interest in." Seeing the preemptive regret on my face, she was quick to add, "Don't start getting worked up, I'm not about to ask you to steal a cargo ship. It's simple: you're going to make your way down to the docks — hopefully undetected, as I would hate for you to die before you can finish your task. Once there, you'll find the ship from the Highlands and a man by the name of Kenes waiting at the base of the ramp. He'll have the package. Be warned, it won't be small, but you should be able to manage. Bring it back to me, and you'll be on a ship by this time tomorrow."

I was skeptical. I knew there was some part to this she wasn't sharing with me, but I also knew there was no use trying to get it out of her until she was ready to share. "Alright. I'll do it."

"I knew you would. I'm glad we could come to terms once again, just like old times." She stood up and waved an attendant over. "Find him a room for the night, one with clothes that don't look like they've been fished out of a mass grave. I'm retiring to my chamber; I don't want to be disturbed again."

The attendant ushered me wordlessly down another hallway, around a corner, and opened a small wooden door for me. I stepped through; the ceiling hung a little too low and the bed leaned at an angle from a broken post, but I was too exhausted to complain. Not that I would ever complain to Meca Khumalo about anything, lest I end up on the wrong side of her magic. There was a plate of candles burning on the table by the bed, and a barred window revealed a deserted low-level street.

Once the attendant had left and the door was closed, I opened the closet to find that it was stocked with clothes roughly my size, but all loose and lightweight in a definitively southern style. I felt the long sleeve of a tunic; it was made of glossy, white, tightly-woven fabric to block the desert sun while staying thin enough to be breathable. It didn't seem practical for the coldness of Excutatian winters, but my current rag of a shirt wasn't much more useful.

Stripping off my shirt and setting it beside the dresser, I climbed into the bed. I didn't know what Meca had up her sleeve, but I had no choice now but to see this through. I blew out the candles.

Chapter Twenty-One

I awoke to a light rapping on the bedroom door.

"Meca Khumalo calls for you at once," said a voice on the other side. I rolled out of bed and dressed myself in the unfamiliar clothes. The tunic hung loose over my shoulders and tapered off at my mid-thigh. I picked up the enchanted bracelet on my nightstand and slipped it into my pocket, not wanting Meca to know about any of my Elemental business. She had her secrets, I had mine.

The servant led me back to the throne room. Candles set on the rim of the fountain cast amber rays across its flowing gold. Between the fountain and the throne, Khumalo and a dozen assistants waited around a wide circle of white sand. All wore thick veils over their faces, staring straight ahead as if they didn't notice me, except for Meca, who flipped up her veil and stepped out of the formation.

"Damion. Not in any rush to set out today, I see — it's ten o'clock, you're almost late. We need to get started right away."

"Get started with what?" I asked, "I thought I was going alone."

"How do you suppose you'll get there in the middle of the day with elves running about and everyone on the street salivating over your bounty? You thought they wouldn't have noticed by now that your body wasn't in the river?"

I broke eye contact to avoid her piercing gaze. "I guess not. What are we going to do, then?"

"In the Ghânt, we have all sorts of tricks you've never heard of. I brought some of them with me," she grinned and gestured to the sand. "Before you go, I'll mask your face so nobody in the world could recognize you. Then, you'll retrieve the package, bring it back here, and I'll undo the spell before I send you off to sea. No more complicated than that."

The idea of being subjected to one of her spells made my heart race, but if everything went as she said, it would be worth the risk. I pushed down my discomfort. "Sounds good. Do you already have a ticket for me to get to Minesra?"

She chuckled. "Do you even have to ask?" She reached into the inside pocket of her robe and held up a paper pass. It seemed legitimate: a one-way trip to the port of Yilioe on the western coast of Minesra, set to depart this afternoon. If I got my job done in time, I could catch the ship and be on my way by sundown. She tucked the paper back into her coat. "Now, shall we get started? I'd hate for this little ticket to go to waste."

She stepped aside, waving me into the circle. I took a deep breath and stepped over the line of sand, my hands clenched at my side. Once I was in the center, she retook her position, completing the circle of women as she flipped down her own veil.

Then, she began to chant. The incantation was in Theineken, the Humanic dialect of the Ghânt, and I couldn't understand a word. The rest of the women in the circle joined in until the entire group was chanting in unison. Meca became more passionate, her voice rising above the others and cutting straight through me, making the room spin. I wasn't sure if the vertigo was a byproduct of the spell or of my anxiety — I had never had magic used on me before, not like this.

Meca reached her hand to an assistant without even a glance, and the woman passed her a round stone tablet. Meca stepped up to me, held it up to my face, and thrust it forward. I tried to lurch back, but the dizziness seemed to hold me still. The stone melted around my face like wax. There was an intense heat and pressure, but thankfully, it didn't hurt.

Meca's voice grew louder as I could feel her draw an item from her waistband. She lifted it to the tablet, and as I was held still by the spell, she began etching onto the other side. It was as if she were carving directly into my face, and if my mouth weren't covered by the enchanted stone, I wouldn't have been able to stop myself from screaming. This process seemed to stretch on forever as the chisel dragged along my skin. Then, with a harsh tug, Meca tore the stone from my face.

I opened my eyes as the chanting stopped. I saw that the stone tablet now had a facial imprint on one side, and as she handed it off to another assistant, I tentatively touched my face. My cheekbones felt lower, my chin a bit further out, my eyebrows sitting higher than I remembered. I felt sick once again, like something horrible had just happened, but Meca only laughed.

Taking a handheld mirror from an assistant, she said, "Damion Excutari? Why, he's nowhere to be found." She held up the mirror, and I saw someone else looking back at me. I gasped softly. Whatever she did, I looked nothing like me. If I didn't know better, there was no way I would have been able to tell that I wasn't looking at a completely different person. I turned my head, and the reflection moved in synchronicity.

I had so many things to say, but the question that came first was, "It can be undone, right?"

Meca rolled her eyes and put down the mirror. "I think you mean to say *'thank you'*, but yes, all you need is to press the mold against your face and you'll be right back to normal. Careful, though. You can only revert back once, so we'll wait until after you've finished my business. Understand?"

"Yes, Meca, thank you. This is incredible."

"I know."

An assistant led me back outside through the underground maze and pushed me out onto street level. The morning sun burned my eyes, but I pushed through it as I joined the bustling crowd on the street level. I was constantly self-conscious of being noticed, but nobody who saw me paid me any mind, and it wouldn't take long to get to the docks.

While I was walking, someone suddenly grabbed my arm from behind. I instinctively reached for my knife, but swiveled to see that it was only some teenager with a notebook and pencil held in his hand. I lifted my hand from the sheathe.

"'Scuse me, sir, I'm an apprentice with the press guild. I've been asking around about what people think of the occupation, what with Prince Damion reappearing yesterday. Have you any thoughts?"

Oh. I felt stupid for almost stabbing this kid because he startled me with an interview, but I managed to gather some words that felt like what a working-class peasant would say. "I, uh, well… I think that I would rather the emperor be in charge — because, you know, elves, right? — but it doesn't matter that much to me. I mean, I get paid the same, don't I?"

My interviewer tilted his head. "You do? Even with the reparation taxes?"

What? I had no idea what those were, and at this point I wanted to get out of this situation before I got tossed into an asylum. "Oh, yeah, I mean, sure, of course. I just get by either way, is what I meant. You know?"

"… right. Sure, I get it. Thank you sir, have a good day." He said, scratching down in his notepad while he walked away, but I didn't move. Reparation taxes? Were the elves taxing Excutatem to pay off their war debts? Well, in fairness, that's exactly what *my* empire had been doing, but it was just another reason I had to get to Minesra and settle this. I needed to end this cycle, once and for all. I wasn't the only one who was losing with the elves in power.

I continued down the street, pushing past pedestrians and dodging carts. The salty air was filled with the hiss of distant waves and seagulls crying overhead. The mast of a ship swayed over the crowd ahead of me, and I came through the last row of shops and hotels onto the dense boardwalk. It was almost noon, so the ship should be arriving any minute.

I should have known better than to expect it to be on time. After half an hour of waiting around in the sun, I saw the green stripes of the Elven Highlands flag fluttering in the distance atop a large cargo ship pulling into the bay. It took another hour for it to dock at the pier.

I approached it as they put down the ramp and began unloading cargo. Meca Khumalo told me next to nothing about who I was looking for, but when I noticed a man standing to the side of the ramp with a large crate beside him, I figured there was a good chance he was my target.

"Are you Kenes?" I asked him. He turned toward me with the least pleased expression I had come across in a while.

"Why would she send *you* to do the pickup?" he asked in a voice worn by years of ocean spray and shouting over waves.

"I was available, I guess. Who knows why she does anything?"

"Fine, whatever. Here's the package. Make sure it gets back to her all right — you know what she'll do if you mess with it."

I nodded and took the box. It was big enough to require both hands to lift it, but proved surprisingly light for its size. As soon as it was in my hands, Kenes went right back up the ramp without so much as a glance back in my direction. It almost seemed like he was a little *too* quick to get it off his hands, but I was short on time as it was, so I decided not to dwell on it.

The hard corners of the box dug into my arms as I pushed through the crowd. I was shocked by how easy this had been. *Once I'm king again, I'll have to pay her back–*

My train of thought was cut off by the box leaving my hands as someone knocked into me. I scrambled to pick it up off the ground, but it wasn't on the ground — someone, dressed in black, was running away with it down an alley. A thief. I immediately sprinted after him, but as I came around a corner, I was thrown into a wall by another man. He had a bandage wrapped around his side, and a third thief stood behind him. The last time I had seen him was the night before, under the glow of my Valkyrie dagger. He didn't seem to remember my face.

"Sorry, it's ours now. Head back to the street and we won't have to cut off your hand."

"That's funny, last time it was *me* that did the cutting," I retorted as I pulled my dagger from my belt. Upon hearing my voice, recognition flashed across his face as he took a step forward and drew his own weapon.

"Well, ain't this something. Nevermind, then — I guess we'll be taking that hand off anyway."

"I wasn't lying last night. That box belongs to Meca Khumalo. I don't think she'll be quick to forgive if you try to steal her property."

"You know, I actually believe you. I just don't care. For Meca, not for Meca, either way the idea of getting you back for last night is just too good to pass up." He flipped his knife in his hand. "Besides, I'm partial to taking that package to Meca myself and collecting whatever it was she offered you. You won't be needing it. What'd'ya say, Pat?"

"Sounds good to me," said the man standing behind him. Patrick was even uglier in the light, apparently.

The boss brandished his knife. I held out my dagger, preventing him from coming any closer. Patrick seemed wary of the blade, but the leader remained completely unfazed.

"I used it before," I warned, "and I have no problem using it again. Give me the box and get lost before you give me a reason to."

He laughed and dismissively waved his dagger. "You don't scare me. I've been working in this district since I was seven years old — I've seen worse than you, and I'm still standing. *You're* the one who should be afraid."

I wasn't afraid, despite myself. I was outnumbered and didn't doubt that they would kill me in a second if given the chance, but I, too, had faced things greater than street thugs. If we were going to fight anyway, I might as well get it over with.

In a flash, I dove toward him, slashing out with my knife. He seemed to be caught off guard by me going on the offensive, and he stumbled backwards, unhurt but stunned. I whirled toward him, stabbing downward, but he countered by cutting up with his knife, forcing me back. Patrick was trying to back him up, but not very well, since he was too afraid to get any closer to me. The leader jutted his knife out toward my throat, but instead of evading, I brought my dagger up and sliced deep into his arm.

He winced and staggered away from me with blood dripping from his fingers. This was apparently too much for Pat, who turned and ran. Now was my chance. His dominant arm was wounded and he was within range for me to– wait, no. Was I really about to kill this guy? I knew that he would return the favor without a second thought, but still…

I held my knife out, threatening him to stay back. "This is your last warning. Don't let me see you again."

I ran off into the direction the third thief had gone with the crate. I turned a corner, and at the end of the alley, I saw him struggling to fit it through a narrow back door, presumably their base of operations. He saw me approaching with my bloody knife and set the box down, bolting inside and slamming the door.

I came up to the box and picked it up. I wasted no time getting back onto the street, periodically checking behind me to ensure nobody was following. I took a deep breath and continued on until I saw the sign for Tricknet Street. The box barely fit down the narrow alley, and by the time I reached the iron door, my hands were red from rubbing against the rough stone. I awkwardly kicked the door as near to the pattern as I could manage, and it was thankfully good enough for the guard. He slid open the visor to make sure it wasn't the imperial authorities, then pulled open the door.

Chapter Twenty-Two

I carried the box back through the maze, bumping into walls in the dark more times than I'd care to admit. When I returned to the central chamber, Meca was waiting on her throne, examining her nails in the flickering lantern light. I set the box down at the base of the gold fountain.

"Here it is. Ran into some trouble on the way back, but nothing I couldn't handle," I informed her as I massaged the red lines on my forearms.

"Good," she said, not lifting her eyes.

"So… what about the ticket?"

Her lips curled into a tight smile as she finally made eye contact. "I haven't forgotten, don't you worry. But first, bring that box over to me. I want to inspect my goods before I make any returns."

Anxiety gnawed in the back of my mind — but no, I knew Meca wouldn't double-cross someone she's dealing with. That would reflect horribly on her business reputation. I picked up the box and set it at the base of the steps leading up to her seat.

"Open it," she commanded. I gripped both sides of the lid and lifted, setting the square of wood off to the side. She leaned over for a better view and grinned. "Perfect. Good work."

Curious what I had just gone through the effort of collecting, I looked over the side of the box. I gasped, almost stumbling backwards into the fountain. I had never seen one with my own eyes, but from the countless descriptions and recounts I had heard, there was no mistaking what was inside the box.

"Meca, where– how– where did you get a *dragon?!*" I stuttered, hardly able to breathe.

"Elvish Highlands. There are no more to be found here, thanks to your family — the Vibrancy of the East attracts them, the human poachers of the West repel them." She scoffed at the horror on my face. "What? It's no danger to you, it won't wake for days. I'll have to bathe it in Ghânt sand to replenish its energy, and you'll be long gone by then. And don't pretend like you've never seen one before. This one is just a baby; we all know about the grown one stashed away beneath your castle."

I backed away from the box and tried to collect myself. "I have no idea what you're talking about. There haven't been dragons in Excutatem for centuries. You can't understand how dangerous they are if you willingly brought one into your *house*."

"I don't need a lying lecture from you, Excutari. Maybe in a hundred years this dragon will be big enough to prove once and for all what secrets are locked away under the castle — but neither of us will be around to see that day, so there's no use fretting." She reached into her pocket and held up my ticket. "Besides, aren't we on a schedule?"

Her implication startled me, but I knew I had to stick to my plan. "I just want to be out of here.

And away from *that*," I said, gesturing broadly to the creature in the crate. I gave the box a wide berth and started up the steps.

Halfway to the throne, she put a hand out to stop me. "Oh, and aren't we forgetting something?" She reached to her side and picked up the white tablet. "You don't want to stay disguised like this forever, do you?"

"Oh, yeah, I guess–" I started, but a flaw in the plan occurred to me. "Wait, no. How am I supposed to get out of here if the disguise is removed? I need to keep it at least until I arrive in the East."

Her smile wavered. "Don't be silly, Damion. There's no danger to you in a crowd. There are thousands of people out there right now, no one will be able to pick you out." She held up the tablet to my face, but I put up my hand to push it away.

"That's not what you said before. I really don't think this is a good idea. Could I just keep the tablet until I get to Minesra?"

"You can't. The magic becomes permanent just a few hours after it's put on, if we don't act quickly–"

"And why didn't you mention that before we did it? Why would you hide that?!"

"Because I could see your nerves shaking through your skin at the thought of using my arts, and I figured that–"

"Meca, no," I asserted, "I did my part of the deal — now give me the tablet and the ticket and I'll be gone. I don't know what you're trying, but I don't want any part in it."

I stuck out my hand for her to give me the items, but she only looked down and frowned. Then, she began to chuckle. "You know, Damion, you're wiser than you were when I last saw you. But you still have a lot to learn."

Sensing the danger in her words, I backed up down the steps until my feet seemed stuck under me. I looked down and saw that the stone step had melted into sand, and I had already sunk to my ankles, holding me in place. Meca added, "It's a shame you'll never get the chance to learn your lesson, but your bounty will make it easier for me to cope."

She rose from the chair and descended toward me with the mask raised. I struggled against the sand, but the more I tried to pry myself free, the deeper I sank. I cursed myself for coming here, and now I was paying the price for my desperation. If she reversed her spell, I would never be escaping this city alive.

I reached for my knife, but didn't draw it. The room was quickly filling with her assistants and guards, most armed with scimitars or foreign weapons with sickening blades and razor-thin points. Threatening Meca would only set them on me, and I couldn't even run, much less fight. I needed to set myself free first, but how could I break out of a magic trap…?

I struck my right arm out toward her — not because I thought it would stop her, but to draw their attention away from my left hand as it fumbled around in my pocket. My fingers brushed against the circular, glass frame. That was it. Meca scoffed at the feeble attempt to hold her back, swatting my hand out of the way as she was just a few steps away from me now. With the mask inches from my face, I worked the bracelet around my wrist and pressed it against my thigh to latch it shut. Instantly, the sand's grip loosened, and I pulled myself free before tumbling backwards down the stairs. Sharp pain shot up my back from the fall as I rushed to my feet and drew my knife, aiming it at Meca on the steps. Her surprise showed on her face; surprise which evolved into confusion, and then fear.

She raised a finger, starting, "I don't know what kind of magic you're working with here, but you better not try anything, or–"

"*I'm* the one holding the knife, Meca. I think I'll decide what I get to try," I growled, my fear of her overpowered by my anger at the betrayal. "Give me the ticket and the tablet."

She stood still for a moment as if contemplating every course of action she could take, but ultimately the dagger compelled her. The tablet was heavier than I expected, but I held it tight as I backed away from her, the ticket pressed up against it. I was acutely aware that none of her guards had made a move. Why weren't they charging me? Meca was out of my range, so I was no longer a threat to her. Could it be…

Keeping an eye on Meca and her backup, I swallowed hard and carefully set down the stone tablet and ticket inside the box, next to the dragon. It didn't stir a bit, and I muttered a prayer to the Elementals that it would stay asleep.

"What do you think you're doing with that?!" Meca boomed. I didn't respond, sliding the lid onto the box and fumbling to pick it up while still holding my knife.

Meca seemed to have all of her guards concentrated at the main exit, but it occurred to me that there was another way out. I broke into a sprint toward the hallway I had been led down the night before. I could hear footsteps charge after me, but I pushed myself hard enough to reach the room first, slamming the door with my foot and pushing my back against it.

I set the box down carefully to the side, then reached out to the wardrobe while the group outside tested the door, trying to get inside. I leaned toward it as far as I could, and I was just able to grasp the outermost corner. Pulling with my entire body, I brought it crashing down onto the door, pinning it closed. I ducked out from under it a second before it crushed me too.

With Meca's forces temporarily held off, I ran to the window. The iron bars outside the pane were worn and rusty, but I didn't figure I could break them with my bare hands. I slid open the glass and shook them, and they rattled harshly, their bolts loose. I rushed to unscrew the bars as the door shook harder with every second. At this rate, they would break it down in minutes. My fingers burned as I twisted the screws faster. Finally, one came out, and I knocked the first bar out of the window. Two more to go.

Their attempts to get in the door only grew more aggressive; Meca Khumalo yelled something to them in Theineken. The second bar fell onto the street outside. As I got to work on the third, I heard the wood splinter behind me. I glanced back without stopping my work and saw that one of the planks had been cracked off the door, and several angry faces leered at me. Hands reached through and began pulling apart the remains of the door just as I knocked the last bar out.

I positioned myself to climb out, but realized I was leaving something behind. I raced to the other side of the room and picked up the crate. Carrying it back to the window, I tried to push it through, but it was just barely too big to fit. I quickly reached around the top, pulled off the lid, and tried again; it scraped the window frame, but fit through as I pushed it out onto the street and tossed the lid after it. I pulled myself up just as a flash of light burst behind me, followed by a shower of wood splinters. A hand grasped at my foot as I climbed out onto the street level, and I slashed at it with my knife. They pulled away, the group flooding the room faltering at the sight of my knife.

I pushed the lid back onto the crate and picked it up, sprinting as fast as my legs could carry me toward the street. I didn't see if they were following me, but I was sure they were. Finally, I reached the safety of the crowded street, disappearing into the sea of merchants and travelers, and made my way to the docks.

I had no idea what time it was, and I could only hope that the ship hadn't left yet. Pushing my way onto the boardwalk, I found a secluded alcove between two buildings where I could set down the box and retrieve my ticket:

A Ticket of Passage:

From the realm of Emperor Jourdan of Excutatem to the port of Yilioe in Minesra; on the ship Melody, of Excutatem, to depart at the third afternoon hour of the fifth day of Onzember.

I looked to the port clock tower, a massive building overlooking the docks. The short hand was almost to the three, the minute hand rounding the top of the clock fast. I whirled around, scanning the ships for the correct one. I saw the name *Melody* printed in fine cursive on the hull of a merchant ship… on the other side of the boardwalk. Shit.

I picked up the box and set off toward the ship, muttering apologies to anybody I knocked into. My feet ached against the hard, sun-bleached boardwalk. Winter clouds had rolled in, blocking out the sun and laying a cold shadow over the bay. I jumped as the bell tower chimed three times, marking the end of the hour, just as

I came around the front of the ship. It was larger than the last ship I had been on, though I hoped that was where the similarities ended.

I ran up to the gangway just as a sailor was pulling it up. I set down the box and waved my ticket above my head, shouting, "Hey! Sorry, got sidetracked. Could you put the ramp back down?"

The sailor heaved a heavy sigh and lowered the ramp back to the ground. I carefully shuffled up the gangway with my box and handed him my ticket. He hardly looked at it before he stuffed it into his pocket and waved me on board.

"Go get yourself settled on the lower deck. That box can go in the storage hold for the trip," he said. Judging by the absence of the dismay and emptiness in his voice that I had come to associate with merchant sailors, he must not have been at this for very long. Really, he didn't seem much older than me.

"Could I keep it with me? I'd rather not get separated from it," I asked.

"Sure, if you want. We won't stop you. It's probably safer to keep it with the other stuff though, 'les you have a lock on that box or it's filled with rocks. Up to you."

I figured he was probably right. Besides, I wouldn't want someone to peek in the box and accuse me of smuggling a dragon — which, in fairness, I was. I noticed another sailor lugging boxes below deck and followed him to the storage hold. I tried to find a good spot to hide the box among the stacks of crates which lined every wall, deciding it was least conspicuous hidden away in the corner. I pulled out my knife to mark it with an X so that I could find it later among the other identical boxes.

Once I was assured that my new dragon — and the tablet that would undo the spell over me, if my blind hope was correct that Meca lied about it being permanent — was secure, I climbed the steps up to the main deck. I couldn't believe that I was back on a ship after the catastrophe of the last one, but I couldn't possibly experience *two* maritime disasters in one lifetime, could I? Well, it would actually be three, with that yachting incident off the Isles of Penelopene on my fifteenth birthday, but we had all agreed never to bring that up again, so it didn't really count.

The rope was thrown down a half hour after three. The ship pulled out painfully slowly at first, but the sails quickly caught wind once we were in the heart of the bay. I stayed on deck until the clouds began to sprinkle rain over the harbor, and I finally climbed down to the bunk deck.

I claimed a hammock on the outskirts of the room and dropped down onto the rough linen sheet. Though larger, the ship wasn't as crowded as the last; after years of wartime embargos, there still weren't many humans with business in Minesra. The bunk level was stiflingly hot and pitch black when the hatch was closed, so when I heard the end of the water pelting above us, I climbed back out onto the deck. I was greeted by a view I had seen countless times before, deeply nostalgic and now melancholy: fog-shrouded mountains rising up on all sides of the bay, city lights from the capital sparkling beneath the darkening night sky. I rested my arms on the railing, only to find it wet from the rain, and decided to stay standing as I took in the view for the millionth time.

The only difference in the view was the black silhouette of the castle, its lights extinguished, leaving an empty space imposed between the roofs and the stars. The image forced a memory back into my mind. It made me want to tear my eyes away, but I didn't. The last time I had seen the castle like this, I was eleven. I remembered the day in reverse order:

Demanding to go on a naval warship to the Isles, never wanting to set foot in the capital again. The crowd parting in horror as I passed. Running to the docks from the castle without bodyguards. Storming out of the castle, not letting myself cry. My father ordering the servants to put out every light in the castle in remembrance. My life shattering in the Imperial Square. The guillotine falling in slow motion. Watching the castle guard bring out my mother in chains. Feeling more powerless than ever, before or since.

Before I knew it, a tear rolled down my cheek, warm against the quickly frosting night air. I didn't wipe it away. I didn't move an inch, just kept my eyes fixed on the city as another tear fell, then more, on and on until I wasn't sure I had any left. Then, I wiped my sleeve on my face and took another deep breath.

I went back down to the bunk level, loud from snoring and waves breaking outside. I crept to my hammock carefully in the darkness. Finding the one I believed was mine, I lay down. I didn't sleep.

Chapter Twenty-Three

Six days later, the coast of the Eastern Continent was in view. The rolling hills and sporadic forests of the Elven Highlands sprawled endlessly atop sheer cliffs that stood tall against the azure sea. None of the natural features compared, though, to the Bastion.

Minesra had rarely historically had a period of peace — a fact Excutatem admittedly contributed to. To defend themselves, they constructed one of the most impressive and expensive engineering feats the world had ever seen, making several generations of Excutaris *really* pissed off.

One of the many Bastions surrounding Minesra, it was an impossibly massive stone block used for surveillance, as a stronghold, as a fortified position to defend from. Its towering rectangular frame was coated with vines and moss, but it didn't show a single crack on its body. Around the base, I could see a town had sprung up, making my brain hurt as I compared the smallness of the townhouses to the sky-scraping grandiose of the Bastion. I had never seen the Bastions in person, but I never really believed the accounts of their hugeness until that point.

The ship glided across the deep waters off the coast of Minesra as we passed towns and ports. Ships on different routes sailed alongside us or cut across our path. Standing at the front of the ship, I couldn't shake the apprehension creeping up on me like the vines on the Bastion. What was I *doing*? Going right into the depths of the enemy homeland, dropping off in a city I had never heard of, populated by elves whose language I didn't speak, with no money and no connections. I found myself wishing for the hundredth time that Cedric was with me — at least he would have been able to speak with the police when I was inevitably arrested. I also found myself wishing I had accepted my mother's offer for an Elvish tutor when I was a kid.

The sailors swarmed the main deck to prepare for docking as we neared the port of Yilioe. Ships I had only seen as dots on the horizon came nearer as we converged on our common destination. I could see masts swaying in the wind from the harbor, and a sea of wooden buildings stretched from the docks into the surrounding plains.

Once docked, I pushed past the sailors into the cargo deck as they all rushed to be the first to unload. I made my way over to the corner where I had stashed my crate. For a moment, my anxiety exploded as I couldn't locate it, but as more boxes were removed from the room, the carved X on the lid was revealed under a stack of crates. I exhaled and pulled the box up onto the main deck, balancing down the ramp onto the pier. I brought it to the far end, where it would be more secluded. I set it down and examined it. I would have expected a box holding a dragon to be made of obsidian and gold and weigh eight hundred pounds, but this one could've just as well been full of flour. It looked so *normal,* I almost couldn't believe what had been sleeping inside of it for the past week.

Tentatively, I lifted the lid just high enough for the sunlight to fall in. The dragon still slept unbothered, just as it had in Meca's palace. The stone that would hopefully undo the disguise spell lay dormant on the wooden floor of the box.

When I heard footsteps on the wooden pier approaching from behind, I panicked, flipping the lid haphazardly over the box and whipping around much more conspicuously than I hoped to be. The footsteps belonged to an elf coming up to the end of the pier. He was fairly taller than me, with golden brown hair braided on one side. He came up to stand next to me at the end of the dock and leaned on the wooden rail.

"Mé hinsè?" he asked me.

"I– um, I'm sorry, I don't understand," I stuttered, embarrassed even though I knew this type of situation was inevitable.

"Enyu? Ilniça… you do not speak Elvenès?"

"Well, no. Sorry."

His brow furrowed. "Do you speak it well, or do you speak it no? Choose one."

My face burned. "I don't– I mean, I only speak–"

I was interrupted by him erupting into laughter. "I'm just joking. I've lived in this port for years, it would be hard *not* to pick up Humanic, and you definitely aren't the first human trader to show up in Minesra unprepared." His accent was fairly pronounced, but he didn't seem to stumble over his words. Awkwardly, I laughed along with him, mostly just relieved to have found someone I could actually speak to before I got arrested or trafficked.

He glanced at the crate, then up at me. His eyes were a shade of green so light it was almost luminous. They reminded me of Cedric's, though Cedric's weren't quite as airy. It made me want to get off this pier to go find him, wherever he was now. Knowing that I was so close, but still nowhere near my objective, was driving me crazy.

"So, what's in the box?" He gestured to the crate at my feet.

I cleared my throat. "Uh, just some… stuff. Nothing interesting," I choked out, forcing disinterest into my voice and leaning against the lid to seem casual. I failed.

"Well, you intend to sell it, I'm sure? Why else would you bring it across an ocean — I could see from the flag on your ship that you're Excutatian," he said. I prayed that he would drop it, ideally after directing me to a hotel or carriage service. Unfortunately, he continued, "Since the war, traders from the West have been… hm… oh, yes, *scammed* more than ever. If you'd like, I can appraise some of your things so you know where to begin your bargain."

He didn't wait for my response, pushing me aside and sliding off the lid before I even processed what was going on. I sprung into motion to keep the lid down, but misplaced my hand, pushing down on the section already off the crate and sending the lid toppling to the ground. I scrambled for it and slapped it back on top, but judging from the elf's expression, there was no use.

"Please," I said quietly, "it's not what it looks like, I–"

"No," he interrupted, "don't even try. You *humans* disgust me. *Drecvesa* belong in the wild, not in a crate, not in a cage, and *absolutely* not in the West!" he scolded, nearly yelling.

He turned to march off in the direction of a customs officer on the boardwalk. I jogged after him.

"No, it *seriously* isn't what you think!" I pleaded, trying to stop him without making a scene. He pushed past me. "I'm not smuggling the… *that*, I'm trying to *return* it! I swear it on…" It occurred to me that nobody here would worship Elementals. "I swear, really, let's just talk about this–"

"We have nothing to talk about," he said, not hesitating a moment in his deadly serious march toward the police.

Desperation bubbling over, I just started to say whatever came to mind. "It's not even the reason I came here. I'm here to see the Silver Council, the dra– the *animal* was an accident. I didn't even want it in the first place."

He took another couple steps, then stopped and turned around. "What, so you expect me to believe you *accidentally* came into possession of a dragon? I've never been to the West; does this happen regularly?!" he demanded sharply.

I tried to stay calm. The longer I could hold him off from going to authorities, the better my chances were of getting out of this alive. "Yes! I mean, no, this isn't exactly *normal*, but my circumstances were unique, to say the least. Please, I don't mean any harm."

He seemed to judge me on a cellular level, analyzing every part of me for lies. Finally, he said, "Let me go take a look at that dragon. For your sake, you'd better not be lying."

We returned to the crate, his suspicious side-eye locked on me the whole way. He didn't hesitate to fling off the cover. The dragon was still there, for sure. I noticed its tail was now wrapped around the enchanted stone — had it always been like that?

"This dragon is unwell," sighed the elf, "from being in the West. Not enough Vibrancy there. If it stayed much longer, it would have surely died, but I suspect it might still recover."

He looked back at me, once again picking me apart. "You know," he finally said, "you have weird clothes for an Excutatian. Let's get this creature somewhere safer so I can decide what to do with you both."

Relief flooded me so quickly I almost fell down. He put the lid back onto the crate and picked it up easily. Without another word, he turned and marched down the pier. I followed.

"Oh, by the way," he said, "what's your name?"

"D– Daren," I stammered. "You?"

"You couldn't pronounce it."

Chapter Twenty-Four

I followed him past merchants on the boardwalk, risking glances to passerby who had no idea what we were carrying mere feet from them. The crowd dwindled as we ventured further from the shipyard into the inner-city streets. After days of sitting around on a ship, my legs were burning after just a couple minutes of walking, and I wanted to make sure we weren't about to walk all the way to the other coast before I even had lunch.

"Where are we going?" I asked Elfguy, which is what I had mentally taken to calling him since he refused to offer his real name.

"My apartment," he replied. "I need to figure out how to release this dragon safely. I'm only stringing you along because you brought it, and I'm not going to do all the work myself."

"That's… fair," I said, trying to sound like that wasn't my plan from the start. Whether for better or worse, this relative stranger, who had just been trying to turn me in to the police, was my best bet at getting anywhere near Mésura.

"At least you're an agreeable dragon smuggler. It's just up ahead."

The city around me was simultaneously completely alien and comfortingly familiar. The elven architecture exhibited more curves and slopes than the angular style of buildings in Exceres, and the unreadable language on the signs made me feel like I was dreaming, confined and disoriented. There were also features exactly like Exceres — banners flittering in the wind, idols in windowsills, vendors scattered around the street. I had no problem understanding *those* things; selling fruit was the same in any language.

"It's this one," Elfguy said, gesturing to a small apartment crammed between two larger residential blocks. He set the box down at the base of the steps and fumbled with a key to unlock the door. He waved me in, not waiting for me to catch up before he stepped through the doorway. I lifted the box and made my way up into the house as well.

The hallway from the door to the kitchen was just cramped enough to be uncomfortable to squeeze through with the crate, but it opened into a common room that was much more spacious than I expected. I set the box down in the middle of the room. Elfguy had already begun lighting up the small fireplace — I didn't think it was particularly cold, but the northwestern winters I had grown up with were probably unheard of in this region.

"Alright," he said once the fire had caught, "let's take a look at this dragon."

He came over and slowly lifted the box's lid, looking down over the beast as it breathed softly on the floor of the crate. Very carefully, and with a detectable sense of nervousness, he reached down and gently stroked the creature's wing. Its long neck twisted in its sleep, making him lurch back away from the box.

"Is it going to wake up soon?" I asked, hoping my suspicions were mistaken.

"Yes, probably," he muttered with a grim tone. "It was forced into hibernation once it was taken away from its territory, but now that it's back in the East, it will begin to wake over the next couple of days. We have two or three if we're very lucky — we need to get it out of the city."

"Well, I'm going to be heading to the capital for my business. Could there be any place to drop it off on the way?"

He scoffed. "You want to release a *dragon* on a highway connecting two of the largest cities on the continent? Are you trying to get someone killed?"

"Then where are we supposed to take it? I can't just go up into the Highlands to drop off a dragon, then turn around and go the other direction until I hit Mésura. Even if I had time for that, there has to be an easier way to do this."

"Well, you brought the dragon, you help me release it. I agree that we don't have time to make it to the Highlands, though. It would be possible for us to get a ride into the eastern plains in two days, return the dragon to its natural territory, and you can catch a river boat down to Lake Tontéres. Mésura sits right on its shore, so the whole thing would take four days, tops. I'm sure whatever business you have can wait that long."

I wanted badly to reject his proposal, but his tone suggested he wasn't asking. I didn't want him to turn me in for rejecting — and besides, I had no other way of getting anywhere on this continent. If it took a four day trip completely out of my way in order to get to Mésura, so be it. At least it would be faster than walking.

"Fine, I'll do it. But you're paying the fares," I said.

"I would take offense to that if I believed you had any money, but sure. It's been too long since I've gotten out of this city, anyway," he said. "We can get a carriage in the afternoon to take us east, but in the meantime, do you want some tea?"

I did want some tea. He set a kettle onto the fireplace and went into the kitchen to mix herbs. I examined the dragon for the first time close-up. Its scales were dark green, the color of moss, but somehow it seemed shadowy, as if it didn't catch light the same way normal things did. It almost shimmered — subtle waves of light would wash down its body toward its tail, which was long and jagged, scratching the interior sides of the box as it flitted aimlessly. The head at the end of its long, snake-like neck was angular, with narrow, closed eyes and a jaw that spanned almost the entire length of its head. I wouldn't want to come across this thing when it was awake, and I *definitely* wouldn't want to come across it when it grows up.

"Hey," I called to Elfguy, "how old do you think it is?"

He shrugged as he poured the herbs into cups. "I'm no expert, but it could be ten or fifteen years. Very rare to find a dragon that young, but they're popular with smugglers since their hundred-ton adult brethren wouldn't fit in a crate. It's why I was so suspicious of you when I first saw it, but smugglers don't usually try to take the dragons back *in* to the country."

It took me a second to process that he just said this little tiny dragon could have been *fifteen* years old. "So, how many years until it grows up into… you know… a *real* dragon?"

He laughed. "If you encountered it in the wild, it would seem like a pretty real dragon to you. But dragons are… weird. There really isn't any way to foretell how fast they'll grow. It could be the size of this room in twenty years or two hundred, there are so many factors it's almost impossible to say. Either way, we probably won't ever know, since I think we both want this thing as far away from us as possible." Then, he turned away from the herbs and crossed his arms. "Now it's my turn for the question. What's that stone *thing* you have in there with it? Did it come with the dragon?"

"Oh, no, it's nothing," I said, reaching in to take the tablet out. The dragon shifted in its slumber, making me withdraw my hands at the speed of sound with the tablet still at the base of its tail. "I just need it for my… business in Mésura. Hard to explain."

"A lot about you is hard to explain, isn't it?" he asked half-jokingly.

"More than you kn–" I was cut off by the kettle squealing as it billowed steam. Elfguy hurried over and took it off the fireplace, bringing it back into the kitchen and pouring it into the prepared cups. He stirred for a minute, then took the herbs out with a mote spoon and brought me the porcelain cup.

I took a small sip of the tea and had a visceral reaction. It was… definitely foreign. It tasted simultaneously cool and spicy, like a minty pepper. I assumed it was something of an acquired taste. I managed to push through the rest of the cup without crying, but I made a mental note to never accept any drinks from an elf again.

Finally, once the cups were empty and Elfguy had gathered his things, I took the crate and followed him out in search of a carriage. He led me down the street until the buildings began to space further apart and I could glimpse pastures through gaps in the apartment blocks. Tipped off by the permeating farm scent, I knew we had reached the stables long before he ushered me to the building. It connected to an expansive grass yard behind it, horses grazing leisurely in the distance. The saloon-style hinged door of the stables carried a sign that read *Hethrès int Amnir.* I tried to guess which word meant "horse" — my money was on Amnir — until Elfguy told me it meant "Carriages for Rent".

"Wait out here for now," he said. "Make sure to keep the box safe, and try not to talk to anybody — I mean, if you even find someone you *can* talk to. I won't take long."

He did take long. I set the box down and sat on top of it, kicking my legs like a little kid. It amazed me how it seemed impossible for anyone on either continent to design a way of renting a carriage that wouldn't take the entire afternoon. I watched as carriages rolled by, drawn by tall, eastern horses like the one that attacked us outside the inn the first night of my escape. I tried to stay attentive, but after so many minutes of waiting, I figured there wouldn't be any harm in just checking out the scenery.

Hopping off the box, I peeked through the gap in the swinging doors and saw Elfguy still talking to the shopkeep in their nonsensical language. As I suspected, I probably had some time to kill. I wandered around the back of the building, the grass of the meadow impossibly emerald. Coastal birds fluttered in the sky, chasing each other or swooping down to pick insects off the fields. The hills rolled on for as far as I could see, thinning into a line in the distance that connected with the sprawling blue sky. My attention was only drawn away from the scenery by the clop of horse hooves around the side of the stable. I figured it was time to go. I turned back and marched over to where I had left the crate.

Panic consumed me for a moment when it wasn't there, but Elfguy called out to me as he loaded it into the back of the carriage. "Sorry for the wait, they tried to charge me a Yil just for a day's travel east. Can you believe that? I managed to bargain it down, but prices have been unbearable ever since Homeis Utlis became Mol Stihirn." He smiled as he closed the trunk of the carriage. "At least Utlis kept *your* people out of the East — with the help of Remius Neiphorous, of course. I guess there are a few good humans left in the world."

I tried to smile back, but I physically couldn't bring myself to make the expression without grimacing, so I just went around the other side of the carriage and pretended to examine its unremarkable craftsmanship. I knew all about Utlis, of course, the leader of the Silver Council who commanded the defense against Acturas's eastern strategies, but it never occurred to me that anybody in the world would be an actual fan of *Neiphorous*.

"Yeah, um," I cleared my throat after my voice cracked on that last syllable, "Neiphorous is definitely there, yep. At least he's not Emperor Jourdan," I finally said. It was hard for me to say anything good about

Neiphorous, even as a lie, so it was easier to disguise it as a jab at my father. Elfguy went around to the carriage door and climbed inside as the driver returned from the stables. I followed, shocked at the furnished interior, even though it was just a linen-wrapped cushion across the bench. What I would have given for Cedric's carriage to have had this, back when Cedric was just a friendly driver and not… whatever he was to me now…

I shook my head. This wasn't the time. I let my thoughts scatter as the carriage rolled to life. There was a time and a place for *that* kind of crisis, and that was after I solved the one that was threatening the future of my empire.

The carriage rumbled from the paved city roads onto the shaky, dirt paths of the countryside, the tall horses making incredible time. I couldn't draw my eyes away from the windows — sprawling hills of grass and wild grain, rivers that looked clean enough to drink from, the sky fading into a sweet purple as the sun dipped toward the horizon. Scenes like this just couldn't be found in the West — at least not for the last several centuries, though it's said that at one point the continents were almost exactly alike. I wished I could have seen Excutatem when there was still Vibrancy in the land — after the dragons fled to the East, it flowed out with them, revitalizing this continent while leaving the West dull and without magic, except for the Ghânt Desert, whose sands stored Vibrancy and allowed magic to be catalyzed. It was a big problem for my father's conquest, stalling him in the South until… well, until the end.

"So," Elfguy said a handful of hours into our journey. "What's your business in Mésura? And why land in Yilioe if you want to get there — why not just take a ship further south and sail up the river?"

"I just have to meet with some people. And my journey here was *spontaneous,* to say the least, so I was working with whatever I could get my hands on," I said, taking my eyes off the outside landscape to look at him. That answer seemed good enough for him, and he dropped the subject. I was sure he was expecting more elaboration from me on the topic, but until he asked, I was keeping that information to myself.

"How about you?" I asked, "what do you do?"

"Nothing too interesting. I work with the Port Estate to try to crack down on smugglers, or at least make it look like we're trying. Can't say we're all that good at it — you bringing back that dragon probably did more good than anything I've done yet."

"Well, I wouldn't know what to do with this thing if you hadn't come along, so I think you're actually doing more here than me. Besides, I'm sure this isn't the first time someone's tried to move a native animal around," I said, trying to be helpful, but instead worrying that I came across as accidentally patronizing.

"Yeah, unicorn horns and feathers from endangered birds, but this is the first time I've ever encountered a *dragon.* Usually the smuggling rings pull out all the stops for trades like this. I can't imagine how you came across it in the first place."

"It's a… long story," I said, thinking back to climbing out the window of Meca's spare bedroom while she blew up the door behind me with magic.

We continued to chat on and off for the next several miles, until there was nothing but a black sky above us painted with glittering constellations. The horses trotted for an hour or so more under lamplight, but eventually the driver decided it was time for us to call it a night.

We pulled over to the side of the road in a lightly wooded area, the dirt path twisting away through the coalescing fog that had settled over the forest floor. The driver went to work removing the horses' harnesses. Elfguy moved immediately to sleep, leaning back against the wooden frame of the bench until I could hear his breathing slow to a steady rhythm. I tried to do the same, watching the stars peek through the shifting tree line above, and not long later, I drifted off.

Chapter Twenty-Five

I didn't know what woke me up. I sat up slowly, rubbing my eyes. The moon still hung high in the sky, and it was just as dark outside, but freshly cold. The fog had thickened, twisting around the trees, snaking through their branches and suffocating the fallen leaves on the ground. I tossed over and leaned back, closing my eyes. I waited for sleep for an annoyingly long while until I accepted that it was no use.

I muttered quietly to myself about never catching a break as I pulled back the handle to the carriage door. It clicked softly as the door popped open, and I climbed out of the cab without waking up Elfguy or the driver. I hopped in place to wake up and shake off the subtle bite of the air around me. I was more than comfortable in weather much deader than this, having grown up pretty much as far north as you could get, but it was jarring compared to the temperate winter day I had arrived in.

I stepped off the path onto the forest floor. The dirt was soft but coarse, crunching under my feet as I ventured further into the woods, still careful to stay within sight of the road. The moon shone bright overhead, but the ceiling of leaves above me blocked enough light for me to stumble on concealed roots and ditches.

It was when I took my eyes off the columns of trees towering around me to look back at the road that I noticed something was wrong. Instead of just one carriage-shaped shadow through the mist, I saw a second approaching from the direction we were going. In the middle of the night. With their lantern unlit. Whoever was driving that carriage didn't want to be noticed. I rested my hand on the hilt of my sheathed knife as I crept closer.

I listened carefully for any sound, but I could only barely make out the squeak of their wheels as they came to a stop in front of our carriage. I squinted, but couldn't see any figures step out through the fog. Crouched behind a tree just a few yards away from the road, I heard a whispered conversation between two people in Elvish, and though I couldn't understand what they were saying, I was smart enough to grasp that it wasn't friendly.

I heard the click of our carriage door opening and another set of boots hit the gravel. *That must be Elfguy*, I assumed, and my suspicion was confirmed by his familiar voice. I tried to interpret his words through his tone, but it didn't make any sense — why didn't he sound scared? I peaked around the side of the tree; I was close enough to see three people standing on the road. One held something up to the driver of our carriage, who sat awake with his hands raised. The other two were standing on either side. But if they were all together, then where was Elfguy?

I heard one of the three arrivals say something to the other two. One of them responded, and I pulled myself back behind the cover of the tree. It was Elfguy's voice, definitely. Was he *with them*? And who were *they* in the first place? I had guessed that the new arrivals were robbers or criminals, but if Elfguy knew them….

I tried to rationalize it. If he worked for the Port Estate against smugglers, maybe he just knew some people of that type and was telling them to head off. But if that was the case, why was he standing *with* them, letting them threaten the driver, and why weren't they leaving? And was I sure I could trust his testimony of who he was in the first place? I cursed myself for blindly believing anything I was told, but at the same time, I had no idea what I could have done differently even if I could go back.

They continued to talk. I heard the driver's voice — clearly desperate. Whatever they were talking about did not have a good outlook for him. I peaked around the side of the tree just in time to see him be silenced with a knife to the chest, and I lurched back to my hiding spot, petrified. I tried to control my breathing, but my heart was beating so hard I was afraid they'd be able to hear it from over there. I heard the thump of the driver's body falling to the ground, followed by a hauntingly calm discussion between them. Elfguy had a lot to say for a minute, and I wasn't sure whether it was my paranoia, or if I had actually heard him say the fake name I had given him. I heard dirt crunching as boots stepped off the road, creeping into the woods.

I jumped when Elfguy shouted, "Hey! Daren! Where'd you go? We're leaving soon! Gotta get an early start today!"

I was relieved he didn't know where I was, but it was replaced by the fear of knowing that he was looking for me. I clutched the hilt of my dagger and stayed pressed against the tree. I didn't risk unsheathing it yet, not wanting the glow to give away my hiding spot.

I heard one pair of footsteps approach from my left side. I readied myself to spring once he came around — it was only a matter of seconds. One step closer, the branches snapping beneath him. Another, leaves kicked up from the forest floor. I was just about to spring to the side and slash out with my knife before I felt a sharp point on the other side of my neck.

"You should take your hand off of that knife, Daren," Elfguy growled. I turned slowly to face the short sword he held to my throat. The other murderous elf stood just out of range of my knife. I lifted my hand.

The third elf came around the other side of the tree and took it from its sheath, awing its glow as he slipped it into his belt. I had to resist the urge to push him off, since he was big enough he could break my arm with his hand. He said something to Elfguy, who nodded in agreement.

"He said it's a nice knife, not the kind you would find from a human smith. We have to wonder where you got it," Elfguy translated.

I stayed silent as the large elf grabbed my arm and pulled me back to the road, Elfguy never taking his sword off me. I searched for any way out, but being unarmed and outnumbered, my options were few. The big elf pushed me against the side of the carriage. Elfguy held his sword up to my chest, the tip an inch away from my heart.

"Look, we don't want to hurt you. We just want to know about *that*," he said, nodding over to the trunk where we stashed the dragon box. "Where did you get it? If you tell us, we'll take it and leave, and then we can both go on with our lives. Otherwise, we'll kill you and take the dragon anyway. Your choice."

"I'm not stupid," I scoffed, somehow more offended than threatened. I had faced so much worse than these guys, it was almost insulting they thought they could intimidate me. "If I tell you, you'll kill me, and if I don't, you'll kill me. There isn't a choice here."

"Ah, correction: If you tell us, we *might* kill you, and if you don't, we *will*. So once again, where did you get the dragon?"

I could've just told them the truth, but then I was surely dead, and stalling would only postpone the inevitable. I had to think of an answer that would throw them off enough for me to get the upper hand. The big thief who had taken my knife was standing far out of reach, Elfguy was blocking me from moving forward at all, and the third elf was flanking me from the right, though I couldn't see if he was armed.

"Fine," I said, "I'll tell you the truth. I work for Remius Neiphorous." I paused as they exchanged a sudden glance, which I took as a good sign. "This dragon belonged to the Excutaris. I was bringing it back as a tribute to the Silver Council, but my convoy was delayed by pirates, and I was forced to take it on a merchant ship. That stone you saw in the box lets me prove my identity: it has an exact copy of my face, you can check it." The other two elves looked at Elfguy, not knowing about the stone, but the understanding on his face seemed to support my defense. For good measure, I finished, "What I was doing in the woods was sending a message to my associates in Mésura. If you kill me, Neiphorous will personally come back to the East just for you."

It was completely unbelievable, but it was wild enough to make him falter. This was my chance, but what do I do? I remembered the knife falling from the sky in that alleyway back in Exceres. I had absolutely no idea what caused that, or if I could do it again, but even if my suspicion was completely incorrect, I had to try. In the second he hesitated, I opened my palm at my side and let my desperation flow into it. The elf to my left shouted in surprise, and I looked down to see a jagged dagger in my grip. Elfguy turned to see what had startled his accomplice, and I flicked my knife up, knocking his sword away as I rushed toward him. I grabbed his forearm and slammed him down into the side of the carriage as his sword clattered to the road.

I saw the other two come at me from both sides, and I backed up toward the woods with my knife raised. Elfguy pulled himself up, bringing his sword back up. I was still outmatched, but at least now I had a weapon and a fighting chance. I thought of running, but I knew I could only get twenty feet at best before I tripped on a root and they slit my throat. I stood my ground with my knife raised, not letting any of them catch me at a weak angle. The elf to my left was smaller than me, and I was preparing to overpower him when the carriage shook.

The three thieves were too fixed on me to notice, but my eyes flickered back and forth between my attackers and the cab. At first, it just shuddered a bit, hardly noticeably. The next time, though, it shook hard, as if it had been hit by some invisible force. I forced myself to ignore it, the murderous marauders in front of me a bigger concern, but when I heard the sound of wood splintering from inside the cab, the blood drained from my face. I shuffled back, more scared now than I had ever been of the elves. The fat elf took this opportunity to charge me. He didn't make it.

Before he could even cover half the distance to me, the carriage exploded, chunks of wood launching in every direction. A form shot out into the night air faster than I could see. The horses which had been watching all of this unfold from the side of the road shrieked and snapped their ropes, disappearing into the mist in an instant. All four of us froze solid.

The dragon swooped down from the sky, snaking between trees as though warming up its wings from the disuse of hibernation. It emitted a deep, reptilian purr as it flitted about the tree line. I stood deathly still and quiet, hoping that it wouldn't notice us. My heart stopped when it swooped to land on top of the wreck of the carriage.

Its long neck undulated like a snake, examining each of us carefully, one at a time. When its eyes came to me, it unhinged its enormous jaw — making me flinch, as I wasn't a fan of being bathed in dragon fire — but only let out a croaking call, like the crackling of an enormous fireplace. I had no idea if that was good or bad for me, but as long as I wasn't broiling alive, I figured it could be worse.

All our eyes were trained on the dragon. My hands shook so badly I dropped my knife. The large elf stepped back, and the dragon hissed at him, its mouth opening to flaunt razor-sharp fangs. The elf to my left seemed to think this was a golden opportunity, lunging toward the dragon and slashing with his knife as if he thought he stood a chance.

Before the elf even reached the carriage, the dragon was in motion. It covered the distance between them faster than I could blink, and I squeezed my eyes shut as he was thrown far back into the ground, his shrieks cutting through the air.

Chaos at last broke out among the remaining three of us: Elfguy took off into the woods, the large elf put up his hands and stumbled backwards towards his carriage, and all I could bring myself to do was creep away until my back collided with the hard trunk of a tree, unable to tear my eyes off of the misted form of the dragon as it tore into the now-silent elf.

The dragon looked up from the corpse as if just realizing we had moved. It locked onto the large elf first, releasing an ear-rending screech and covering the distance to him in seconds. I only watched, mortified, as he was lifted into the air and then launched into the ground by a creature not even a quarter his size, one that I was able to carry around in a box. He didn't even have time to scream, only forcing out a strangled gurgle before he was silenced for good. A moment later, the dragon looked up again, eyeing the area until it landed on me.

Its eyes reflected blue in the moonlight, shimmering ethereally through the fog. Staring into them filled me with pure, concentrated dread, the kind that made my ancestors build fortresses and castles to keep them away just to be able to sleep at night. The dragon didn't fly to me; instead, it stepped tenderly off of the elf's corpse, creeping toward me achingly slowly.

I wanted to run, but knew there was no use if it could move faster than an arrow and kill faster than one, too. I clenched my fists, remembering the lessons I had taken as a child for this exact purpose — I mean, dragons weren't a regular issue in the West, at least not these centuries, but they were fresh enough in our collective memory that everybody in the aristocracy knew the warding gesture by muscle memory.

When the dragon came within five yards of me, it roared and reared back as if to pounce. Just as it left the ground, I thrust my hand in the air, palm facing out, my first three fingers bent into a claw. The dragon immediately pivoted, collapsing to the ground in panic before launching back into the air, disappearing in the other direction.

Knowing it would be back once it realized I wasn't really who I made it think I was — one of the ancient dragon hunters of the pre-Elemental age whose sacrifice of two fingers in training forever instilled a terror among dragons of three-fingered humans — I wasted no time bolting into the tree line. I stuck my hand out and willed the knife into it, and I felt my fingers curl around its hilt. I kept it in my hand as I tore around trees, over ditches and branches and roots that threatened to take me down. I had no idea if it had caught onto me yet; I figured that once it had, it would only be a matter of time before I was being ripped into just like the elves back there.

I heard a swirl in the highest leaves of the trees a few dozen feet behind me, and I glimpsed back just in time to run straight into the side of a tree. I crumpled to the ground, my vision swirling and the side of my head leaking blood onto the dirt.

I heard a mass drop a few feet to my side, leaves scattering on top of me from the landing. I was too disoriented to turn, but I didn't need to, because the dragon conveniently positioned its head right above mine, boring into me with the cold, frighteningly luminescent blue hue of its own crescent eyes. I thought for a second I was hallucinating when I heard a whispery, muffled voice in my head.

"*Yummba e etriticka humbe suom,*" the dragon said. I didn't know what language it was speaking, but I knew just from the power of it that it was absolutely ancient, possibly as old as the Divine Language itself.

"Ersa junes mia hidarthum," I said on the off chance that the dragon would understand. "*Please don't eat me*".

The dragon reared back and flapped its wings, portraying some mythical reptilian emotion I was not familiar with. In my head, in the Divine Language, it said, "*You speak the tongue of those my fathers swallowed whole. Perhaps I would swallow you whole, if only I were as large as the Old Flames.*" It followed up promptly with a not-hallucinated hiss.

I didn't like the idea of being swallowed whole. I responded out loud in the Divine Language, "I never killed your kin. Those wars were done long ago, I have no tie to them."

"*You speak of ties, but not of the blood-tie within you. I smelled it even in my sleep — you are stained with the spilled blood of my lineage. You have no place in the East, human king,*" it hissed, its tone deep with hate. I had no more panic left in me to rely on, all of the life-threatening emergencies of the past weeks wearing down any sense of self-preservation that might have guided me. Instead, I was guided by another force.

Thoughtlessly, like the words weren't my own, I said, "If you kill me, then she will never be free."

The dragon roared like a landslide, leaving my ears ringing. Luckily, I didn't need them, since the dragon spoke right into my thoughts.

"You cannot negotiate her freedom — even if it were your place to decide. I've been listening, fallen king. I know what has become of your empire, and I know that you are in no place to bargain."

My response seemed to come from a source much deeper in my mind than I had ever dared to venture. I didn't know who was speaking, but it wasn't me. "The chains cannot be broken but by my hand. I alone bear the mandate of the crown. If I am slain, she will be sealed away until the death of the realms. Weigh the cost of your revenge carefully," I warned in a voice that wasn't my own. I was once again afraid, but not because of the dragon. I felt disassociated from the scene altogether, like I was a spectator watching the exchange unfold from a distance. I didn't know what any of this meant, but prayed it didn't make the dragon any angrier.

The dragon growled a low, scratchy hum. *"I have no desire to spare you. Alas, your line of mortal wretches will not end here. I will let you live this day, so long as you shall free the hostage once the time comes. I may grow slower than my cousins, but I will still be large enough to tear your castle apart if you forsake your oath, soon enough for you to see it first hand. Is the deal made?"*

I felt a mysterious weight on top of me. I knew whatever I said next would be decisive, not just in this moment, but in the overall scheme of an ancient conflict thousands of years in the making. I hoped the Elementals would understand, and I hoped my decision wasn't as selfish as it felt.

"Alright," I said with confidence I didn't know I had left, "I agree. I will free her, if I live to return."

The dragon hummed once again, prying into me with its gaze. *"Then you shall live to return."* With that, it took off into the sky, leaving nothing but a shower of leaves in its wake. I lay still for a moment, breathing hard.

What have I done? I hadn't even worn the crown yet, and I just made a decision I had a feeling would be one of the most consequential since Obelevon the Dragonslayer, my several times great-grandfather, chased them from Excutatem in the first place. What secrets had he hid? I rolled onto my side and found my knife on the ground. I slipped it into its sheath, then leaned on the tree as I shakily stood. I set off the way I had come, praying that the Elementals wouldn't cast me into the Trench for betraying a legacy I didn't know existed.

Chapter Twenty-Six

I retraced my steps to the road under the moonlight, my legs aching from running and my everything else aching from everything else. I stepped out of the tree line. The ruins of our carriage lay alongside the elves' — theirs was undamaged, but with but no horses to draw it. The door hung ajar. It was clear it had been emptied, with empty bags and shattered boxes strewn about.

"Fucking Elfguy," I muttered. Of all the people I hoped the dragon came across next, he was near the top of my list, right below Neiphorous and whoever it was that decided I should be the one to cross every legendary beast that existed. I approached the wreck of our old carriage, its wood beams splintered from the inside. The enchanted stone still sat at the bottom of the dragon's shattered wooden cell, thankfully unbroken. I retrieved it from the box and held it up. I was exhausted from dealing with magic in any capacity, and I wanted nothing more than to leave this fake face behind me.

I had no idea what I was doing, but it's not like I could go to the Ghânt and find a witch to help me. I held the mask up to eye level, looking into the face-shaped indent. *What's the worst that could happen?* I thought as I hesitantly pulled it hard onto my face. I expected to once again feel the stone melt around my face, but instead, it snapped my facial features back in place in an instant. I panicked at the unexpected jolt, peeling it off as quickly as I had put it on.

My skin burned from the transformation. Bringing my fingers to my jaw, I flinched as they grazed the sensitive flesh, but the shape felt decidedly normal. I wouldn't know for certain if it worked until I looked into a mirror, but it at least *felt* close enough.

Suddenly, my hands felt lighter. I stared in awe as the tablet crumbled to sand around my fingers, the particles drifting away into the fog. Whether it was undone or not, there was no turning back now, so I just had to hope my dumb luck carried me yet again.

With nothing else to do but wait, I began to walk down the dirt lane. My eyes had long since adjusted to the darkness when I saw the first sparks of pink sunrise arc across the sky.

I walked until the mid-morning sun had risen well into the sky and the wreckage of the cab was long gone behind me. I slouched from exhaustion, dragging my feet with every step, but I couldn't stop. Straining my eyes ahead of me, I froze: The outline of a town stuck out across the straight edge of the horizon.

It took me another hour to reach the village. I was sure I looked about as bad as I felt, but I was only grateful to be out of the woods, away from the dragon and the marauding elves. Townsfolk paid me worried glances whenever I caught their attention, but none bothered me. Now that I had made it to a town, the hard part would begin: I had to find a way to the capital.

To make matters worse, before I had even reached the town center, an elf lightly clad in leather armor intercepted me with his hand to my chest.

"Túr obeshu hothlorèn," he demanded.

I blinked, and he seemed to correctly assess that I didn't understand.

"Does… does anybody here speak Humanic?" I asked futilely. He blinked this time. We had apparently come to an impasse — me wanting him to help me get to Mésura, him wanting to know my business in the town, neither of us having any idea how to proceed.

"Eurrrr… té… ventres… in… ilthe… notra… mius… Iutrelthon," he said patronizingly slowly, as if talking at a snail's pace would miraculously bring me Elvish fluency. He gestured for me to follow him, and having neither a reason for suspicion nor a real alternative, I did.

He led me through the winding streets of the village until we came to a stop in front of what I took as the town hall — it was the largest building I had seen, and the best kept, with a small garden out front and large windows on all sides. He held open the faded door and followed me in once I passed over the threshold. The entire interior was one large room, stiflingly musty with the windows closed and a persistent old carpet smell despite the bare floor. A small desk sat at the opposite end of the room, occupied by an ancient elf scratching a quill on parchment.

The officer spoke, informing the older elf of our arrival. "Iutrelthon, get humên ventrest hice elima gothai. El thaeren if Elvenès."

The elf behind the desk, presumably a mayor of some sort, nodded and waved my guide over, leaving me standing awkwardly by myself. The mayor pulled himself up from his seat to examine me with disinterest, as if he had been around for so long that nothing could surprise or intrigue him.

The mayor said something to me in Elvish. His voice was worn down but clear, not raspy or whispery like I expected from somebody of his age. I began to respond that I didn't know what he was saying, but he put up his hand to silence me.

Taking a cane that leaned against his desk, he shambled to a cabinet on an adjacent wall. He pulled open the glass door with a thud, setting his cane down as he leafed through boxes and bits of paper. At last, he retrieved a large blanket of ink-stained parchment and unfolded it to present a map. The officer scrambled to take the paper from the mayor as he returned to his desk.

The officer splayed the map on top of the desk and smoothed over its crosswork of creases. I came closer. For such a small town, their map had many fewer inaccuracies than I expected.

The mayor locked eyes with me and spoke again, tracing along the map what I assumed were directions or instructions. Not understanding exactly, but assuming I knew what he was getting at, I put my finger down on Yilioe and drew east along what I presumed to be the route I had taken with Elfguy, ending at the large dot representing the town.

The elf nodded, then put his own finger on the town and continued the journey east toward the river. I nodded. Then, he traced his finger down the river to a large black splotch I knew to be Lake Tontéres. Again, I nodded, putting my finger on the dot labeled, in fine calligraphy, *Mésura*.

The elf leader turned toward the officer and muttered something. The officer responded; I stood silently, waiting for the verdict. Then, the officer looked at me and rubbed his fingers, a universal sign to ask if I had cash. I shook my head solemnly, then turned out my pockets, hoping they got the idea. If I couldn't pay them back, I could at least win them over with pity.

The older elf turned to his subordinate, confusion showing on his face. The officer said something to him, and he nodded, then rubbed his chin in thought. They exchanged more words as I stood waiting, hoping they wouldn't just shrug and kick me back out onto the street. After some deliberation, they appeared to have reached a consensus: The elf sat back down as the officer came around the desk and escorted me out of the room.

He led me down the street, passing small houses and quiet shops. Villagers peeked out from windows or doorways to catch a glimpse of the human who had arrived unannounced with no business. We reached the bank of an immense river, the deep water rolling lazily. A bridge connected this half of the river to an adjacent town on the other side. A boathouse sat on stilts half over the water, but it seemed too small to hold any actual boats, so a line of small canoes and sailboats were tied beside it on the shore.

"Ané!" the officer shouted, announcing our arrival to the elf woman who emerged from the hut. I waited behind as he greeted her and began a lengthy explanation, filled with surprised interjections and side glances on her part. I didn't like them gossiping about me in a foreign language, but it didn't last long before she nodded, albeit somewhat reluctantly, and waved the officer off.

As he turned back down the street, the elf lady approached me, dusting off her hands and untying her orange hair. "Ané," she said, putting her hand on her chest. I blinked, failing to grasp her meaning. She rolled her eyes and gestured to herself again, repeating the word

"Oh, *you're* Ané?" I realized. She nodded at the sound of her name. I pointed to myself and said, "Damion."

I realized too late that I shouldn't have used my actual name, especially when it was probably so notorious across the entire continent. It was a fairly common name for people in my generation, though — every parent wanted to name their son after the heir to the empire — so I would just have to roll with it and hope she never put the dots together.

She led me up the steep ramp to the boathouse and pulled open the twine screen door. The room was muggy and quiet, the only sounds being the muffled rushing of water below and the creaking floorboards as we filed in. The sole source of light came from the screen door, casting mysterious shadows in the far corners of the cluttered room.

Ané busied herself by tinkering with some device on a workbench at the far end of the hut. I decided to take a look around, though there wasn't much to see: pencil drawings hung on the walls, diagrams of boats and a map of the Eastern Continent that, unlike the last map I saw, was *well intentioned,* but not necessarily *accurate.* My eyes wandered to the cluttered shelves lining the walls, each overflowing with essentially anything one could ever need to sail a boat — linen, oars, hooks. Ané set down her project with a disappointed sigh, and I could finally see what it was: a broken compass, the kind imported from the Southeast that used some sort of magical north-oriented rock to point the way. I hadn't seen one in years, the trade embargos of the war tanking supply in the empire.

I mindlessly scanned the shelves, hardly even processing the variety of things I saw, until my eyes fell upon something unlike the rest. A coin. It was engraved with an image of a glowing ship hovering above waves. Judging from the grime and dullness of the copper, I imagined it was almost as old as the mayor, but couldn't have been worth much if they just left it sitting on the counter. I picked it up, examining it with mild interest. On the back were four lines of Elvish verse in fine cursive.

Ané sighed with disappointment and set down the compass. Then, her head shot up in my direction. Without thinking, I slipped the coin into my pocket so that she wouldn't see me messing with it, but I soon realized that she wasn't looking at me — she was looking past me, at the narrow doorway. I heard the footsteps before I saw the silhouette of an elf against the late morning light as he clambered up the ramp.

He paused in surprise when he saw me, obviously not expecting to find a human in his shed, but Ané pushed past me and began to explain. She nodded back at me; he shot me an irritated glance, then looked back at her to continue their incomprehensible conversation.

After she explained the situation of my sudden arrival, she waved for me to follow them as they stepped out of the boathouse. The three of us walked along the riverside to a sailboat tied to a post in the sand. It was clearly designed for two people, but we could manage — and I wouldn't be complaining about comfort as long as it got me where I needed to go.

"If you're wondering why we're bringing you with us," he began in practiced Humanic, making me jump. I hadn't expected anything in this town to speak it. "Lord Iutrelthon decided that since we're already going south, you can come along. You're lucky he isn't making you pay. Old age has made him more generous than I would be."

"You speak Humanic?" I asked cautiously.

"You think because we're a small town, we have no contact with the rest of the world? I travel to Mésura or Yilioe every month — I've been dealing with humans there for the last ten years. Ané comes, too, but she only trades with our elven customers."

"Right, sorry," I conceded, not wanting to get on the wrong side of the only person in this village I could even talk to. "And I appreciate the ride. Maybe once I get to Mésura I'll be able to scrounge up something to pay you back."

He shrugged, then went back to checking the supplies in the boat. "I doubt that, but at least it doesn't cost us anything extra if you're just taking up an extra space. Just don't expect us to make you dinner, because it'll be a long journey."

"How long should it take?"

He sighed, obviously tired of the questions. "We should reach the mouth of Tontéres by midnight if the currents and wind agree with us. It would be too dangerous to sail through the lake overnight, so we'll pause there and finish the rest by noon tomorrow, hopefully."

I nodded even though he wasn't looking at me. I was grateful for the free trip, though I quietly hoped he wasn't serious about not giving me anything to eat for the next twelve hours. Content that the boat was ready for our departure, he finally stood.

"I'm Tetre by the way. Ané's older brother."

I was surprised by the complete lack of resemblance: Ané was fairly tall, whereas Tetre was hardly my height; Tetre had dark brown hair, Ané's was red. I did see a similarity in their eyes, though — his were darker than hers, but they were the same rich brown.

"Nice to meet you, Tetre," I responded, "my name's–"

"Damion, right? Ané told me. Pretty unfortunate to be named after *that* guy," he joked. "You know, you both left Excutatem to come to the East around the same time. That's actually pretty funny. Do you happen to have any castles back home?"

I started to laugh along with him before I processed what he had said. "Wait," I interrupted, my brow furrowed, "Dam– *he's* in the East? How do you know?!"

"Don't ask me, it's just a rumor. Some people are saying that he got on a ship to Minesra with the help of a mob boss in Exceres. They questioned the people on the ship, but nobody saw him, so it's probably not true. Besides, he'd have to be stupid to come *here*."

I didn't disagree with him there. I began to regret impulsively changing my face back when I did — I could have really used a disguise right about now.

Ané and Tetre noticed an elf approaching from the road and went to greet her. She wheeled a long box on a cart behind her. I looked between the boat and the box; I couldn't imagine how it would fit in there between the three of us. The elf with the cart dropped the box at the edge of the beach. She looked at me and asked a question to the other two; they nodded. I focused on the box, avoiding their gaze.

Tetre and Ané both took a side of the box and lifted it off the cart. It definitely didn't seem light, but Ané must have been stronger than she looked, since they guided it over to the base of the boat without much struggle. They set it down on the sand and shook out the remaining weight from their arms. Tetre dug around the various scattered supplies within the boat for a tightly-knit tarp and a thick rope.

He handed Ané the tarp. She wrapped it around the box, and Tetre wound the rope around it several times before tying it into an elaborate knot. Ané tested it to make sure it held as Tetre secured the other end to the boat. I was shocked when they lifted the box once again, walked to the edge of the river, and, on three counts, flung it several feet into the water, launching water into the air. I expected the box to shoot straight to the bottom of the river, but once the ripples settled, it floated on the surface as if it were hollow.

"What's in there?" I asked Tetre.

"None of your business," he said, wiping off his hands. He seemed to be taking every opportunity to make sure I knew that he didn't trust me, which I admitted was a fair judgement. "But since you asked, we're bringing a unicorn horn to an auction in Mésura. It's too big to fit in the boat, but they float, so we just trail it behind."

I was dumbfounded that I just watched some elves haphazardly chuck a *unicorn horn* — one of the most valuable commodities from the East — into a river, but it didn't seem at all out of the ordinary for them as Tetre climbed in over the side and readied the rudder. Ané waved me over and gestured to an open spot at the front end. I stepped into the boat and adjusted myself to fit in the tight space. Finally, Tetre untied the rope holding the boat to shore and let the current pull us onto the river, their magical cargo trailing behind.

Chapter Twenty-Seven

It wasn't long before boredom took over. The boat rolled painfully slowly when the wind died, and the current didn't seem to be in any rush to get to Lake Tontéres. Ané busied herself with the sail while Tetre steered from the back, and whatever words were spoken were in Elvish, leaving me with nothing to do but dangle my hand in the river and watch the clouds drift by.

Growing up in a region mostly dominated by dark forests and cold mountains, the endless lush meadows around the river seemed almost impossible in the dead of winter. It might have been snowing in Exceres while I was getting a sunburn in the East. The elves seemed completely unbothered by the heat, though: Despite being just as pale as me, they never seemed to burn, which just felt unfair.

I didn't think about much of anything as the boat continued to drift down river. Occasional concerns would try to intrude about where I was going and what I was going to do once I got there, but I forced them out of my focus. This cycle continued until the sun dipped beneath the horizon and the enormous blue sky dwindled into black. I looked up to the stars and saw… none. No moon, either. Startled by the potential cosmic horror unfolding above me, I turned to Tetre, illuminated in the dim, wavering glow of his lantern.

"What's going on with the sky?"

He glanced up and blinked. "What do you mean? It's still there," he said. Ané just reclined on the side of the boat, uncaring about whatever we were talking about.

"But where are all the stars? The moon?"

He looked up again, then sighed like he was ashamed to be sitting on the same boat as me. "Do you not have *clouds* in the West?"

I squinted at the sky. Invisibly black clouds had swooped in above us, blending in seamlessly to the darkness of the night behind them. *Guess that answers that*, I thought, pretending I wasn't embarrassed to have immediately assumed the celestial bodies just disappeared. I mean, it was just clouds.

I was just letting myself relax when the first thunder crash echoed across the plains. I sat up as Ané said something to Tetre, who nodded.

"We think it might rain," he translated. "If it gets bad, we'll need to pull to shore and wait it out. This boat can't handle that kind of weather."

I didn't like the idea of having to wait any longer to continue my journey, but I also didn't like the idea of being in a *second* boat-related disaster. He didn't wait for my input as he fished around in the dim light for a map while Ané wrestled with the sail against the shifting winds. There was another clap of thunder, and out of the corner of my eye I saw a distant cloudbank erupt with lightning. For a split second, it revealed the fury of the skies above us, and docking the boat for the night seemed like a much better idea.

Tetre scanned the map as best he could with it clutched between his fists, the wind fighting to steal it away. He called out to his sister, but she shook her head. He retorted, frustrated, but she clearly wasn't willing to back down. Tetre turned reluctantly to me.

"The map says there's a town not far downriver. If we open the sail, we should be able to get there and beat the rain, but Ané thinks it's too risky and that we should steer to the shore now. That makes you our tiebreaker. Try not to get us killed."

I didn't like being put on the spot, but I had made a lot of difficult decisions so far. Surely I could manage this. "It would probably be better to get to the town. Pulling over will stop us from sinking, at least, but if we make it to the town, then we won't be caught out in the storm."

Tetre nodded smugly and relayed my decision to Ané. She shot me an exasperated glance, but relented, unfolding the sail so it could catch the incoming winds. The ship veered to the side as we picked up speed, but Tetre steadied it with the rudder. It was right at that moment that the first raindrop pelted me in the forehead. I wiped it away and prayed silently to Signel that we'd reach the town in time.

The gale tore at the sail, and Ané held the rope with all her strength to keep it secured. Thunder shook the skies, and dry lightning arced down to the plains in bursts of violence. Tetre compared the map to our surroundings, trying to judge how much further the town was, but more raindrops thudded against the boat, and he slipped the map back into his leather bag to protect it. Thunder crashed again, shaking the frame of the boat. The rain followed.

It was hard to see, hard to *breathe* under the torrent. The sail flitted helplessly as Ané pulled it down, deciding that this was far enough, and Tetre didn't argue this time. The boat rocked on the churning river, taking on water from the rain and waves lapping over the side. Tetre tried to maintain control as best he could, but the current was no longer cooperating.

He angled us so that the rushing water carried us toward the shore, so fast I began to worry we would crash, but at least we'd still be on land. My attention was drawn to a rumble far upstream, but it quickly grew louder than the thunder as it neared. We all looked up at once. We could only stare in horror into the darkness, not seeing the source until a lightning strike revealed it — closing in fast, a wall of water barrelled toward us.

I barely had time to brace myself against the sides of the boat before the wave overtook us. My ears rang with the crack of the boat shattering as I was swallowed by the water and sent spinning into the depths. I thrashed wildly for the surface — or, at least, the direction I *thought* was the surface — clinging onto whatever breath I had managed to take before the impact. A jolt of pain sent me deeper to the riverbed as a sharp wooden fragment hit me in the chest. My lungs burned and my arms ached from fighting against the current, scrounging for anything to grab ahold of.

I was struck again by another piece of debris. I grabbed it to push it away, but held on as I felt it was *rising*. It felt like some sort of long, swirled rod — definitely not a piece of the boat, but if it was somehow bringing me back to the surface, I wasn't letting it go. I held it close as it cut seamlessly upward through the current, and I finally broke through the waves, gasping for air. Rain pelted me, and savage waves still fought to pull me back down if I dared let go of the lifeline in my arms.

I kicked my feet toward the shore. I didn't know how far I had to go as I squeezed my eyes shut from the onslaught of water, but I fell into a rhythm, focusing on nothing but holding onto the rod and pushing myself further. I ignored the soreness, not letting it slow me down. I seemed to swim for an eternity against currents and waves that wanted me dead, but I managed to channel one final burst of energy as my fingers grazed wet sand.

I grasped for the beach, but the sand broke off and fell away into the water, so I jammed the rod into the shore for leverage. I pulled myself forward until I managed to grab onto a rock on the shore, holding on to it as I broke free of the river and collapsed onto the sand. I heaved hard, blinking rain out of my eyes to no avail. I wanted to lay there and wait out the storm, give myself a chance to rest, but I forced myself to sit up.

I reached down and felt for whatever it was that had saved my life. It was several feet long and smooth, almost bony, with ridges swirling up from the base toward the pointed tip. I had felt something like it before, but it wasn't until a lightning bolt lit up the riverbank that I saw it clearly. I almost laughed at the absurdity of it.

The unicorn horn was buried halfway in the beach, pure marbled porcelain beneath a thin layer of sand and river grime. I had seen them before in the castle — my father had a secret collection in his chambers, believing their magic would ward off assassins. I tried to pry it out of the ground, but it proved too slippery and heavy to even budge, so I could only leave it sticking out of the sand as I pushed myself to my feet. I climbed up the beach, clinging onto whatever handholds I could find in the rocks at the top of the ridge.

The rain cascaded over me, trailing down my face and dripping from my nose in a steady stream. My adrenaline gave way to exhaustion, only worsened by the freezing water that soaked me to my core. I wiped my face on my wet sleeve and squinted through the darkness for any sign of Tetre or Ané, but I couldn't make much out through the rain. If Tetre's map was correct, there should be a town close downriver.

Soaking wet, freezing, and with no sign of the storm letting up, I set off along the river. All I could do was hope that things wouldn't get worse. I was usually not that lucky.

Chapter Twenty-Eight

My boots squelched in the mud as I trudged along the riverbank, having long since given up trying to shield my face from the rain. After fifteen minutes of marching, I came across the wreck of the sailboat — thankfully without the bodies of any elves strewn among the annihilated hull. Still, that meant I was once again on my own.

Through the apocalyptic weather, I scanned ahead as far as I could for any sign of civilization — a light, the roof of a building. Nothing. I began to worry that the map had simply been incorrect, that the town was miles downstream and I would be stuck out here for longer than I knew.

I tripped on nothing and fell to one knee. The sodden earth muddied my already soaked clothes, but I didn't pull myself back up. I couldn't keep going on like this.

A lightning bolt in the distance shot light across the fields, glinting off a piece of metal on the ground in front of me. I picked it up and squinted hard, but couldn't make out what it was. I reached to my sheath and pulled out the Valkyrie dagger, holding it up to the object.

The silver light of the knife gleamed off the copper surface of the coin I had accidentally stolen from the boathouse, the ship impressed on its front now shadowy and imposing. It must have fallen from my pocket. I held it closer, examining the words on the back of it carefully in the dull light.

"Set-er mon-eh-lay tu-fair ahem-bolay estis," I muttered, sounding out the syllables in my unpracticed, culturally insensitive Elvish accent as if it would bring them any meaning to me. With no use for it, I went to slide the coin back into my pocket, but froze when lightning struck just up river, bathing me in light. Except, it didn't come and go in the blink of an eye — it lingered. In fact, it grew *brighter.* I faced the light and squinted in the sudden brightness. I couldn't believe what I was seeing.

A boat was floating down the rapids of the river. Not a sailboat, either; a *ship*, the kind you would see traversing the open ocean, with sprawling white sails and a ram on the front. The entire vessel was bathed in a shimmering glow, launching light in front of it like the most powerful lantern in the world. I had to blink to make sure I wasn't hallucinating.

The ship cruised to a stop along the shore where I stood. It didn't sway an inch on the wild waters, or drop any sort of anchor. Peering down from the deck was a man dressed in eastern sailing vestments completely unsuitable for the weather — short sleeves and no hood, like he was sailing under clear skies. He pushed a plank over the side, and it planted firmly in the mud at my feet. Bewildered, I looked around me. I was surrounded by nothing but the same dreary, rain-stricken meadows for as far as I could see. My options were either to climb onto the magic ship, or to wander the plains for what could be days. I set my foot on the plank.

The ramp was too steep to stand on, so I had to crawl up to keep from tumbling over the side. Once I neared the top of the ramp, the sailor reached forward, grabbed my forearm, and pulled me up the rest of the way. I spilled over onto the deck of the ship unceremoniously, but hurried back to my feet, watching him pull the ramp back up. The ship immediately rolled into motion.

I whirled around to examine the deck and found in sight but the sailor. Even stranger, the rain no longer fell on me; I could still see and hear the storm raging in the fields, but the ship seemed somehow exempt. I turned back to the sailor who stood at the railing, watching me in turn. I got the impression that he was waiting for me to do something.

"Well?" he said. His voice was rather soft for a sailor, though he had a clear eastern accent — not Elvish, but unlike anything you'd hear in Excutatem.

"... I'm sorry? I don't actually know what you want from me," I said.

He blinked. "You read the script, though, did you not? You know that you have to offer payment, yes?"

"What do you mean 'script'? I don't remember–"

He interrupted me, his patience evidently worn thin. "The coin. I know you have the coin, I can sense it. You read the words on the back, but I gather you didn't know what they meant. No problem! I'll explain."

He walked to the larger part of the deck and gestured broadly to the ship. "This is my ship. Beautiful, isn't she? Lovely aura about her. And since *you* had one of my coins of invocation, *you* get to decide where she goes! Just pay up, and we'll be on our way."

I stared at the sailor as he flaunted the ship's supposed power. I wasn't sure whether I could trust him, but if this ship would really go *anywhere* I wanted, then this was exactly what I needed.

"So… I just have to pay you and you'll take me to Mésura?" I asked as I reached into my pocket to retrieve the coin.

"Exactly!" He smiled to reveal a set of strangely white teeth. I held the coin out to him, but his smile fell.

"What do you want me to do with that thing?"

My eyes darted between it and him, confused. "I thought I had to…?"

He stood in silence for a second before bursting into laughter. "Oh, you thought you could *pay* with the coin? I'm afraid that's not how it works, traveler. Try again, and this time with something more worth my time."

I lowered my arm, the coin clutched in hand. "I thought the coin was what I would use to pay for the trip. I mean, usually things like this are bundled up like that — one artifact that does everything, you know?"

He scoffed. "No, I don't know. That's a horrible business model. What, if you sent a letter to a guild asking for a repair to your shutters, would you expect that letter itself to suffice as payment? Of course not. That's silly. Very silly."

I couldn't argue with that. The last thing I needed was to get kicked back out into the rain. "Okay, sure. So what do you want? I don't have much else to give," I admitted.

"That's no problem! Most of the people I pick up are starving, dead broke, or *actually* almost dead. I'll just take a portion of your soul and spirit you to your destination — you *do* have your whole soul intact, don't you?"

"Hold on, hold on," I said, backing up, "that's a pretty big leap. My soul isn't really for sale. Can you take something else? I have… uh, I have…" I looked over myself, wondering if he would value my muddy, water-logged boots as much as my mortal spirit. On second thought, I kind of hoped he wouldn't.

"Sorry, no. Besides, I'll only take a small part, just enough to add to my collection. You probably won't even notice until you die, and when you're dead, you won't care that you're missing a little bit, now will you?"

"I think I will, actually. Still want to keep my soul."

"I'm afraid that's not an option." His face darkened as he stepped toward me.

My hand shot to my dagger. I could try to fight him, but I was on *his* ship, and I didn't know the extent of his magic. If I was going to figure out a way to get away from this guy, I needed to know who — or, more precisely, *what* — he even was.

"Let's just wait a second," I said, backing away from him. "At least tell me who you are. I need to know who I'm working with before I, you know, give them my soul."

He didn't stop his approach, but he smiled, patting his chest. "The elves know me as 'Kuthrîs', but obviously I won't tell you my *actual* name. They call me a 'demon of the water'" — he included the air quotes — "but I'm actually *made* of water. Just water that likes to collect."

My blood ran cold. I wasn't familiar with elven demons, but if they were anything like the ones back home, I was in a much more serious situation than I thought. It didn't matter if it could get me to Mésura in the blink of an eye — it wasn't worth the cost.

I stalled with the first thing that came to mind. "So, uh, how did that little village get the coin? I feel like it–"

"If you're trying to put off your fate, at least ask me a question I can answer. I have no idea how they got the coin. I really don't care. Please at least ask more interesting questions if it's how you want to spend your final moments."

I backed into the railing. I glimpsed over the side of the ship, the waters below roiling black in the storm. I risked a glance back to Kuthrîs — he was nearly on me. I sucked in a deep breath and pushed myself over the side.

I was knocked sprawling back onto the deck, my skin burning where I hit the glow that surrounded the ship as if it was a barrier keeping me in Kuthrîs's domain.

The demon chuckled. "Good try, but that won't work. I went through all the effort of picking you up, I'm not leaving without a sale. Now, I think I've had enough of this — time to pay up."

There was nowhere for me to get up without practically running straight into him. He knelt down at my side and grabbed my face; I put up my arm to protect myself.

He reared back, howling and screeching as he clung to his arm. I lay frozen on the ground. The Elemental bracelet that hung from my wrist glowed a deep, glassy red which quickly cooled to nothing more than a black shadow within the crystal. Kuthrîs growled to himself as he staggered away from the divine force, his hand smoking and oozing black blood from a very real wound that I couldn't believe was inflicted by a piece of jewelry. But he wasn't dying. I knew that he would rebound, and at this point, I suspected he would be wanting more than a piece of my soul once that happened.

I rolled over onto my stomach and staggered to my feet, but didn't run. I had nowhere to go. I drew my Valkyrie dagger quickly and faced Kuthrîs, who had now recovered from his burn.

His voice was pained and rough as he pointed at me. "I should have known! *YOU* are a conspirator, is that it?! Sent by the usurping western gods to end me?" His eyes glossed over, then melted down his face as pure water. His next words came out in a new voice, this one deep and warbling like he was speaking from the river. "*I won't have it.*"

He stuck out his arm and water cascaded from his sleeve, not spilling to the ground, but extending out to form the staff of a trident. The weapon drizzled water from its three points, pooling a small puddle on the ground at his feet. He reared it back to spear it at me, and I threw myself out of the way, but barely fast enough — the residual rain water on my sleeve quickly stained red from the cut it left. The water-based weapon collided with the wooden deck of the ship, collapsing into a puddle on the floorboards. By the time I was back on my feet, he had already replaced it with a second trident.

Kuthrîs held up his new weapon in front of him to keep me at a safe distance. Now that I knew his tricks, though, I had to strike first. I dove toward him. He swung at me, but I escaped the pointed tips as I rolled to his side. The pole of the trident hit me hard on the back, surprising me at how solid a weapon made of water could be. It knocked me forward, but I caught myself, slicing back with my knife to parry his next swing. Both our weapons clashed off each other, stunning us, but I recovered faster.

As he was raising his trident back up, I charged him, stabbing for his chest. He put up his hand to block me, and my knife sliced straight through two of his fingers, turning them to water which spilled to the ground.

"Nice try, human," Kuthrîs jeered as he stepped back to examine his hand, "and next time, try aiming for my head — it's the only part of me that you could actually hurt."

I thought it was awfully convenient that he would share that. I brought up my knife to the side to knock away his trident, but he deflected it, jutting forward faster than I could dodge it. The outer point left a shallow puncture in my side, the water immediately washing away the blood. I grimaced, but had no time to examine the injury as he launched it again at me. I leapt back as the trident hit the spot I had been standing. It fell apart again against the deck.

Watching him remake the trident, I noted that he seemed slower, more concentrated. If I could keep this up long enough to wear him down, I could… do something. Anything. I didn't have time to plan it out, since the demon was stabbing the trident straight for my throat.

I turned to the side, letting it slip past me. Out of instinct, I grabbed the pole of the trident, but my hand only came away dripping as it went *through* the water making up its staff. Cut off from the source, the entire length of the weapon up from where my hand passed through came undone and splashed to the ground. Kuthrîs waved the remaining half of it in frustration, struggling to get it to reform. It was obvious now that his water was spread thin. I was getting close, I just had to hold out a little bit longer…

Before he could strike back against me, I lunged at him. He staggered back, bringing the staff up, but I parried with my knife. I swiped at his head, but he blocked me by materializing a dual trident in the blink of an eye. The demon fell to his knees from the effort it took to make the new weapon, paler in the face and water dribbling from his mouth like blood.

The energy of sustaining two weapons made him sluggish, and I jumped up faster than he could counter me. I stabbed down into his skull.

Water gushed from the wound and spilled in torrents onto the deck. I stumbled back, not wanting to get any of his water on me, and watched him writhe around as his life force spilled out and seeped into the floorboards. He dissolved from the head down into nothing but a wet mark on the floor.

Breathing hard, I looked around. *Is that it?* It seemed… I mean, with the bleeding cuts from the tridents, I wouldn't have called it *easy,* but did I actually just kill a demon? I noticed a trapdoor in the center of the deck. Not knowing what else to do, I walked over

— avoiding the demon puddle on the ground — and pulled it open.

The inside of the ship didn't glow. It reeked of mildew, like it had been floating at sea unattended for a hundred years. I *really* didn't want to go down there — nothing good could come from the bowels of a demon ship.

I held up my dagger. The glow revealed a small staircase leading to a lower deck. The stairs in question were twisted and scratched, like a wild animal had been locked down there for some time, but if a pack of hungry wolves waited patiently at the bottom, they were awfully quiet at the moment. The ship was still cruising along, the storm raging just as strong beyond its boundaries. There was no other way off that I could see. It was worth a shot.

I lowered myself down onto the first step. It groaned and sagged under my weight, but I continued my descent one step at a time, guided by the silver light emanating from my knife. The creak of the steps conjured images of whining, invisible spirits; the heavy smell of rot reminded me of the catacombs under Exceres, its decaying stones and pervasive, miasmic air. All of my senses warned me against venturing deeper, but my legs seemed to have made up their mind, and I continued down onto the lower deck.

The darkness encroached on me, making me feel watched from every angle. I instinctively couldn't take my eyes off of it, in case there was a predator lurking just beyond the dagger's light. I took a tentative step into the void, then another. Soon enough, I had inched anxiously into the center room. It appeared empty, although the unspeakable horrors my imagination was cooking up would argue the contrary.

When a little paper note came into the range of my guiding light, I jumped out of my skin, gasping to catch my breath. It was just a piece of paper lying face-down in front of me. I approached it carefully, reassuring myself that I had a knife and a protective bracelet and a pedigree of people who went up against way bigger obstacles than a sheet of paper, and I bent down to examine it.

It was yellowed and torn at the edges, and strangely soggy — not quite soaked, but as if it had been handled by wet hands. There were no words I could see, so I picked it up and flipped it over.

The paper was blank on both sides. The message came from behind my ear, though, in a very alive and very familiar voice: *"I win."*

Chapter Twenty-Nine

I lurched forward at the sound of Kuthrîs's voice behind me, but the rotting floor couldn't bear the impact, and it caved in under me. I screamed as I fell into an even deeper blackness, my knife and only source of light slipping from my grip. The wind was knocked out of me as I landed in some sort of shallow pool on a lower level. I rolled over onto my hands and knees, fumbling for my knife, but its glow was nowhere to be seen.

I nearly panicked about losing my only weapon before I remembered the enchantment on it. I held my hand out in front of me, willing the knife into it, waiting to feel the leather band around the hilt in my palm… but nothing. I tried my other hand. Still no sign of it. I cursed. *Now* wasn't the time for this.

I clambered to my feet and peered into the darkness, fidgeting with the bracelet on my wrist as if it would ward off any dangers lurking around me. The room was warm, humid, and smelled like murky ocean water locked away for far too long. I wiped sludge from the floor off my face onto the side of my shirt, which was also wet, so not much of an improvement.

Trying to stay quiet, I stepped forward. The water splashed softly, but in the midst of the dead silence around me, it was deafening. I moved further. I squinted my eyes and listened as closely as I could, but I couldn't make out any details about where I was.

Then, the water moved. I thought at first it was swaying with the ship, but the floor was stable. No, the water was moving on its own, rushing around my feet toward the opposite side of the room. I swiveled around and strained my eyes, but it was no use. I could hear more water rush over, heard it splashing against itself as it did *something* that I fundamentally understood water shouldn't do on its own. I distanced myself from whatever was gathering over there. I was defenseless — against what, I couldn't see, though I had some good guesses.

The standing pool below me had lowered several inches, leaving little more than a cast of slime coating the floor. My footsteps thudded loud as I backed up straight into something hard and sharp behind me.

In my terrified state, I shot away from it and screamed like a child, but when the sound settled, the room was still. Nothing jumped out from the darkness and grabbed me. There were no watery tridents impaling me. Trembling, I crept closer and held out my hand, unsure if I even wanted to know what I had bumped into.

When my fingers grazed it, I pulled my hand back immediately out of reflex. It was rigid, rough from the hard water permanently stuck onto it. Holding my breath, I reached out again, and delicately grazed its surface. I felt it narrow into a sharp point at the end of some sort of rod bent inward toward an upright centerpiece. I had no idea what to make of it. Feeling the middle section, the whole thing seemed to be a ridged column with several pairs of the rods in rows on either side. It was strange; it almost felt like a–

I gasped and fell backwards, my back colliding hard with the floor. I scrambled away, slipping on the residual water on the floorboards.

"What– what the– what the *fuck* is that?!" I gasped, hoping I was wrong, hoping I hadn't just closely examined a skeleton's ribcage. I pushed myself back onto my feet and fumbled through the darkness away from the skeleton with my hands held out in front of me. I had no idea if there even *was* a way out, but I couldn't just stand around until I became the next set of bones forgotten down here.

I heard a splash below me as I kicked up water. I guessed this was where the water had amassed. I didn't want to check it out — nothing good could come from that. I heard the distinct sound of sloshing water, not below me, but in front. I stifled another scream when a voice chirped in front of me.

"Welcome back!" Kuthrîs greeted, his voice waterlogged and choppy. "You haven't held up your end of the deal, human. I really would've taken you anywhere you asked — from the hull of my ship, with the rest of my collection. I see you've found my altar. If I had known you'd be so touchy, I would've washed up the bones for you."

I staggered backwards, petrified. "Kuthrîs," I cautioned, "we have no deal. I'm protected — you can't hurt me. Just let me go, and we can both move on from this."

The demon let out a gargle that I assumed was laugh-adjacent. "You are not protected. You scorched my hand with that revoltingly pretentious divine bracelet, but my tridents cut through your flesh just fine." There was a clap as two waves of water collided. "Speaking of, what a rare and powerful piece that is! Where did you get it? If I could lay my hands on it, I would be delighted to loot it off of you. Consider it a fee for the trouble you've put me through."

"I don't owe you anything," I snapped back. "We never came to terms. And I'm not even at Mésura, so if there ever *was* a deal, it's *you* who isn't holding up his end–"

I was cut off by the ship rocking into motion, weaving around curves along the river faster than any vessel I had ever been on. It only seemed a matter of seconds before it slammed to a stop, throwing me to the ground.

With wet satisfaction, Kuthrîs declared, "Since you insist, here we are. Mésura. You won't get to see it, but I only said I'd *bring you*, not that I'd let you leave. Now, it's your turn."

"No– we never came to a deal, you can't–"

Drops of water flicked onto my face. I wiped them away and held my hand out, not wanting the demon to be launching any more of his liquids on me. From much closer to my face than I expected, I heard Kuthrîs gurgle.

"My ship, my rules."

He launched out, engulfing me in a column of water. I thrashed around, choking on the salty, bitter mass. My fingers occasionally broke free of the orb of water, but I couldn't seem to get any traction to pull myself free. I once again failed to summon my knife as the air in my lungs burned from panic. It wasn't long before I was too exhausted to fight any longer against the crushing force of the demon's water. I let my arms drift in the swirling liquid.

Before I blacked out, a sudden flair of a new kind of pain pulled my attention to my wrist: burning. I squinted through the murky water and saw a faint glow, barely visible, radiating from my bracelet. I remembered what Exolirus had said when he gave it to me; if being submerged in magically charged demon water was overloading it, I needed to get it off me.

My vision darkened as I forced my arms to work, pulling at the clasp on the back of my wrist as the glow brightened. The metal burned hotter, small bubbles rising from its surface as it began to rattle. My fingers smoldered as they fumbled with the clasp, and it finally broke free of my wrist, sinking in Kuthrîs's murky depths.

In a flash of light like a lightning bolt, I was launched across the room, rolling to a stop with my head spinning from the combined impact and near-asphyxiation. I pushed myself up to my knees, hacking to clear the taste of grime from my mouth. Looking down, I noticed I could *see* my hands. I craned my neck up to find the source of the light.

Silver flames danced on top of the water that lay scattered across the peeling floor from the blast. Light undulated across the sunken walls of the room, revealing a derelict ship's cabin, furnished with only a few fallen chairs and a rotting table still laden with empty bottles. In the ceiling was the hole I had fallen from, the floor slanted down around it like a funnel into a horrible arena. Then I noticed the altar.

Against the wall sat a massive skeleton on a pedestal. Its arms were spread to the sides, palms open to the ceiling as water dribbled from between each finger. In the center of its rib cage was a silver coin. I rose unsteadily to my feet and approached it cautiously — it must have had some sort of connection to Kuthrîs's power.

Behind me, Kuthrîs was reorganizing himself. I saw that he was really a huge tower of brown, sickly water, several feet taller than me. A line of divine fire roared between us, keeping him from coming near me — at least for now. At the top of the column of water, with its glowing blade obscured by the grime, was the hilt of my knife. *So that's why I couldn't summon it.*

Kuthrîs's water form convulsed against the wall, trying to recover from the explosion and avoid the flames. His agonized groans boomed throughout the room. I ignored them, stepping up to the altar and examining the coin. It looked remarkably like the summoning coin, but instead of a glowing ship, it was marked with a bony hand reaching up from the waves. I saw why he chose the ship insignia as the summoning coin — better for marketing.

I reached for it, but froze when Kuthrîs roared with laughter.

"Go ahead, try to remove my heart. Just touching it would liquify you in an instant. I have lived many hundreds of years on this continent, and yet your hubris astounds even me to believe *you* could destroy me."

I pulled my hand back. Surely he was bluffing — he lied about his weakness before, I couldn't believe he was now telling the truth about his supposed power. Still, I wasn't going to risk turning into a puddle. I looked at him, at the silver flames between us, at my knife held captive in his liquid mass. I was out of options. I had to do something.

Grabbing one of the skeleton's ribs, I spat, "You should have let me go when you had the chance."

I pulled the altar down from its pedestal. It crashed into the ground, bone fragments scattering across the floor as I dragged it to the fire. Kuthrîs howled, bounding toward me as fast as a rip tide, but he was forced to retreat as the flames singed him in a burst of steam. The heat stung me, too, as I came within range, but unlike Kuthrîs, I wouldn't evaporate. With both hands, I hefted the entire rib cage into the blaze.

As soon as the flames licked the bones, they crumbled to ash, leaving nothing between the coin and the cleansing holy fire. It glowed red hot, and I saw Kuthrîs, too, was boiling. He almost screamed, but the sound couldn't escape as his figure warped, whole chunks of water sloughing off and evaporating. The coin melted to pure copper which pooled along the floorboards — along with Kuthrîs, who entirely collapsed, unable to maintain any semblance of a form. All of the water that had been contained within him spilled out, extinguishing the fire, but it was already done. No sign of Kuthrîs or the coin persisted as the room was once again plunged into darkness.

I stumbled as the ship swayed. The patter of rain sounded above me, I realized I had a new problem. I ran to the side of the room and hugged the wall as the ship rocked wildly. I was finally sent toppling back as the hull collided with the rocky shore. I covered my head with my arms as chunks of the roof fell to the ground and sections of the walls caved in, flooding the cabin with water. The ship keeled over onto its side as it ran up on shore. Everything fell still.

I gasped for breath and to make sure I wasn't bleeding or dying — two things I was doing a lot of these days. I summoned my knife to my hand, and it finally complied. Guided by its glow, I carefully maneuvered through the hole in the wall which used to be the ceiling, the one I had fallen through before. Walking along the wall to stand right below the trapdoor to the deck, I jumped up to grab onto the frame, grimacing as the splintered corner dug into my palm. I pulled myself over, but didn't account for the fact that the deck was *also* on its side.

I tumbled straight off and rolled down the deck hard, barely able to grab ahold of the railing to slow my impact on the ground. I landed in the sand, thankfully; my head hit the ground half a foot from a sharp stone on the beach. I lay still under the drizzling rain for several minutes, letting the cold water wash over my face, before I stood.

My legs aching, I climbed up the ridge from the beach and stood on the moonlit plains as the storm clouds finally parted. Far in the distance, I could see a sea of lights cut through the nighttime darkness, a city larger than I had ever seen.

I had reached Mésura.

Chapter Thirty

The full moon bathed the city in an unearthly glow. I had never seen so many lights at this hour of night — even the dark shadow of the lake was punctuated with the lanterns on ships and the beams of three lighthouses. Mésura sprawled for miles on its shore, the torchlit bell towers, column-supported high-rises, and defensive buttresses making the city grander than I had ever imagined. The mountains around Exceres had always made it look smaller by comparison, but Mésura seemed to tower over the lake and meadows beneath it. The domes of palaces rose high above the sea of apartments, but it was the temple that I couldn't take my eyes off of.

The Reterluyn Fil — Cloud Temple — towered above the city center at an impossible angle, threatening to fall at all times onto the most densely populated area in the Eastern Hemisphere. It never did, though; it had been frozen in the air for thousands of years by Aeverial magic. It was an ovular spire of silver and marble, jutting up toward the star-filled sky.

That's where I needed to be, the seat of the Silver Council. I had learned about this city from our ambassadors to Minesra, but I had never expected to be going — at least, not without a convoy of ships and a reception festival after we conquered it. Anxiety nagged at my insides.

This is stupid, isn't it? Obviously.

I'm going to get arrested and beheaded, won't I? Probably.

Do I have a choice? Unless Exolirus pulls up with his gold wings and says that the Cardinal Elementals changed their minds, nope.

But are the Elementals always right? … if I answered that, it would probably be blasphemous. Whether or not I had a choice, I had made it too far to back out. I mulled over plans of what I was going to do *other* than get arrested and beheaded.

By the time I reached the outskirts of the city, it was already early morning, and I was barely holding myself up from exhaustion. I cut through an alley connecting the muddy fields to the paved road of the city. Dozens of people were on the street despite the early morning hour, but I figured if I kept my head down and stayed out of the way, I wouldn't have any problems. Humans weren't as uncommon in the East as elves were in Excutatem; nobody would pay me any attention.

I wound deeper into the city, the temple disappearing behind rooftops and apartments which blocked most of the sky. The street level was completely unlike Sitika — a constant stream of carriages and carts flowed smoothly through wide streets walled by smooth windows on shopfronts, ornate ceramics and decorative robes on display inside. Morning bells chimed almost constantly in the distance, echoing through the smokeless air. I held my hand up over my eyes, pretending to be shielding them from the rising sun, but really to hide from all of the gazes I felt on me. *Nobody will think it's you,* I assured myself, *none of them would even know what you look like—*

I jerked back. When I looked up, I saw myself looking back at me. The wanted poster on the street sign was tattered from rain, but still a freakishly good depiction of me. I cursed under my breath. With these around, staying out on the street much longer would only get me caught.

I ducked back into the nearest alley between two high-rises. I needed to get somewhere private. At first I thought to go to our embassy and see if anyone there might be willing to help me, but there was no way it was still operating, and that would only bring attention to me. I didn't have many options beyond that, but I couldn't just stay crouched in an alley all day…

Stepping back out onto the street, I examined the wanted poster again. It looked fairly old, so I dared to doubt that I would still be in the forefront of people's minds. If I didn't draw any attention to myself, nobody would be able to pick me out of a crowd until I revealed myself to the Silver Council — I hoped.

My eyes drifted off of the poster and onto a newer flier plastered below it. In the center of the page was an elegantly-drawn rod which unmistakably resembled the unicorn horn that had saved my life in the river. The text on the flier was in Elvish, but I found a Humanic translation in the small print at the bottom: There was an auction happening tomorrow in the city, and a unicorn horn — *that* unicorn horn — was the main event. I knew I had to go. Ané and Tetre, if they had made it, would be there, and seeing as I was the only person who knew where the horn was, we might be able to help each other.

The address on the flier was 1340 Runilar Ev., and judging by the name *Runilar* printed on the street sign above it, it must have been just down the street. It was the best place I could have been to get in contact with the Silver Council without delving completely blind into the heart of my enemies' homeland. I ducked out of the crowd and onto Runilar.

I started down the avenue, scanning the gold-plated address numbers above the doors. The street was empty, which made me more comfortable, but also more exposed. I had to find this auction house as soon as possible and get off the street — I clearly didn't have enough money to set foot here, and that would make it harder to come up with a good excuse.

I followed the even numbers up the street, passing 1302, 1304, 1306… Up ahead of me, I could see a tall, wide domed building. Something told me it was my objective. I picked up pace toward it.

Before I had even covered half the distance, I could hear boots trailing behind me. *It's probably nothing,* I assured myself, but when I glanced back, I saw I was being followed by an elf decked in orange leather armor. A police officer. I snapped my head back in front of me and tried to calm my heart rate. He wasn't actually *following* me, right? He was just on patrol. I did my best to maintain my pace and resist looking back at him, and he didn't seem to be trying to catch up with me. I took several deep breaths. *1326, 1328, 1330.* I came to the door of 1340 Runilar, the domed building I had been aiming for, and reached for the handle.

"*Nietra!* Halt!" the guard shouted at me.

I just about melted to the ground. I faced him, the blood draining from my head. "Y-Yes? Is there a problem?" I asked, failing to stabilize my quivering voice.

"What is your business in the auction house? You do not look like you have the money to buy a single thing," he demanded, his accent clearly accusatory. None of these elves seemed to be holding back with the unsubtle jabs.

"I wasn't going to buy anything," I defended, taking my hand off the door handle.

"Then what were you going to sell?" he asked. My heart skipped a beat. I obviously didn't have anything valuable.

"Oh… I was, uh, gonna sell…" I stalled as I reached into my right pocket. Nothing. Fumbling around in my left pocket, I was surprised to find my fingers brushing against a small metal disc. I took the summoning coin out of my pocket and uncomfortably held it out. "This. I was going to sell this coin. I don't know what it is, but it looks like it would go for something."

He seemed unimpressed by the dull copper coin. He reached out and plucked it from my hand. Holding it up to appraise it in the sunlight, I watched his eyes go wide. He forced it back into my palm and pointed at me. "You don't know how dangerous that coin is. You must be careful — do not read the incantation." I wished someone had given me that heads-up yesterday. "But alright. Go sell this coin and be free of it, the auction house will guard it better than you."

I nodded and went to enter the building, but he stopped me once more by putting his hand on the door. When I looked up at him, he was studying me deeply.

Finally, he said, "Have you been in Mésura long? I feel sure that I've seen you before."

"Uh– yeah, I came in on a ship a couple days ago. Merchant guild." I hoped my voice didn't sound as suspicious as it felt.

He paid me a lingering glance before nodding. He turned and continued back down his patrol route as I stood shaken by the close call.

Desperate to get off the street, I pulled open the wide mahogany door of the auction house. I was immediately struck by a wave of frigid air, unlike the warm equatorial weather outside. I slipped through the doors and into the massive chamber. My footsteps echoed off the polished tile floor to the reception desk, the marble statues lining the walls watching me coldly. Behind the desk, a spectacled elf busied himself with a thick ledger laid out in front of him.

He looked up as I approached and closed the tome. "How may I help you?" he asked me in a precisely practiced accent, the expensive Humanic I'd hear in the castle back home.

"I'm not sure if you could help me, but I'm looking for some people. Do you know if Ané and Tetre made it here?"

He blinked before removing his glasses and wiping them off with a handkerchief. After sliding them back on, he leaned forward to examine me more closely.

"If I may ask, what business do you have with Mr. and Ms. Patima? You are surely not from their town." His words were purely questioning, but I detected more than a little pointedness behind them.

"I have information for them. It's fairly urgent."

"In that case, I will be happy to take a message and deliver it to them at the earliest convenience. May I have your name?"

"No– I mean, I think that it would be best to speak to Tetre in person. I don't think a message will suffice."

"I suspect it will. Do you have a message, or shall you be leaving now?"

I saw the sentries guarding the interior doors had shifted nearer to me. I guess it was fair — an unknown, exhausted human stumbling in and demanding to speak with some merchants would definitely be an irregularity.

"Alright, I'll leave a message. Tell him…" I wasn't sure what to say. I didn't want to over-share, but I needed to convince him to see me in person. I continued, "Tell him that I know where it is and that I'll be waiting for him outside. Please make sure he gets it, it really is very important."

The receptionist just nodded. I sort of expected him to write it down or immediately set off to find Tetre, but he just looked at me expectantly. "Anything else?" he asked, "we're really quite busy."

I looked around at the empty lobby and took the hint. Without another word, I turned and walked back out onto the street. I found a secluded spot between the auction house and the jewelry store next door where I could wait for Tetre in the shade, out of the way of the growing daytime traffic.

I watched elves and occasional human merchants pass by, completely oblivious to my presence. If there had been a wanted poster with a huge red arrow pointing right at me, I doubted anybody would even notice. Some kids chased each other down the alley, nearly running right into me and not paying me a second glance.

After twenty minutes, I heard the auction house door open and peeked around the corner. Tetre stepped out first, followed immediately by Ané. I came around the corner to greet them and was met with Ané's fist to my jaw as she yelled something incomprehensible at me. I staggered back, holding the side of my face as the sharp pain dullened to an ache. Tetre put his hand on her shoulder to hold her back before she could come at me again.

"Damion," he said quietly, "we didn't think you made it. What do you want?"

Geez, nice to see you too. I decided to cut to the chase. "I know where the horn is. I would have brought it, but I don't have the upper body strength of a troll."

"Well, I appreciate it, but I doubt you came all this way just to tell us where our horn is. What do you *really* want?"

"I just need some help," I said. I tried to elaborate, but it occurred to me that I didn't even know what I needed. Money? Directions? A hotel room? Was I even in a position to be asking that type of stuff from him, especially after it was *my* vote that caused the boat to crash? "I need to figure out how to get in contact with someone. An ambassador, I think his name starts with an L... Lucan?"

Tetre turned to Ané in confusion and muttered something to her. In the jumbled mass of syllables of her response, I made out "Lucciun", the ambassador who helped Cedric's mom in Ramethus. I pointed and nodded, confirming to her that he was the one I was referring to.

"Why do you want to see the ambassador?" Tetre asked me.

"Nothing important," I lied. "I just have business with him to settle. I went to see him in Ramethus, but he had apparently been replaced." I didn't know if I had shared too much, but he didn't seem to think too hard about it.

"I'm not sure where exactly you would find him, but we can visit the Reterluyn and ask. It wouldn't take too long, but we better get that horn after."

I froze up. I couldn't go to the capitol; one of the government officials or diplomats there would definitely recognize me. "Well, actually, I think we shouldn't do that. I mean, we have to cover a lot of distance today."

Tetre frowned. "So what do you propose, then? Do you want to meet the ambassador or not?"

"I do, it's just… why don't you and I collect the horn now, and Ané can go get a meeting for me with the ambassador. I would prefer for it to be arranged outside of the temple, if we could, since it's not an *official* meeting."

Tetre seemed skeptical. He turned to Ané and relayed what I said to her; she didn't seem entirely sold either. They discussed back and forth for a handful of seconds before Tetre looked back at me.

"Alright, fine. I don't know your angle here, but as long as I get that horn before tomorrow, I don't care."

Having come to our agreement, Ané set off into the packed streets toward the capitol as Tetre and I made our way to a stable at the outskirts of the city. As I had grown accustomed to, I waited outside while Tetre went in and bargained for a ride out to the river. I was surprised when he came around the back of the stable not with a carriage, but with a huge, solo horse. It was bigger than any horse I had ever seen; its saddle had room for two riders *and* a storage pouch, which was conveniently unicorn horn-sized.

"Are we riding *that?*" I asked.

"No, I'm riding this. You're walking behind us," Tetre shot back. I didn't know how to react until he broke into a smile. "Yes, we're riding the… I don't know what you would call it in Humanic. In Elvish we call it a *dophetresia,* which means something like 'horse of the plains'. It's much faster than western horses when we're cutting across the meadows."

I didn't necessarily *want* to ride the big plains horse, but if it got us there and back on time, I wouldn't complain. A stable worker brought out a ladder for us to climb onto it. Tetre went first, both to demonstrate how to mount the creature and to claim the front seat. I followed; the ladder was unstable and rickety and I had a pressing sense that the horse would immediately reject me and jettison me twenty feet, but when I threw my leg over its side and settled myself, it hardly even acknowledged the added weight. The stable owner shared some last words with Tetre before handing him the reins.

Tetre led the horse carefully across the street, dodging pedestrians and carriages, toward the expansive grassland beyond the city limits. He called back to me, "*Dophestresia* can't walk well on roads. Hold on tight, though, because once we're in the open plains, there's no slowing it down."

I really hoped he didn't mean that literally as I wrapped my arms around his waist. As soon as the horse came over a stoop and saw the miles of still-soggy meadows and plains, it released a jovial *heeeiung* and broke into a sprint. At least we would get to the horn before evening.

Chapter Thirty-One

The horse hardly slowed as it thundered down the plains. Its hooves landed so forcefully they splashed mud on me from seven feet below. It was hard to judge our speed relative to the ever-unchanging sea of plains, but whenever I looked at the ground and saw nothing but a blur of green whisking by, I'd instinctively tighten my arms around Tetre, despite his objections. The constant pounding of the horse's hooves made my whole body numb. Even though it was moving faster than any carriage I had ever been on, it felt like the longest trip of my life.

We slowed to a trot — thankfully, Tetre hadn't been serious about the horse's unstoppable nature — once we reached the bank of the river. The water was still high and rushing, as if desperate to get this added volume out of its system. I wasn't sure how far Kuthrîs's ship had taken me from where I first climbed out of the river. All I knew was that when I had gotten on, there was no sign of life, and when I had gotten off, Mésura was pretty much right in front of me, so I figured we had traveled quite a ways while I was fighting for my life against a demon.

As if he could read my mind, Tetre leaned back and asked, "How did you get back, anyway? Ané and I went to the town we had been talking about. We waited for you for a bit, but when you never showed, we just assumed you didn't make it and moved on — no offense."

"None taken," I said, taking some. "I… walked." I realized as soon as I said it that it was completely unbelievable, if not obviously impossible. I hoped he wouldn't press, but with not much else to talk about, he turned around and gave me a judgemental stare.

"No way. Don't even try. There's no chance you *walked* from the river all the way to Mésura, overnight, in the rain, after almost drowning. How'd you do it?"

I racked my brain for any excuse or explanation that didn't require me to explain the truth, but none came. Defeated, I reached into my pocket and pulled out the coin. At first, he didn't seem to know what it was, but when he read the text on the back, blood drained from his face..

"How did–" he started, but I interrupted.

"I took it from the boathouse — it was an accident, trust me. I had no idea what it was, but I guess I accidentally summoned some ship. It took me downriver to the city before I got off. All there is to it." I suspected he knew that it wasn't the whole truth, but whether he didn't believe me or was just too scared to ask more, he fell silent.

We continued upriver, scouring the rocks and sand for any sign of the porcelain-white rod. It occurred to me that it might've been washed away, down the river and out to sea. I would have to hope for the best, because I didn't know what Tetre would do if we had to turn around empty handed.

I was just beginning to get nervous when Tetre stopped the horse and pointed across the riverbank. I saw it glimmering in the sunlight, still buried in the wet sand.

"I told you it was here," I said. Tetre only knocked my shoulder as he commanded the horse to kneel so that we could climb down. Getting off was probably scarier than getting on, especially without a ladder, but the sodden ground proved a fair cushion to stop me from breaking my femur.

Tetre and I circled around the horn. He examined it closely before directing me to stand at its base while he would lift from the end sticking up. He counted down from three — as soon as he said *lift,* I pushed up with my legs the way I saw dock workers lift boxes twice my weight. It broke free of the ground, swaying between us as we shuffled back to the horse. The hardest part was lifting it above our heads to slide it into the horse's saddle; it almost fell back and impaled Tetre's face once or twice.

Once it was fastened in, Tetre knelt down to boost me back up onto the horse. I maneuvered myself back into my seat, but Tetre seemed to have no problem climbing onto the horse by himself. With both of us settled in, he gripped the reigns and turned the horse back in the direction we had come.

As the horse barreled back toward the city, I had no concern: I had settled my business with Tetre and Ané, I was going to meet with someone who could actually help me bargain with the Silver Council, and I was one step closer to completing my mission and finally ending the nightmare of the past months.

As the city came into view, though, I noticed something strange dotting the horizon. We slowed; the sound of the hooves rumbled in the distance, and it became obvious that it was a group of riders racing to meet us. We came to a stop in the middle of the field as they approached, and my heart dropped. They were soldiers. All were clad in white armor, marbled steel that gleamed in a way that heralded doom for any enemy of the elves — in this case, me. These had to have been the Dayguards of the Silver Council. They could only be here for one thing.

My heart raced as cold dread boiled in me. They quickly encircled us, drawing spears. Tetre looked back at me with panic… and resolve. He knew why they were here. Our horse stepped back nervously, but he pulled the reins, halting it.

The Dayguard leader, as I could tell from his uniquely ornate headdress like the feathers of a graceful and deadly bird of prey, trotted forward on his own horse. He shouted something to Tetre, who only nodded before kneeling the horse and gesturing for me to climb off. I didn't want to, wondering if I could somehow get control of our horse and make a break for it, but their spears looked awfully sharp, and I had nowhere to go even if I *could* get past. A soldier beckoned Tetre over and let him climb up onto his horse. Tetre offered me one last look I couldn't decipher — concern? Disbelief? Regret? — before they raced back to Mésura, leaving me completely on my own.

"Damion Excutari!" the commander shouted with near-glee. "Former king, present fugitive. By proclamation of the Silver Council, you have been charged with nine hundred thousand counts of accessory to murder — one charge for every elf killed by your father's campaign — as well as one count of murder of a Minesran official, one count of conspiracy against the Silver Council, and two counts of resisting arrest." Though his face was obscured, I had no problem detecting his grin. "You are hereby under arrest. You will be informed of your trial date as soon as the Silver Council is made aware that you are in our custody." He shouted something to the other soldiers in Elvish, and they closed in on me.

As the first soldier reached me, pulling me off the horse effortlessly and throwing me to the ground, the commander added, "I have to say: You made it longer than anyone expected. But all evils, no matter how persistent, must be brought to justice. At last, you will be."

Chapter Thirty-Two

I was brought back to Mésura with a bag over my head and my hands bound in chains. They had confiscated my knife, and it wouldn't come to me no matter how much I called it. I wasn't sure whether the head covering was to stop me from escaping or to keep my arrest out of the public's attention, but it felt uncomfortably like I was being paraded around as they weaved through the streets in a tight formation.

They came to an abrupt stop in a quieter area. The horse knelt down, and I was pulled hard to the pavement, not even able to sit up before I was forced back to my feet. I was led into a building by a firm grip on my forearm and a blade pressed between my shoulder blades. I stumbled over a threshold, which just got me yelled at in Elvish by an unseen guard and shoved harder.

A rough hand stopped me sharply, then led me forward slower than before. I didn't realize why until I almost tumbled to my death down a staircase. Going down a spiral staircase blindfolded reminded me of descending into the lower levels of Kuthrîs's ship, except this time it was the reality of danger that scared me, not just the possibility. I had no defense, and I was fairly sure there wouldn't be a way out of whatever awaited me at the bottom. I shuffled down the stairs as carefully as they would allow me, wishing I could at least get a railing or wall to ground myself, but my only support was the leather-gloved hand gripping my shoulder.

When I reached the lower level, I fell forward from the sudden end of the stairs. Then, it was back to being pulled along. From the smell of torch smoke in the humid, stale air, I knew that I was underground. A dungeon, probably. I was almost proud of myself for making it as far as I did before finally getting captured, but that sense of defiant victory didn't stick around as I was aggressively shoved to the side, followed by the sound of an iron door clanging shut. I staggered, but managed to stay on my feet.

A guard banged on the bars and yelled something at me. I backed up, wanting to be as far from the elves as possible. Seeming to grow impatient, the guard knocked on the cage door and repeated his command. Not knowing what else to do, I crept over toward him. Without warning, he reached through the bars and grabbed my arm. I pulled away, but he held me up against the iron bars separating us, only releasing me after he unclipped my chains. Once they finally fell to the ground, I distanced myself from the bars and used my now-free hands to pull off the hood. I whirled around to take in my surroundings.

I stood in the center of a small cell, furnished only with a basin of water and a wooden bench draped in linen I hoped wasn't the bed. Three of its walls were made of large, smooth stone bricks; the fourth wall, facing out onto the torchlit hallway, consisted of rows of floor-to-ceiling iron bars and a door held shut by a padlock bigger than my hand. The guard who delivered me to the cell stood on the opposite side of the bars, eyeing me triumphantly, before checking the lock on the door and walking off down the hallway.

Motionless, I stared at the bars. I had expected this to happen all along, but now that I was here, it felt unreal, like I was spectating someone else's life through their eyes. After everything, I still ended up in the cage. It was all for nothing.

I drifted to the bars and gripped the steel. There wasn't a bit of rust on them — in fact, they almost looked polished. I pulled halfheartedly, and just as I expected, it didn't budge whatsoever. The elves wouldn't make the same mistake as Meca Khumalo. In a last, futile attempt, I stuck my hand through the bars and called for my knife. It didn't come.

Holding the bars, I looked down the hallway, but couldn't see any trace of the guards. I called out, but there was only an echo as a response. Damn it. I tried again.

"Hey, don't just leave me down here!" I shouted futilely. "I just need to talk to someone, we can get this all sorted out! Get me Ambassador Lucciun!" There was no response. I knew that even if there was a guard to hear me, they probably couldn't understand what I was saying. Hollowly, I called out, "There's really no need for this!"

I let the echos settle. No one came. I knew that there was no getting out of here alone, and that if I could get *one* person on my side, I might be able to escape my fate. I opened my mouth to call out again before another voice interrupted me.

"…Damion?"

I froze with my mouth still open, but no sound escaped.

"Damion? Are you down here?"

I knew that voice. I would know it anywhere.

"Cedric?!" I shouted a little more enthusiastically than was called for in the enclosed space. I had been captured, maybe betrayed, thrown into a stone dungeon with more charges against me than I could count, and yet I suddenly felt nothing but relief.

I heard Cedric, only a few cells down from mine, rush to the bars. "What are you doing here?" he demanded. "I thought you were dead! They told me you…" His voice cracked before he finished the last word.

I managed to force a jaded laugh. "No, not dead yet. It sure has felt like it sometimes, though." I was aiming for it to be funny, but it just came across sad. I, too, felt tears creeping up. "How long have you been here?"

"… I don't know, actually. They threw me on a ship once I recovered enough from the battle at the castle, but time is hard down here. It feels like it's been ages."

From where I was, holding onto the bars, the stone walls and ceiling, the dim lighting and smoky air… I could see where he was coming from. I'd bet this place would take a toll after a couple of days, and I felt sick at the idea of Cedric being stuck down here while I was out fighting demons. There was a long pause. It was broken by Cedric, his voice hollow and quiet.

"Damion…" he murmured, "I hope you didn't come here to rescue me. I wish you had just stayed away after the battle. I might get pardoned at my trial, but…" He cleared his throat. "You won't, Damion. You know that. You shouldn't have come."

His words resonated, but only left me with a deepened sense of resolve.

"Don't worry about that. I didn't come here for you– wait, no, I mean, I *did* come here for you, but I have another reason. I need to meet with the Silver Council, and if I could just find that ambassador — Lucciun — he could arrange that. *That's* why I'm here, but obviously it's not quite working out."

He seemed surprised. "Lucciun? You think he'd help you?"

"Well… yeah, why not? You thought he'd help us back in Ramethus. Isn't he at least our best bet?"

He seemed to consider. "I guess so, but I wouldn't expect him to be too fond of you. Maybe if he knew you were with me, he'd be more inclined… but we'd have to get him down here first, and I don't have any ideas for how to pull that off."

"Well…" I started, "I guess we'll just have to think of something else then." Cedric was silent, and I tried to think of something encouraging to say, but the weight of my situation came crashing down on me. Finally, I settled on some words, though they weren't quite so inspirational.

"Cedric?" I said.

"Yeah?"

"I just wanted to say that I'm sorry. For all of this — everything. I'm the reason you're here right now, I'm the reason you got arrested, I'm the reason you left your whole life just to get dragged around with me and Acturas. He was the soldier, and I was the prince being hunted, but you saved my life over and over again while I've only put yours at risk. If it weren't for–"

"Stop," he interrupted.

I lost my train of thought. "... what?"

"Just stop. I'm old enough to choose how I spend my life. You didn't 'drag me around', I *chose* to follow you, and I knew the risks ever since you introduced yourself as the crown prince in that bar when we first met. I saved your life because I *wanted* to help you, not because you somehow manipulated me into it. So you're right, I wouldn't be here without you, but that's just because if we never met, then I'd never have found anyone worth fighting for. I would do it all again if I could go back. All of it. So stop blaming yourself."

"I– do you mean that?" I asked, not really believing what I just heard.

"What? Of course I mean it, you think I just said all that as a joke?"

My face burned, but I still wished I could see him face-to-face. "No, I just… I really can't believe it. Why would you do that for me? Risk everything?"

He scoffed from behind the bars of his own cell. "Why? Why do you think I would do that, Damion?" He paused, but I wasn't sure if it was for dramatic effect or to prepare himself to continue. "I did it because I love you. I've loved you since we were on the pier in Semmerfall. I'm not gonna lie, at first I was just trying to see how much money I could get out of you, but when I saw you in the lake… I didn't know what it was, but I felt like I would do anything for you." He fell silent as if he finished his speech, but added something as an afterthought. "Oh, and speaking of…"

I heard him reach into his pocket and dig around for something. "I really don't know how I've kept it this whole time, but ever since we started off, I could never let it get away from me. Thankfully, the elves didn't think it was worth confiscating. Here," he said, and I heard the patter of a small stone across the floor. In the flickering torchlight, I saw the outline of a tiny white pebble, hardly noticeable, as it came to a rest in front of the bars of my cell.

I squeezed my arm through the bars and took it. It was as white as snow, almost perfectly rounded, and no bigger than the tip of my finger. I had no idea what I was holding at first, but remembering that night in Semmerfall, I recognized it as the pebble Cedric took from the beach. I clutched it in my hand. There was nothing I could say that would convey the whirlwind of feelings it brought.

I took a deep breath and steadied myself against the wall, squeezing the pebble into my hand. I finally found words. "I love you too, Cedric."

There was a pause. Not long, but heavy. Then he spoke, as warm as the water of a lake on a different continent on the other side of the world.

"I know."

Chapter Thirty-Three

I was awakened by the echo of boots marching down the steps. I had fallen asleep against the stone wall, the exhaustion of the past days catching up to me all at once. The rock was still gripped in my hand, but I stuffed it into my pocket and scurried to my feet.

The soldier stepped into view, his eyes trained on me. He came to a stop outside my cell.

"The Silver Council has elected to expedite your trial. It will take place in one hour, in the Reterluyn Fil, where you will be tried for your abundant crimes and, once convicted, sentenced. Do you have any final arrangements before you are brought to justice?"

I suddenly felt dizzy, like the cell was on the deck of a ship in the center of a deadly storm. I guess my time was just about up. I tried to think of something to say that was noble and king-like for my last words, but I was interrupted by Cedric.

He muttered something to the guard in Elvish. The guard snapped at him, but he kept talking, his voice rising as he argued something I couldn't understand. The guard shouted again and smacked the metal bars, but Cedric's tirade didn't pause even for a second. I was confused and afraid, but no longer for myself. *What is he doing?* Was he trying to get himself killed?

Cedric continued his taunting until the guard finally snapped, drawing a sword from his belt and marching over to Cedric's cell. I couldn't see him, but his verbal onslaught never faltered, only becoming more taunting as the guard brandished his blade and clashed it against the bars. A metallic clang pierced the air and left the room ringing. After a handful of seconds, only a soft vibration lingered as the brunt of the sound was absorbed into the stone, but it was quickly replaced as Cedric continued his tirade.

My fear had now turned into sheer panic. I knew what he was doing, but I didn't know how to stop it. I couldn't let him sacrifice himself to save me. Before I had a chance to speak up, though, the soldier had already picked a key off his belt and was unlocking Cedric's cell, sword at the ready and rage steeped onto his face.

"*NO!*" I shouted as I raced to the bars of my cell. I flattened myself against them, but I couldn't see any of what was transpiring. I heard the clashing of a scuffle, grunting, a yelp, and then a groan as a sword clattered on the stone floor. Not a second later, a figure tore out of the cell. Cedric raced in my direction with something clutched in his hand, but couldn't cover half the distance before he was tackled to the ground by the now-swordless soldier.

I could only watch as Cedric and the guard wrestled on the ground of the dungeon. Cedric brought his elbow back to connect with the other elf's cheek, but winced when the soldier wrapped an arm around his neck. Cedric thrashed under him, but the soldier only squeezed harder. I tested the bars again, desperate to do anything to help, but they held as firm as ever. I looked back at Cedric, and, to my surprise, his eyes locked with mine as his face began to flare into darker shades of red. Breaking his arm free, he thrust his hand in my direction, and whatever he had been holding scattered across the floor to land just within the bars of my cell. It was small, pointed, and iron; at first I thought it was a tiny knife, but when I scooped it up, I saw it was something much more valuable. A key.

I snatched up the key and pressed myself up against the bars, squeezing my hand between them to maneuver the key into the lock. Unable to see where the keyhole was, I could only slide the key around on the surface of the lock to find it while Cedric fought uselessly to shake off the guard's grip around his throat. I could tell we were both becoming more desperate with each second that passed; me, panicking to find the keyhole, and Cedric, trying to catch any breath he could as his attempts to resist grew weaker.

Scratching the entire surface of the lock with the key, I came to an assumption that I couldn't believe. There was no keyhole. Where was the keyhole?! It made no sense to me how it could be possible, but I didn't necessarily have the chance to call a timeout while I figured it out. Obviously the key had to go *somewhere*, and if the keyhole wasn't on the front of the lock, then where would it…

I looked across the hall, past Cedric and the guard, to the cell directly in front of mine. It confirmed my suspicion — the lock on the cell door had no opening for a key on the front. Not on the sides, either. That left only one place for me to try.

The lock was bolted tight against the bars, very different from the loose-hanging ones back home, but I managed to slide my arm down to work the key against the bottom. I nearly lost hope when I felt nothing but solid steel, but, abruptly, the key slipped upward into the slot concealed on the bottom of the lock. I twisted it around in my fingers, the gears and pins grinding as it disconnected the steel door from the wall. Finally, with a metallic crack, the door fell ajar.

The guard looked up at the sharp sound, but he didn't have time to stand before I charged from the cell and threw myself into him, knocking him off of Cedric into the stone ground. Cedric immediately broke into a coughing fit as he pushed himself away from the elf soldier, his face quickly returning to its usual shade as he rubbed the bruises across his neck.

I didn't have time to check on him, though, because the soldier was getting back up. I weighed the odds in my head — there were two of us and one of him, but he was wearing armor and Cedric was still recoiling from being choked out on the floor. We could run, but where would we go? What was waiting at the top of the staircase? Neither of us even had a weapon.

Knowing that we needed time to regroup and that the guard was the biggest threat at the moment, I looked for a way to hold him off until we had time to escape. Not wanting to give him any time to recover, I charged him again, pushing him up against the wall as his armor clashed against the stone. He brought his fist up and suddenly my vision was flaked with red, my ear ringing, but I only grappled him harder as I propped my foot up on the wall. With as much force as I could muster, I pushed off from the wall, pulling him in the direction of the open cell door.

Though he stumbled initially, I was only able to bring him halfway to the door before he regained his footing. I tried to no avail to push him the last couple feet, but he stood firm, fighting more against my grip on him with every second. He was bigger than me, and I knew that once he recovered from his surprise, I wouldn't stand a chance.

A metal crash sounded from one of the cell bars and cascaded throughout the dungeon. The guard and I turned to find Cedric standing at the open door of his cell, the guard's discarded sword in hand. He aimed it away from the bars and toward our fight, and the guard and I let go of each other.

I broke away from the guard and ran to stand behind Cedric. Brandishing the sword, he shouted an order in Elvish and gestured with the blade toward the cell door. The elf soldier stepped towards us, hands raised as if to defuse the situation, but Cedric jabbed toward him with the sword and repeated his command as the guard stumbled away from the blade. Finally, seeing no sign that Cedric would relent and not wanting to be skewered by fugitives, the guard stepped across the threshold of the cell door.

I didn't waste any time covering the distance to the door, Cedric right beside me with the sword to back me up if the elf tried to turn the tables. Cedric forced the guard further into the cell as I grabbed a bar and slammed the door shut, then fumbled with the lock until it was secure. Only once the padlock clicked shut did I allow myself to take a deep breath.

Cedric rubbed the dark bruise across his throat while holding the sword aloft with his other hand, still pointed at the guard fully confined within the cell. The soldier paced a few feet from the bars, not wanting to come within range of the sword, but obviously looking for a way out.

"We have to get out of here," I told Cedric. He nodded, understanding that it couldn't be long until more soldiers came to investigate the hold up.

"Do you know how to get out of the fort without running into any more guards?" he asked me. I didn't like his use of the word *fort*. It didn't cast an optimistic outlook on our chances of escape.

"I was blindfolded when they brought me in, I have no idea what it looks like up there." I looked at the guard, watching us talk. I lowered my voice. "We could take him with us… you know, as a–"

"Hostage?" Cedric finished for me. I cringed at him saying the word aloud, not wanting to admit that the thought had crossed my mind.

"No, more like a guide. Just to give us directions so we don't walk into an ambush."

He shook his head. "There's no way he'd be helpful, it would just complicate things."

I nodded and turned away, not wanting him to see my face redden. "Yeah, sorry. Let's just get out of here before any more come." I regretted even suggesting it. A lot had changed since I last saw him, but I couldn't let myself go down that path.

I didn't wait for him to respond, marching away toward the stairs. I stopped just before the first step, breathing deep and readying myself. Then, with Cedric behind me, I set up the spiral staircase and into the elven fort.

Chapter Thirty-Four

We reached the top of the staircase, but hesitated before stepping out into the hall. There were no sentries guarding the stone arch which led out of the dungeon onto the main floor, but I had no clue which direction we should turn to get out.

I whispered to Cedric, "Which way do you think has less guards?" He glanced in both directions, then hesitantly nodded his head to the left. It was an obvious guess, but we didn't have much else to go on. My heart pounded as I leaned forward, peaking both ways to make sure the coast was clear. Then, fueled by the combined rushes of adrenaline and regained freedom, I stepped out into the hall.

We started left, but I stopped as if I hit a brick wall. It was a sense in my gut, a tingling that made me stop dead in my tracks. Cedric had moved past me, and he turned around to shoot me a worried, questioning look. He nodded his head back, urging me to continue down the hall, but the foreboding was impossible to ignore.

I turned around, looking down the opposite direction. There was something we weren't noticing,

I was sure of it. Left of the dungeon, a set of double doors led to an unknown section of the fort. What was that sound coming from behind them…?

My eyes widened and I grabbed Cedric by the arm, pulling us both into a sprint down the opposite direction. We rounded a corner and collapsed against the wall just as the doors were flung open. Multiple sets of armored footsteps entered the hallway, a hundred feet from where we stood deathly silent.

An unseen voice reached the entrance to the dungeon and called down; I could hear our captive guard shout back in response. In a frenzy, they rushed down the stairs to his rescue. I'd hoped we'd have more time — once he told them what had happened, the entire place would be on lockdown.

I pulled Cedric further down the hall, away from the dungeon and the elf soldiers. I moved just short of a run, not risking the sound of my boots drawing attention to us.

The hallway was empty, continuing for a hundred feet before ending at a T intersection. One of its walls was punctuated occasionally by a door, the other lined with windows — barred, so there was no chance of escape from there. Not that I wanted to jump out *another* window to escape an elven facility.

Without stopping, I peered out the window to my right and saw that the fort was on the coast of the lake, so large I could have just as easily mistaken it for an ocean with no hint of its other shore on the horizon. I overlooked thousands of merchants and artisans amassed on the docks. My heart sank. Even if we could get out of the fort, trying to sneak through the crowds undetected would prove impossible, and the lake only limited our opportunities of escape.

Cedric leaned in and whispered, "We could try to get on a boat. That would give us a better chance than running on foot."

"Do you know how to sail a boat?"

"I can figure it out."

He didn't sound sure.

We rushed down the hallway until we reached the intersection, the path ending as it branched out to both sides. My heart raced as I leaned past the corner, glancing down the hall to the right. When I turned to look left, I immediately sprung back, my hand clutched against my mouth to stop myself from yelping.

Quietly, to Cedric, I said, "It's clear to the right, but there's a sentry to the left. We might be able to go to the right when they're not looking."

He swallowed and glanced back the way we came. "Well, we mi–"

He was cut off by an echo from the direction we had come. We both spun around to find that the empty hall was filling with the clatter of several sets of marching boots drawing nearer to the corner.

No longer having the luxury of time to discuss our plan, we immediately turned back to the intersection, Cedric readying his sword. I peeked around the corner at the guard I had seen earlier. The soldier stood like a statue fifteen feet from the corner. If we tried to escape the other way, he would only need to turn his head and we would both be done for.

I was about to make a break for it when Cedric stopped me. Holding out the sword for me to take it, he whispered, "You go right. I'll go left and distract him." Seeing the obvious horror on my face, he cut me off before I could reject the idea. "I'm not important, Damion. If we both get caught, then this was all for nothing, but if you get out, then whatever happens to me doesn't matter."

I moved to stop him, but he had already stepped out of whispering range, leaving the sword in my hand as he crept closer to the corner. He seemed ready to make a break for it, and once he did, I would only have a few seconds to escape in the other direction. I forced myself to prepare to leave him behind as the footsteps behind us drew nearer to the corner. It was only a matter of seconds now.

Cedric stepped out — but immediately drew back and pressed himself against the wall. A voice had called down the hallway in Elvish. I obviously couldn't understand what was being said, but judging by Cedric's alarm and the patrol suddenly raising his spear and running down the hallway as fast as his armor would allow, there was something important happening. I had no time to investigate, though, since Cedric grabbed me and led us around the corner in the opposite direction.

Panting, we slipped out of the corridor into a divet in the wall which served as the threshold of a deep-set doorway. I heard distant shouting, along with a chaotic din which rose up from the docks.

Through heavy breaths, I asked Cedric, "Did… did you hear… what's going on?"

He nodded, but took a moment to swallow and take a deep breath before he responded. "They were talking really fast, and I'm not too familiar with their dialect, so I couldn't catch most of it… they mentioned a–" He caught himself and seemed to reconsider. "Nevermind, I must've misheard them. That wouldn't make any sense."

It pissed me off that he would choose the exact words which most piqued my curiosity while choosing not to give any actual information, but I didn't have the breath to inquire more.

I said, "We have to keep moving. Whatever it is, they'll be done with it soon. I mean, it's a whole *fort*. I don't think anything could occupy them for long."

We slid out of the doorway and examined our surroundings. The hall was the same as any of the other ones we had seen, but I noticed a sign on the wall.

"Do you think it's directions?" I asked Cedric.

He hesitated. "I can't read Elvish," he responded quietly, suddenly sounding more self-conscious. It occurred to me that I wasn't even sure if he could read in *Humanic*.

I thought for a second. "Do you want me to… sound it out? And you can try to interpret?" I didn't want to come across condescending, but it was hard *not* to when you're offering to sound out letters to somebody like they're a child.

Even still, he seemed to accept that imminent death was more important than pride. "Just promise that you'll at least try at the accent, it's actually kind of important."

I nodded and looked over the sign. An arrow pointing to the left read *Aeme Poie, émara hostenn,* and *gothaiar,* and an arrow pointing to the right read only *yeha.* I cleared my throat and gave my artistic interpretation of the syllables.

"Okay, it looks like… Ay-m poy, eh-mara host-en, and goth-ay-ar? Any ideas?"

He looked insultingly deep in thought — I really *did* try the accent — before he said, "I think Aeme Poie might be an armory, so that could be helpful, but if there are any soldiers there, we'd be way worse off. The other two are government offices and a courtyard — I don't know if any of those could help us. What's to the right?"

"I just looks like yee-haw," I responded, accepting that it was no use even trying.

"Sounds like… I think it's the word for *exit?*"

I almost laughed at how easy it seemed. "Wait, so that's it? We just go down there and leave?"

"I mean, it probably won't be that easy — all the guards seemed to be going in that direction, so we'd risk running into some of them. It might be safer to go deeper into the fort, since the guards are mostly at the front." I realized by the way he was watching me that he expected me to make the decision.

I weighed the options in my head, feeling the mounting pressure of both my decision and the chance of being caught standing in the hallway while thinking it over. Would it be stupid to run in the same direction we just watched an armed guard go, probably to join a couple dozen more of his friends? Yes. Would it be better than taking our chances running further into the elven fort…?

"We'll go for the exit. They'll probably be occupied dealing with whatever is going on inside. If we're careful we can just…"

"Walk past them?"

"Worth a shot."

He looked down the length of the hallway. We both flinched when a crash boomed from outside, as if a building had caved in. More shouts and screams followed, and apprehension filled me at the idea of walking into *that,* but I stayed firm in my decision. It was just a better cover for us to escape, nothing more. We would get out. We would be fine.

I repeated those phrases in my mind as I wordlessly set out down the hallway, Cedric following, toward the crashing and screams outside the walls of the fort.

Chapter Thirty-Five

We wound from hall to hall, the chaos outside growing clearer as we neared the fort's main gate. It didn't help that I still had no idea what we were even heading toward, but no matter what it was, it was better than hanging around here.

We turned a corner and stopped in our tracks.

Directly ahead of us spanned a long corridor that ended with an iron gate massive enough to easily fit a plains horse through. The doors were fortified with metal plates, and a small unit of guards stood in a defensive formation in front of them, spears raised. One elf in polished armor stood in the back of the formation and shouted orders, though they didn't seem to be doing much more than waiting.

The whole room rumbled with sporadic quakes interspersed with shouts and screams from outside the closed gate. I wondered why these guards weren't outside helping, cursing my luck that not even an impossibly opportune crisis could clear the guards out of our way.

I looked at Cedric. He met my eyes and shook his head, telling me what I had already figured out: We couldn't get through here. I scanned our surroundings — there was no alternative exit I could see from here, and the only other hallway in the chamber just led back into the fort.

Not seeing any other option, I indicated the other hallway to Cedric, and he showed no objection. We began to move, but before we had even covered half the distance, a shout from behind us made us spin around. A group of soldiers was storming down the corridor, led by the guard we had locked up in the dungeon. He did not look happy to see us.

Cedric raised the sword and pushed me behind him, although we were now being cornered on two fronts as the formation in front of the gate took notice of us, tipped off by the shouting. Our only shot now was to make a break for it, but as I started toward the doorway, another set of guards came scrambling around the corner. They froze when they spotted us, as if they hadn't been aware we escaped.

I stood back-to-back with Cedric, only one of us armed, as armored elven soldiers closed in on all sides. I could hear my heartbeat in my ears, and I called one last time for my knife. It didn't come. The commander who led the formation raised his lance at us and shouted in Elvish.

Cedric risked a glance away from the approaching soldiers and called back to him. I could tell from his tone that he was trying to diffuse the situation, but he couldn't hide the shakiness in his voice. Once again, I found myself completely powerless to protect anybody in the face of real danger, and this time I wasn't even able to be included in the conversation. I started to mutter a prayer under my breath, but stopped after the first syllable. It was useless, I knew that;

Elementals were limited in the East, and it's not like they would come to my rescue every single time I got into a mess.

The guards brandished their swords and spears, ready to drag us back to the dungeon — or, more likely, directly to my trial and subsequent execution. The commander issued one last command, gesturing to us with his lance, and the guards all at once moved in to apprehend us. We were so clearly outnumbered, Cedric lowered the sword. It was better to avoid a fight than die losing.

Seconds before they reached us, a metallic thud echoed through the hall. All of us spin around to face the iron gate. The newly arrived guards seemed confused; the guards who had been in formation looked petrified. All of us stood in complete silence, now unified under a strange pact of shared bewilderment and gradual fear, which only mounted when another slam against the gate made us recoil. The soldiers who had been guarding the gate stumbled back into the connecting halls. Cedric once again pushed me to stand behind him, but I had no chance to before a third collision spawned a deafening squeal of straining iron and sent dust tumbling down from the rafters above us.

The impact seemed to knock the officer out of a trance. He raised his lance and screamed a command at all soldiers present, including those who hadn't been in his formation in the first place. They all immediately mobilized, creating a fortified row of spears and swords at the end of the entrance hall. I was about to use the opportunity to grab Cedric and make a break for it, but the commander turned his blade on us, balancing between commanding his troops and stopping us from getting away.

Another hit on the gate. It was obvious the iron plates of the doors were weakening under the pressure, which didn't make sense, since they were obviously designed to hold strong under siege attacks. Could there *actually* be an invasion out there? Could an entire army sneak up into the heart of elven territory in the nick of time for me to escape?

Cedric turned to the captain and whispered a question to him. The officer didn't even look in his direction. Another impact sent an entire plate crumbling to the ground and let smoke pour in through the crack. Cedric repeated his question. The officer shot him a weary glance, more irritated than angry, but refocused his attention on the gate without offering an answer.

I saw a flash of movement outside the crack in the plating, and another collision followed shortly after. The hinges creaked, and the doors were shook inward with a sharp snap, nearly breaking open entirely. Only one or two more hits and they would be completely done in. His patience clearly gone, Cedric shouted his question to the officer for the third time. Finally, the officer relented, spinning toward Cedric and grinding out the words "efta él drecvesa inthol" through gritted teeth. One of those words felt familiar to me, but I couldn't place where I had heard it. Judging by Cedric's reaction, though, it was bad news.

His face went entirely pale. His voice small, he told me, "I thought I had misheard them when they said it earlier… I didn't think it was *possible,* I just–" He was cut off by another slam against the gates, more plates denting or falling free from the gate entirely. I didn't even look, too invested in what Cedric was saying.

"What is it? Just say it," I demanded, hoping he would snap out of his terror.

He locked eyes with me, taking multiple deep breaths as if to work up the courage to say the words. "It's a d–"

He never got the chance to finish. One last death blow against the gates marked the end of our defenses. The hall immediately flooded with the squeal of iron crumbling on the stone floor, guards shouting or screaming or praying, and, above all, a deep, rumbling hum which rebounded off the walls. I knew that sound. There was nothing else like it. I had only ever heard it once, in the forest, when–

A dark form swooped into the corridor, diving straight toward the line of guards. The formation broke immediately as all of the soldiers — even the officer — abandoned their post and fled. Most pushed past each other down either of the connecting halls; a few collapsed against the floor and covered their heads, or crouched against the wall in frozen terror. Cedric and I only stood still, watching as the figure covered the entire hall in just a matter of seconds. It came to land on the ground in front of me.

The dragon's reptilian head swiveled around, analyzing us. I had hoped I'd never see its unnaturally blue eyes, unforgettable and paralyzing, ever again. It passed its attention between me and Cedric as the echoes of the fleeing guards grew distant down the halls of the fort. It seemed to linger on Cedric for an abnormally long time before finally hissing at me, spinning around, and bounding off the floor. It shot out through the broken gate as abruptly as it had come.

We both hesitated, but a shout in Elvish from down the hall spurred us into action. Not sparing a glance down the corridor, I grabbed Cedric's arm and pulled him toward the gate.

The fallen door clattered as we stepped over it and out of the fort. I was immediately suffocated by a wave of heat and smoke, using my arm to shield my eyes as we ducked back against the wall of the building. Squinting, I saw rows of buildings consumed by fire. Through the haze, I could see the forms of soldiers scattered across the street, most unmoving. Shouts and screams still rang out from unseen sources down the avenue, but I saw no sign of the dragon that had liberated us.

I coughed and pulled my shirt up over my nose. Leaning in to Cedric, I shouted over the din, "Where do we go from here?"

He peered through the smog both ways before shaking his head. Obviously, he didn't have any better ideas than I did. I cursed silently. Finally, taking a deep breath and then immediately coughing it up, I chose to turn left and follow the street until we could find a good hiding spot or escape route.

We stayed low as we passed by burning buildings and fallen soldiers. I almost couldn't believe that such a small dragon could wreak such havoc, but then again, I had good reason to be afraid of it when I first uncovered it. I guess the elves had become as complacent as Excutatem about dragon preparedness — they usually stayed deep in the Highlands to the north, or the Sacred Lands further east, or some other lands far away from the capital city.

I led us around a corner, away from the destruction around the fort. The smoke was lighter on the side street, and I was able to see down the rest of the avenue. I stopped in awe. Down the street, sunlight

sparkling off its silver frame, loomed the Reterluyn Fil.
It was even more grandiose in the day, almost blinding
in the light, entrancing me with its ornate architecture
and sheer scale. Birds flitted about its higher levels and
swooped in to land on angled balconies; I could hardly
believe a tower like this could exist.

My stupor was broken as Cedric pushed me into
a crevice between two buildings and ducked next to me,
peeking out down the street. I started to ask him what
he had seen, but he put his finger to his mouth, shutting
me up without ever taking his eyes away from the base
of the tower.

I heard countless armored footsteps echo off
the stone street in a marching formation from the silver
tower toward the fort we had just escaped from. Cedric
stayed low behind our cover, watching the soldiers
approach while I squeezed myself against the shallow
alley wall.

I held my breath as the first row of soldiers
passed, none of them discovering us despite only
needing to glance to their right to blow our cover.
Another row, and I tentatively let myself exhale. More
and more rows of guards marched down the street
toward the fire and chaos, most armed with long spears,
some carrying iron nets or crossbows. In the middle of
the formation, an old elf in robes of blue fabric seemed
to have a whole row to himself — a mage of the Silver
Council. I wondered if he had been at any of the battles
between Excutatem and Minesra in the northeast during
the war, back when they had gotten desperate enough
to throw their best sorcerers into the front lines. Had he
been deployed with Neiphorous when they conquered
Exceres?

I finally allowed myself to breathe normally once the unit passed us, not one soldier looking over to see Cedric crouched down and the human fugitive-enemy-prince-emperor trying to sink into a stone wall. I was about to say something when Cedric once again silenced me with his hand. My heart raced, but I stayed quiet, listening closely as the light smacking of sandals against stone approached.

As the elf neared us, Cedric readied his sword. It was probably just an out-of-the-loop civilian wanting to see what all the commotion was about, but if they noticed us, then what? They would blow our cover, but what could we do to stop them? Somehow, I felt more nervous as they approached than I did about the entire battalion which had now disappeared around the street corner.

The footsteps closed in on us, and I clenched my eyes shut, not even wanting to see who it was until they inevitably passed us and we were safe. I listened to the scuff of their footsteps on the cobblestone road as they continued closer, praying they would pass us by. My hopes were dashed when they came to a stop in front of our hiding spot.

I opened my eyes. An elf dressed in heavy, white fabric stood a dozen feet from where we hid, his hands behind his back. Judging by his aloof demeanor, I had a sneaking suspicion he expected to find us here.

"Prince Damion," he said with a nod toward me as a greeting. "And I take it *you're* Cedric…?" Cedric seemed taken aback that someone knew of him, nodding just slightly. The elf continued, "I am Homeis Utlis, Mol Stihirn of Minesra, but I figure you both already know of me." He spoke with a deliberate Elvish accent, though he clearly had enough experience speaking Humanic that I assumed he could drop it entirely if he wanted to. I looked at Cedric, not knowing what to say. He didn't seem to have any ideas either.

To me specifically, he said, "The Silver Council has been looking for you for quite a long time now. I'm so glad we are finally in contact, but I'm afraid I must hold the explanations until we're in a more secure area." He stepped back and gestured out with a hand toward the tower. "Shall we?"

I exchanged another glance with Cedric. *Trap?* he mouthed silently to me. I nodded. Obviously it was a trap, but I couldn't figure out his angle. He seemed unarmed, outnumbered, and *way* too important to be baiting fugitives by himself. Besides, if he knew we were here, why not just send the soldiers? Would he put himself in danger just for an unnecessarily elaborate ambush?

I stepped past Cedric and onto the street. He rose slowly to his feet, holding the sword aloft, but clearly waiting to see what I would do. I approached the elf, trying to gauge his intentions, but he seemed completely unthreatened. I passed a glance both ways down the street and saw that it was almost eerily empty except for the three of us. If he was willing to come out here all alone, then I figured he would be worth at least hearing out. I faced the Mol Stihirn.

"Lead the way."

Chapter Thirty-Six

Cedric offered me an overabundance of nervous glances as we followed Utlis down the deserted street. The Mol Stihirn seemed completely unfazed by the sword keeping distance between us as he beckoned us along with no clear urgency. The arched gates to the tower were closed, and I imagined what threats were hiding behind them. Instead of the main entrance, though, Utlis led us down a narrow lane beside the temple.

He called back to us, "We'll use the back entrance. The street is cleared of guards, but the lobby is fortified on account of — well, you know." He raised an eyebrow. "Funny timing, isn't it? For a dragon to attack the city at the exact moment we were going to bring you here? Of course I'm not suggesting you've somehow allied yourself with a *dragon,* but it worked curiously well in your favor."

I didn't respond. I didn't need them knowing that the dragon was probably not, after all, a coincidence. I felt he somehow already suspected, but I didn't trust him enough to explain, and I didn't want to implicate myself in the carnage behind us.

He stopped at a seemingly unremarkable crack in the tower's outer wall and placed his high hand on it, tracing its length. Finally, he came to a small, circular engraving in one of the upper stones and positioned his index finger in the center of the circle. He whispered a phrase under his breath and the sigil glowed blue, sending two streaks of azure light coursing through the stone wall in either direction to form a rectangular outline. Keeping his finger placed in the circle, he pushed on the wall, and it swung open like a door, revealing an unlit hallway inside.

Utlis went first, stepping over the threshold and waving us in. With one last uncertain glance, Cedric followed me into the tower, the door grinding shut behind us as the enchanted light faded away and left nothing but a solid wall in its place.

I followed Utlis's footsteps through the dark, narrow passage. He led us around invisible corners and warned us of incoming stairs until we eventually reached the end of the hall, marked by a non-magical door with soft light seeping beneath it.

Utlis stopped before the door. In a low voice, he said to us, "This is a good time to mention who you are about to meet. You probably don't know many of them, but all of them know you — or, I should say, know *of* you, mostly in connection to your father and your rather infamous escape from Exceres. They all understand why you are essential to us, and each has agreed to allow you to work with us toward our mutual goals, but I must warn you to be careful not to provoke any of them. The war affected some more than others, and a few are still tentative to offer you amnesty. Just remember that."

I didn't like the sound of that, but had no time to ask him to explain further before he twisted the door handle and pushed it open. I squinted against the sudden rush of brilliant light. Beyond the doorway lay an expansive chamber, its walls rising along the tower's angle toward a domed ceiling. High-set windows focused sunlight into the center of the room and glared off the expensive metals and jewels which adorned the furniture. A long, semicircular desk was occupied by a fair-sized assembly of elves who I assumed to be the Silver Council, each writing or talking to those in neighboring chairs. Utlis shut the hidden door with an echo that drew all attention to us.

Since we had entered on the side of the room, Cedric and I followed Utlis in uncomfortable silence around the desk and into the center of the room. I tried to present confidently as I had been trained for my entire life, but I couldn't bring myself to make eye contact with any of the elves gathered. One did catch my attention, however; a human, one who looked strangely familiar with his auburn hair cut short in a distinctly western fashion. I was sure I knew him, but I wasn't sure how.

"Meuni Ubelemica e Tyer," Utlis began in a voice that had been practiced for decades to fill entire rooms, "ui melecui Min Emara e Ecsecutatema, Damion Excutari. Rememi omader, eha ui fetestuia él Humênica."

He gestured to me and proceeded, this time in Humanic, "I understand you are all hesitant to invite an Excutari into our affairs, but we must stand united against our common enemy. We have already come to understand that Remius Neiphorous cannot be trusted to rule in the West — please do not let old bitterness cloud your judgment in matters such as these."

Most of the councilors nodded in resolve, but I couldn't take my attention away from the human. Unlike the others, he seemed… irritated, almost frustrated. I was distracted by Utlis stepping forward and outstretching his palm to the floor.

"Now, we must first begin by informing the prince of our plan." He muttered another incantation as the floor began to shimmer, but he was cut off by a voice to our right. It was the human, now stood up from his seat.

He said something to Utlis, his Elvish marked by a thick Humanic accent, and I could tell from his tone that he was *not* happy. A flicker of annoyance crossed Utlis's face, but he masterfully masked it behind a forced neutral expression. I felt a hand on my arm and turned to see that Cedric's nervousness had been replaced with defensive anger, also directed toward the human.

While the redhead had spoken in Elvish, probably to keep me from understanding, Utlis responded in Humanic. "We've discussed this a dozen times by now. You already agreed–"

He was cut off by another round of arguing, accented by a few too many broad gestures toward me. The other councilors rolled their eyes and whispered to one another, but the human didn't seem to take any hints. Utlis tried to respond, only to be cut off again, until finally he snapped a harsh, "*Aeres, enough.*"

There was no more arguing after that, but if there was, I wouldn't have heard it over the racing of my heart. Aeres… could it… yes, of course, it had to be him.

Despite myself, I found myself approaching the redhead — Aeres — at his desk. Now his resentment toward me made sense. And now the feeling was mutual.

"You…" I began, drawing Utlis's attention away from his spell yet again, "you're Aeres of Felfort, aren't you? How'd you manage to get *here*? You deserve to be in that dungeon, not sitting with the Silver Council."

"The only fugitive in this room is *you* — oh, and that guy who follows you around. Forget you're not in Excutatem?" His voice was laced with fire — literally, sparks flew as he spoke. So it really was him, then. Not many Elementalists in this part of the world.

I almost laughed at the absurdity of it. Of all the people I expected to come across ever again in my lifetime, he was near the bottom of the list. "All this time, you've been hiding out *here*? And after my father had been sending the Hall of Elements down to the Ghânt looking for you. We should've known you'd go running to the elves like a coward–"

"Once again, there's only one coward here, and it's not me. Fleeing the country the second word broke that we were closing in wasn't what I'd call 'kingly' — and it's a shame, too, because I would have *loved* to see you at the battle."

My mind was suddenly clouded by rage. "How could you help Neiphorous?! Didn't you know what he'd do to Excutatem?"

He grimaced. "I hate Neiphorous too, but I hated your father more. I wasn't about to pass up the chance to go back to Exceres and settle our score. I stayed deployed there for a while — you're lucky I got recalled to Mésura before you showed up with your pathetic attempt to retake the city, because I still had some fire saved up for you." He snapped his fingers, and a burst of fire flashed in his palm to drive his point.

The thought of him using the Elementals' magic to attack his homeland was too much for me. Forgoing all better judgment, I broke out towards him, content to take him on unarmed even if it only left me with a nasty burn scar to show for it. I was stopped ten feet from the desk by Cedric wrapping one arm around me, pulling me back, as he used the other to put the sword between me and Aeres. I was going to shout something profane at the rogue Elementalist until Cedric kicked me in the leg and hissed something to the effect of "shut the fuck up". I wearily stepped back.

Utlis stepped between me and Aeres. "I know you both have good reasons to be spiteful toward each other, but our cause is too important to allow bitter rivalries to tear it apart. You don't have to like each other, but you *will* be working together. At least until we're finished."

Aeres looked like he was about to retort, but seemed to let it go for now. I also stayed silent as Utlis once again returned to the center of the floor and outstretched his palm, uttering a spell under his breath. Below us, the floor glowed again until it had been replaced by a stone map of the entire world, large enough for him to stand in the center of the Median Sea. Its surface was intricately detailed with lines and colors, displaying two continents and the countries on them.

Utlis walked to Minesra and pointed a finger at Mésura, casting a gold dot down on the map over the city.

"We're here. Our plan is to send forces back to Exceres," he set another dot on top of the city in the northwest, "and force Neiphorous to surrender so that we can replace him with somebody more… reasonable. Somebody who knows how to lead, and understands western politics, and will be accepted by the people of Excutatem — so it obviously can't be an elf. Not that we would want to govern an occupied territory on another continent in the first place. You would have to be mad to try that," he added with detectable passive aggression.

"Why do we have to invade *again?* I thought most of Neiphorous's troops were elves, can't you just call them back?"

Utlis exchanged a bitter glance with a few councilors. "A few are still loyal to the Council, yes, but you know firsthand the effect Remius has on his followers. We gave him too much power, and I fear there's nothing we could say that would weaken his grasp on them. We have to fight to get them back."

He continued, "And so, we'll send our army up through the Pass of Hamandar, what you know as Jennira's Pass." He drew a line with his finger and cast a gold streak across the map, tracing north to the point where the continents' nearly touched. "Once Neiphorous catches wind, though, he'll immediately try to stop us, which is why *you* will be going separately."

He drew a different line, this one branching out of Mésura, following the river out to sea, and then arriving at a port south of Exceres. I hated where this was going.

"Could I *not* go on another ship?" I pleaded, "I've been on too many ships in the past few months."

"If they find out you're with us before we reach Exceres, then you and everybody involved are put in danger. If you're captured or killed when Neiphorous tries to stop us, our whole plan falls apart, you and your supporters die, and we have to find a replacement that won't be immediately overthrown or start a revenge war. I'm sorry, but you're taking the boat."

"What if I'm recognized on the ship?"

His brow furrowed. "It's a Minesran naval warship, everybody on board is aligned to the Silver Council. They'll be on your side if we tell them to be."

"You're really dedicating a whole warship just for me?" I had forgotten that civilian cargo ships weren't the only option.

"It's not *just* for you, but yes, you're important enough to warrant a transport of your own."

"... what do you mean it's not 'just' for me? Who else is going?"

He hesitated. "You see, your safety is our top priority. It's the reason we're arranging this ship in the first place. We have to keep your team small, since you need to travel light without being noticed, and the one who is most equipped to defend you is..."

I pieced it together based on the scowl the redhead wore behind Utlis. "I swear to the elements, if I have to trust Aeres with my life I would rather *walk* to the West."

"Our options are too limited to change our plans now. An elf would only draw attention to you, and he knows the country better than any of our soldiers. And if Neiphorous somehow discovers you and sends assassins, Aeres can fend them off better than any soldier. I trust you two can put aside your tensions for long enough to make it to Exceres in one piece.

I glared at Aeres. He glared back. It seemed neither of us was happy about this, but if it came down to fighting with *him* and fighting alone, I... actually, I would rather fight alone. It would be less embarrassing. But it wasn't my call.

I pointed to Cedric. "And would he come with me?"

"If you want."

I took a deep breath. This was it. If their plan worked, then this whole mess would finally be over and I could return to my life. And if it failed… then the mess would still be over. It would just be a lot less fun to talk about.

"So when do I leave?"

He glanced awkwardly at the councilors. "We really thought you would arrive here much sooner than you did. We could only delay our plan for so long before we were forced to begin without you, so we prepared the ship to leave at dawn. Tomorrow."

Vertigo washed over me. It seemed like I *just* got here, *just* found Cedric and some semblance of a structured alliance, and now I was being launched back into the fray like an extremely unlucky ball in the world's longest and most violent game of catch.

He added apologetically, "If we had known you'd be here, we really would have put it off a few days so you can become familiar with the plan, but there are limits to how much we can play with armies and ships before people start to talk."

I wished they would have pushed those limits just a little bit further, but if these were the cards I was dealt, then so be it. It's not like I could go demanding they put off their military operation so I can catch up on sleep. I only had one more thing to ask.

"Let's say I go west, fight off Neiphorous, take back Exceres. What happens then?"

"Then you're emperor."

I sat on the bed across from Cedric in the upscale apartment they had issued us for the night. Something had weighed on me since our introduction to the strategy, and I had to clear it up before tomorrow.

Without looking at him, I said, "You know, you don't have to come with us."

"What'd you say?" he asked, water dripping to the floor as he wiped his face with a towel over the basin they had filled for us.

"I just said… I mean, if you would rather stay here, I would completely understand. I just don't want you to think that you *have to* go or I'll be disappointed or upset. I won't."

He put down the towel. "I'm going."

"Seriously, if you don't want–"

"I'm going, Damion. Cut it out."

I wanted to make sure he understood the stakes, but I knew he already did. I wasn't even totally sure if I wanted him to come — I wanted him to stay here, where it was safe, but that would mean ending my journey alone. I decided to let it drop. There was no changing his mind, either way.

As we prepared to sleep, though, one last thing occurred to me.

"Cedric?" I said to get his attention. He stood defensively in front of me, ready to shut down any more of my concerns about him coming with me.

"Remember what you said in the fort? When we were trying to sneak past the guard?"

He looked at the ceiling, trying to remember. "You mean that thing about how you're more important–"

"Yeah, that." I caught his gaze. "Don't say

anything like that again. You've been through just as much of this as I have, and neither one of us is getting sacrificed. I mean it."

He laughed awkwardly and looked down. "Okay, sure. No more sacrificing myself, I guess. If you insist."

"Good," I said with finality. With that, I lay down on the softest bed I'd had in weeks and fell into a long-awaited sleep.

Chapter Thirty-Seven

The ship docked at a port thirty miles south of Exceres — close enough that we could take our time travelling before the army was set to arrive from the North three days from now. I waited with Cedric at the top of the gangway while elf soldiers disguised in civilian clothes unloaded cargo onto the deck, pretending to be a merchant ship so they wouldn't raise suspicion.

"Where is he?" Cedric asked. I rolled my eyes.

"Maybe he fell off on the way. It's not like we would've noticed," I quipped.

A sudden voice from behind made me jump. I whirled around to see Aeres, a leather bag slung over his shoulder which contained everything the Council decided we'd need to make the journey.

"Aw, you were worried I fell off the boat? That's sweet," he mocked with fake flattery.

"Not worried — hopeful, actually. Let's just get off this ship," I replied, turning away and leading us down the gangway onto the crate-laden pier. We found an isolated spot beside a stable and stopped to regroup. Aeres dropped the bag to the ground and began sifting through it, announcing what the Council had allowed us.

"Looks like we got a Stendar, some bread and water, a jar of Leornic oil for injuries, and… that's it." He shook his head. "Did they seriously send us on a military campaign with a bag of kitchen supplies?"

"We won't need much. Most of the trip is just going to be in the back of a carriage, anyway," I said just for the sake of disagreeing with Aeres. I was also put off by the basic supplies we were working with.

"I've survived on less than this for longer than we'll have to. I'm just worried that *you* won't be able to make it a mile without spending half our gold on liquor."

"You know I made it all the way from Exceres to Mésura on my own, right?"

"I did too, and I was *also* being hunted an empire that wanted me dead, so don't–"

He was cut off by Cedric dramatically sighing as he backed up. "I didn't spend the last week on a ship just for you two to argue over who had the most tragic life. We're never gonna make it to Exceres if you spend the whole time arguing like this."

My face flushed and Aeres fell silent. I stepped out toward the stables, but turned back when Aeres reached into the bag and called out, "Hold on, I almost forgot…"

First, he produced a familiar steel dagger which I remembered as being very good at killing Sirens. Cedric immediately snatched it from his hand, appraising it as if he were afraid it was fake.

Aeres explained, "It was confiscated when they arrested you in the castle. It's best that you two be armed, but the Council didn't want you having any weapons until you were way out of Minesra. Just to be safe. Unfortunately, that means Damion will get access to a deadly weapon, which is a nightmare to everyone in a mile radius." He reached into the bag and pulled out another blade, this one longer and heavier. I couldn't stop myself from smiling as he held my Valkyrie dagger out to me. He jumped back in surprise when it flew into my palm.

Finally, he retrieved one last item — a short copper rod, no more than a foot in length. I was about to remark about how it wouldn't be great for fighting until he pressed a mechanism and it sprung open from both sides, revealing the rod to be the handle of a double-bladed spear. Both edges glowed red hot, which seemed overkill since each was already as long as my arm and sharp enough to cut stone. He looked at me to make sure I noticed — I just pretended to be unimpressed and ignored that my own magic knife suddenly seemed way less cool.

With Cedric and I armed and Aeres's fire death staff hanging in rod form from his belt, we took our money and set off to find a carriage which would take us to Exceres.

That night, we sat around a campfire and gnawed on the stale bread the Council had so graciously provided for us. The carriage driver was already asleep on his bench, clearly not wanting anything to do with us, which made it all the easier to talk about our plans.

"So, once we reach Exceres, I'll just stay behind and out of trouble until the fighting is done?" I asked as if I hadn't had the plan drilled into me a dozen times before leaving Mésura. I didn't necessarily *want* to be on the front lines, but it still felt a little anticlimactic after all I went through to get here.

"That's the idea. It's for the best, anyway — we can't have the prince getting a scratch, or accidentally maiming one of our men with that knife of yours."

I scoffed. "Like it would be much better having *you* around. Better be careful not to forget which side you're on and join Neiphorous again–"

The fire burst ten feet in the air, sending me scrambling back to avoid getting my eyebrows singed off. Aeres jumped to his feet and walked directly through the flames toward me, pointing at me like he was about to turn me into ash. Before I was eviscerated, though, Cedric sprang up and pulled me back to my feet, whirling around to face Aeres.

"What is your problem?!" Cedric demanded just short of yelling. The driver stirred in his sleep, but he didn't wake up.

Cedric turned back to me. "And you! Ever since we left Mésura, you two have either avoided each other like the plague or seemed ready to fight to the death!" He looked back and forth between me and Aeres. Both of our eyes fell. "So?"

I swallowed. "So… what?"

"So *what is your problem?*"

"It's his fault," we both accidentally said at the same time. I locked eyes with Aeres. Neither one of us wanted to explain it.

I sighed. "Okay, so, you've probably noticed Aeres is an Elementalist. His host is Infernus — you know, the fire and all that. Before the war, he was in the Hall of Elements, and since his patron is a Cardinal Elemental, he was pretty popular. My father even invited him to dinner at the palace a couple of times.

Anyway, we put a lot of faith into his loyalty, but as soon as the war started, he abandoned–"

"*Deserted*, not 'abandoned'," Aeres interjected, "and it's not like I just up and left. Your father was asking me to invade Hulland. I'm from Felfort — not that you know where that is. It's less than a day from the border. It would be like pillaging my own home town, and whenever I tried to talk to Jourdan, he–"

"*Emperor* Jourdan. My father wasn't a perfect person, or a beloved leader, or a respectable king, but he was still the *king*, and by betraying him, you betrayed all of us."

"I *was* loyal to the king, but I had stronger loyalties to defend." Without another word, he extinguished the fire with a flick of his hand and walked off toward the carriage.

Cedric and I stood in darkness and silence for a few moments. Then, quietly, Cedric said, "You know, I think he has a point."

"He completely betrayed us, Cedric. He betrayed the Elementals."

"I don't believe in Elementals."

"And he betrayed you, too. He didn't have to support the war — I mean, I didn't support it either — but going to the *elves*…?"

"*I'm* an elf."

"You're *half* an elf, and you're still Excutatian. Minesra was your enemy, too."

Cedric was silent for a second. Then, quietly, he said, "Did I ever tell you what happened to my mom's town in Illiera when the war reached them?"

Now I was silent. After a moment, Cedric stepped away and walked to the carriage. I stayed where I was.

The next morning, we were back on the road. As we continued north, we passed through more towns and cities, and so we had to be more careful about being spotted. I had my face plastered on every poster on this coast, but, as far as everyone knew, I was still at large in Minesra, and Cedric was in prison.

I was quiet for most of the day's trip. Cedric and Aeres made small talk between each other and the driver, but I couldn't stop thinking about last night. Why was I being so hypocritical about this? I was the first one to criticize the war, but the second someone actually *did something* to oppose it, I went up in arms over whatever my father told me to believe. I wouldn't be able to keep this level of immaturity if I was going to rule anything.

In the afternoon, we pulled over at a small town to feed the horses and stretch our legs. I decided to follow Aeres to the only bar in town while Cedric stayed behind to help the driver tend to the horses.

I pushed through the swinging double doors to see Aeres ordering at the counter. It looked like he was the only patron; a thin layer of dust coated most of the tables. I came up a comfortable distance beside him and leaned against the bar. He sighed when he noticed me.

Aeres started before I could get a word in. "Listen, I don't care what you think about me, but you can't keep bothering me about it–"

"That's–"

"It was *eight years* ago, too. How long are you going to hold a grudge–"

"Just wait and–"

"Do you really have nothing better to do–"

"Can you stop talking for a second?!" I snapped before I could stop myself. I cleared my throat; it was a pretty counterproductive thing to say to someone I was supposed to be apologizing to.

I took a deep breath and continued. "Sorry, I didn't mean for it to come out that way. I just… I just wanted to say that I feel bad about the way I've been acting. I mean, it's not like you've been super warm and friendly either, but I'm starting to realize we have a lot of the same problems."

"What, like the war your–" He glanced at the barkeep searching for a bottle on a shelf and lowered his voice. "Like the war your family started that forced me into exile in Minesra? Is that one of your problems?"

I whispered, "You mean the war that cost both my parents their lives and almost ended my bloodline? The one that *also* sent me into exile — and to *Sitika*, which is, like, way worse by comparison. The war wasn't good for me, either."

He opened his mouth to respond, but was cut off by the bartender sliding a drink in front of him. The barkeep looked at me expectantly, but I shook my head. He seemed disappointed, especially since I was probably his second customer this week, but he walked off to go sweep the eternally dusty floor.

As Aeres started on whatever drink he had ordered, I finished my remark. "I'm not saying we have to be best friends now, but I think it would just be easier if we didn't hate each other as much as we do. Just think about it."

I stood up to leave, but he grabbed my arm. Taking a second to swallow another sip, he said, "You know what? Sure. It's probably best if we try to get along, anyway — it'll be hard to fight together tomorrow if we both want each other dead." He put down an empty glass and stood up. Then, he added, "But we still aren't friends. Don't make any more problems for me."

I nodded. Those were acceptable terms.

I led the way back out to the street, where Cedric and the driver were tying the reins onto the horses. If all went according to plan, we would pass the Wall of Obelevon tonight and reach the outskirts of Exceres by morning. Tomorrow evening, this would all be over — one way or another.

Aeres climbed into the carriage and Cedric waved me in after him. It was time to go.

Chapter Thirty-Eight

Exceres was not how I had left it.

Billows of smoke cut through the city skyline. The sentries that usually lined the top of the wall were nowhere to be seen. Arrows protruded from the side of the massive gates which hung bashed open, streaked with black scorch marks — Aeres had experience breaking through the city's defenses. Shouts and clangs of battle resounded from inside, while the elven soldiers that remained outside the wall were in a state of equal chaos.

Cedric and I waited in the elven command tent, out of the way of soldiers and their spears as they rushed into battle. Four Minesran generals strategized in the back of the tent in Elvish, not interested in me at this stage in the plan. For the time being, my job was to stay out of the way until the city was safe to bring me in.

"Your hands are shaking," Cedric commented. He sat next to me on the ground, since the tent wasn't furnished with anything besides the table the generals crowded around.

I pulled my hands into my sleeves, but we both knew it wasn't because of the cold. I tried to think of something to say to lighten the mood, but I couldn't take my mind off the battle.

"There's something I need to tell you," I said. He looked at me expectantly while I found words. "I wanted to…" I looked to the back of the tent. I didn't know how much Humanic those commanders spoke, but this needed to be between me and Cedric. I leaned in and dropped my voice to a whisper. "Actually, let's go find another spot. Somewhere quieter."

We walked to the edge of the tent. The elves inside didn't even look up from their discussion, and no one paid us any mind as we slipped out, dodging sprinting medics and frantic messengers. As we wandered further from the gate, the sounds of battle grew distant, and no more elves lingered in the abandoned suburbs of the outer-wall city. We walked the empty streets in silence as I scanned the wall.

"It's actually funny," Cedric said as if to himself. I stopped.

"What?"

"This is actually the first time I've been to Exceres. I mean, I used to take people up here all the time when I was a driver, but I never got this close to the wall. They weren't the type to have business in the inner-city."

I couldn't help but laugh. Cedric's first time to my hometown was during a military siege — and that somehow wasn't even among the strangest things about us. "Once this is all over, you'll actually get to go *past* the wall. It's nicer in there. And the castle's pretty cool, too."

Cedric looked down, failing to hide the redness in his face. "A castle does sound pretty good, come to think of it. Anyway, you had something to say, didn't you?"

"Oh, right." I looked up at the wall again and found what I was looking for. I swallowed despite the dryness in my mouth.

Sensing my apprehension, Cedric added, "So… why do you keep looking at that pipe?"

I opened my mouth to answer, but didn't know where to begin. I decided to just tell the truth.

"I'm going to kill Remius Neiphorous."

Cedric stared blankly at me. "What?"

"I'm not following the elves' plan. Remius is the biggest threat to everything in my life — he stole my empire, killed my father, tried to kill me, *almost killed you.* I can't risk him escaping again. I need to finish this myself."

He didn't seem to comprehend what I was saying, as if the idea were so insane the words didn't even make sense together. I knew it was crazy, but I had already made up my mind. Finally, he asked, "Are you sure? It's not like he has anywhere to run, once the elves get him–"

"Even if the elves catch him, he'll just be shipped back to the East for a trial where he has more allies and better chances of escape. I can't let that happen."

He didn't take long to consider it. "Then I'm going too."

I knew he'd say that, but it didn't make it easier. "No. This is between me and Remius, I'm not going to let you risk your life for this."

He didn't seem to accept that answer. "How is it different from all of the other times I risked my life for you?!"

"It's different because now I have too much to lose."

"I do too."

"Yes, you do," I said, pulling a slip of paper from my waistband. I had written it in the carriage on the way up here, while Cedric was asleep and Aeres completely uncaring of whatever it was I was writing. I pressed the paper into Cedric's hand.

He didn't bother unfolding it. "Damion, you know I can't–"

"It's an imperial decree. My first one, so I'm not totally sure if I did it right, but it'll probably hold up. Since I don't have an heir, I have to name my successor in the event of my death."

He rolled his eyes. "So you want me to go deliver this decree to whoever's replacing you while you run into a battle with Neiphorous? How is that–"

"It's you, Cedric."

"What's me?"

"My successor. It's you."

Silence fell between us. I hoped the statement would do enough talking, since I wasn't sure I had it in me to say more without completely breaking down. Cedric wiped a tear from his cheek, holding the paper like it was made of gold. Thankfully, he nodded.

"Okay. But you have to promise me I'll never need to use this."

"I'll do my best. Promise me you won't put yourself in danger trying to help me."

"I… alright. I better see you later."

"You will."

"I love you."

"I love you too."

With nothing left to say, I marched up the hill to the drainage pipe. I stepped up to the stone circle, claustrophobic flashbacks appearing in my mind of my unceremonious escape from the castle the very first day. I looked back at Cedric, watching me from the street. The next time I saw him, I would be king. Otherwise, I would never see him again.

I wouldn't let that happen.

I climbed to my feet and wiped grime off my clothes, my knife clutched in my hand. The kitchen was empty, as I expected it to be. I took a deep breath to calm my nerves. *Am I really doing this?* The surrealness of it all crashed over me at once. I was going to stand up to Neiphorous, and no matter what became of that, I'd be taking my destiny into my own hands.

I crept to the door and tentatively pushed it open, cringing at the squeal of the hinges. I paused to see if any guards would come running to investigate, but the whole hallway seemed deserted. I stepped into the hall and turned left, toward the spot I assumed Neiphorous would await his last stand.

Slowly, with immense care to avoid detection by any soldiers who might be patrolling the building, I snuck through the maze of corridors. I knew the layout of the castle intuitively, electing to follow less direct routes since the larger ones would surely be filled with guards.

Creeping up to the last turn, I froze — not because I heard something, but because I still heard *nothing*. I would have expected scores of soldiers at this point, Neiphorous throwing everything he's got to protect himself, but it almost seemed as if Neiphorous had abandoned the castle entirely. Was that his plan all along? To trick us into focusing our effort into storming the castle while he fled out a back door and escaped? I didn't put it above him to pull something like that once he realized it was a lost cause.

I peaked around the corner. Not one soldier guarded the chamber's ornate gold doors at the end of the hall. Normally, this would have been ideal, but it only made me more anxious. My heart pounded as I marched down the hall, no longer sure there was anyone to sneak around. If I alerted a soldier to my presence, at least I'd know I was in the right place. When I reached the doors, I hesitated for a moment before grabbing the handle and pulling one door open while raising my knife in anticipation.

The room was hauntingly lit as rays of midday light streaked through the stained glass windows and rested on the three thrones at the far end of the room — one for the emperor, one for their spouse, and one for the heir. Only two had been used for the past decade. I lowered my blade and stepped into the room, each footfall heavy and loud on the marble floor.

I approached the throne on the left, the one that had been mine when I was prince. A thin layer of dust coated its surface, leaving the jewels that lined its velvet headrest dull and sunken. A pang of sadness shot through me as the throne that was once a promise of power now seemed to be a symbol of my downfall. I wiped my hand over an emerald, sending dust floating off and disappearing into the shadows. The gem glittered green against the misuse of the rest of my chair — but it wasn't my chair, not anymore.

I turned to the center throne, a much grander seat with gold finishes and so many jewels they would leave marks on your skin if you leaned too hard into it. I stepped up to it. Though my heart had been racing when I entered, it was steady as I climbed the three steps which lifted the throne higher than the others. I closed my eyes and fell back onto the velvet cushion.

I immediately sprung forward, my eyes wide and darting around the room. "Who's there?!" I called out. The only response was the echo of my own voice, accentuating the emptiness of the room as if mocking me. I knew I heard someone say—

"*Come down,*" the voice repeated. There was no echo off the walls, because it was channeled directly into my mind. I didn't know what it meant, but Neiphorous could wait.

I nearly tripped down the steps from the throne as I raced out of the room, flinging open the doors and stepping into the hallway. I had no clue what its source was, but I knew it must have been nearby. At the far end of the hall stood the castle gate, sounds of battle still slipping in through its gaps. It didn't sound like anyone was particularly close to breaking in, so I had time.

I was about to settle for running aimlessly around and hoping I accidentally stumbled across it when I caught something. It was like a rumbling, almost too deep to perceive. I could barely hear it over the noise of the battle, but, realizing that this hum was *also* in my head, I covered my ears. With the outside sounds drowned out, I could get a feel for its direction, the hum pulling me toward it from within.

I dashed to the left and pushed open a side door, following the hallway around a corner, down another hallway. As I ran, the rumbling grew slightly louder. I was getting closer.

Finally, I came to a stop. My breath caught, both because of my exhaustion from running and from the fact I was now standing in front of the dungeon gate. The iron grate door groaned as I pulled it open. I drew my knife for light and began down the spiral staircase into the stale darkness below.

I reached the bottom and swallowed to clear the taste of mildew from my mouth. The soft glow of my knife lit up the narrow walls, each lined with rows of rusty bars on cells empty of people and furniture. The humming was no longer just in my head, clearly emanating from the impenetrable darkness in front of me.

I crept forward to a point in the hall and froze. I hadn't had the displeasure of being down here very much in the past, but if I remembered correctly, there should have been a wall where there was now nothing but a void. I held my knife out into the darkness and saw that there were steps leading to a level beneath the dungeon. I tried in vain to stop my hands from shaking as I stepped down.

This staircase was different than the last — it had no sign of wear from years of use, no water damage or moss or erosion. It wrapped around an empty so wide I didn't even realize it was a spiral until I reached the next level. I thought about what this could possibly lead to, but my imagination was drowned out by the humming, now fuller and louder than ever in the enclosed space. After descending for a shockingly long time, I stepped down onto a level surface.

I could tell by the echo of my footsteps that I was in a vast chamber, but there was nothing within the glow of my knife but the floor directly below me. I couldn't see what lay in front of me, but I knew it was the source of the rumbling. Slowly, I stepped towards it, but stopped at once. As soon as I moved, the rumbling stopped. I squinted into the black abyss in front of me. The only other light came from two softly luminescent gold spheres floating at eye level a few dozen feet from me. It was only when they blinked that I realized they were eyes.

My stomach dropped. I felt like prey that had been baited into a predator's lair. I stepped back toward the stairs, but scattered forward when I bumped into something that hadn't been there before. I backed up to the side, slashing my knife wildly through the darkness, and heard a voice speak to me — not in my head, but out loud.

"Welcome home, Damion," Remius Neiphorous said through the darkness. "We've been waiting."

Chapter Thirty-Nine

Neiphorous's boots scuffed on the stone floor as he approached through the darkness. I couldn't break eye contact with the invisible creature. It only seemed to be watching, not an immediate threat to me — at least, not in the way Neiphorous was.

"Where are we?" I demanded. I hated that he seemed to know more about my own castle than I did.

"Dungeon," he replied insultingly simply.

"You know what I mean. What is *that?*" I gestured with my knife toward the creature. Its eyes flickered between me and a spot in front of me where I assumed Neiphorous lurked. He stayed right in front of the stairs — the only way out was through him.

Remius chuckled to himself. "*That* is a prisoner your family has held here since Obelevon was on the throne. And it's the weapon I'm going to use to finish what your father started."

"I thought you wanted to *stop* my father," I said, "wasn't that your plan? To use his war as leverage to force the elves to finally help you take over the empire?"

"You're close, but you're missing the main point. I didn't kill Jourdan because I wanted to *stop* him. I killed him because I was going to *replace* him. I'm going to accomplish what he never could — *I* am going to conquer Minesra, *I* am going to unite the continents, and the only way to do that is with her."

"Who is '*she*'?" I figured he was referring to whatever was down here with us, but wished he would wrap up his villainous monologue and get to the point.

There was a pause. Then, quietly, he said, "Let me show you."

I heard a grinding sound on the wall as if he were pulling something. Suddenly, with a sharp click, a dozen braziers lining the room burst into flames all at once. Now lit up, I saw Neiphorous in light armor with two swords, one hilted at each hip. He stood by a lever which turned on the lights — magically? Why would there be magic in the castle? *How?* There hadn't been magic in Excutatem since the dragons–

I collapsed back against the wall, my knife clattering to the ground as I released a squeal I had never heard from myself before. Twenty feet in front of me lay a dragon half the size of the entire room. Its tail was curled beneath it, but it had to have been a hundred feet long from tail to head. Shadowy gold scales coated its entire body, and its eyes glowed orange through its chains.

Around its entire body, binding its wings and forcing its legs to the ground, were massive crimson chains, so large they could be used for a ship's anchor. The chain around its neck was held down by a weight, preventing it from rising more than a few feet from the ground, and a muzzle covered its entire face with only narrow gaps for the eyes.

"This," he gestured with delight to the dragon, "is Hythraga. She's been imprisoned for centuries beneath the castle, right underneath your feet, and yet you were oblivious for your entire life. A nice metaphor for your entire pathetic bloodline, your loss of the glory and might that allowed your ancestors to bring *her* here. Your family has grown weak, and in the natural order of things, a stronger force must kill it and take its place."

He drew a rapier from his hip. I grimaced; I had faced that sword before, and I remembered the damage he could do with it. He began to march toward me. I reclaimed my knife from the ground and backed away from him.

"What does any of this have to do with me? You've been here for weeks, why not just take the dragon and forget about me?" I asked, not even attempting to hide the shakiness of my voice.

It might have been the flickering of the firelight, but I thought I saw his eye twitch. "Because," he began venomously, "only the emperor can break her bonds, and no matter how much I conquer, no matter how many I kill, I will never be emperor until *you* are dead. I had hoped to catch you with your family so I could end the bloodline in one swoop, but you slipped from my grasp time and time again. Now, there's no more escaping."

Neiphorous continued closing in. I pushed myself as far from him as I could get, but the room was a massive dome, and if I followed the wall any further I'd be a little too close to the dragon for comfort.

Remius stopped ten feet from me. He raised his rapier at my head and said, "I'll give you one final offer. Surrender now, and I'll spare your group — Aeres, that traitorous snake, and whatever the elf's name was. He's so forgettable."

I gritted my teeth. I wanted to protect Cedric — and Aeres, too, I guess — but I knew better than to trust anything coming from a Neiphorous. I remembered the promise I made to him before we left Mésura — *neither one of us is getting sacrificed.* I wasn't about to break that promise, and Remius wasn't the only one who could lie to get the upper hand.

"Fine," I conceded, forcing defeat into my voice, "I'll surrender, if it means you won't hurt them." I opened my arms, leaving nothing between his sword and me.

He huffed in approval. "At last we're being reasonable! But I'm afraid that knife will have to go. Can't have you trying to trick me into getting close to you so you can stab me, though I doubt you could land one hit on me without hurting yourself in the process."

I nodded, swallowing my smile. That was exactly what I wanted him to say. Carefully, I tossed my knife toward him, but deliberately overshot so it landed a few feet behind him. He rolled his eyes, but made no move to pick it up.

He swished his sword in the air, then continued his approach, the blade pointed directly at my heart. I clenched my fists, my palms sweaty as my heart raced. Once he was within killing distance, he drew the sword back, but paused.

"And just so you know," he said, a grotesque smirk etching its way onto his face, "I was never going to spare your friends."

With that, he moved to finish me off, but his sword never reached me. Instead, he screamed in pain and shock as my knife lodged itself in his leg in response to my call. I ran around him and drew it from his thigh, leading to a new slew of screaming and cursing as blood spilled to the floor.

"I figured," I muttered as I shook blood from the blade. I wasted no time slashing my knife down toward him, but he kicked out with his uninjured leg, hitting me in the shins and knocking us both to the ground. He pushed himself up unsteadily, blood pooling beneath his boots, but he only seemed invigorated by the wound.

"You always choose the most painful path toward the same fate, don't you?" he spat. With his left hand, he drew his second rapier from its hilt.

Fighting Neiphorous at all would be a struggle, but bringing a knife to a sword fight would be a death sentence. I made a break for the stairs, but he intercepted me, slashing a shallow cut in my side that forced me away from him. It seemed like his leg injury wasn't going to handicap him as much as I had hoped, though I noticed his forehead was glistening with sweat that wasn't there when I first arrived.

I held my knife up and backed away, almost tripping over my own feet to keep my distance from him. If I could keep this up, he'd tire himself out enough for me to get a strike in, or at least flee. I backed up further into the room, not taking my eyes off him, until I felt a hot breath on my back.

I veered away. I was so focused on avoiding Remius that I had almost bumped right into the dragon. The entire time, it had been silently watching, its eyes trained on me with an intensity that I didn't quite understand. It had called me down here, didn't it? What did it want from me? I had no time to think on it, since there was a sword swiping at my head. I ducked, then barely avoided his second blade by tumbling to my side and kicking away from him, but when I tried to stand, he knocked me back to the ground with his blood-soaked boot.

Through ragged breaths, he gasped, "You… could… never… defeat…" The last word was mouthed, but he didn't seem to have the breath to say it. On my back, I pushed away from him, but bumped hard into something behind me. Neiphorous raised his swords, and just as he brought them down, the entire scene faded away.

I looked around, dazed. *Am I dead?* The empty void around me seemed kind of anticlimactic for an afterlife, but when I looked down I could still see my body. That probably meant I wasn't dead, but then what happened?

The answer came as a shifting mass behind me. I lurched to my feet. Turning to face what I had bumped into, I found myself staring directly into the massive face of the dragon — Hythraga — completely unchained. I knew I should have panicked, but she only stood still, her wings folded at her side, watching me. She didn't seem dangerous.

I spoke first with a strange tranquility. "Did you save me?"

In my head, but also out loud, she said, "Nay, thy body be still where it were. I brought thee here, into my mind, only to speak." She paused for a moment to examine me. "What is thy name?"

"Damion Excutari," I said, my family's name hanging heavy in the air.

"So thou art indeed an Excutari. I knew this when you set foot in my cell; a presence such as thine I have not felt for many hundreds of years. And thou art king?"

"Well… yes. Sort of. Remius Neiphorous wants to steal the throne, and it looks like he's winning."

She made a rumbling sound that almost felt like laughter. "His kin and thine have fought for the throne since I flew through the skies of Heniphrost. I beheld from high above as the great Jennira swapped out the last Neiphorous king on the throne, beginning the glory of the house of Excutari. And now I may see the cycle begin anew, all with the same tired eyes."

I thought about how long ago it had been that the first Excutari queen killed her husband, Godrik Neiphorous III, and replaced him on the throne. A sickening feeling rose in me as I imagined how long she had been imprisoned. "How long have you been trapped beneath the castle?" I asked. "There aren't supposed to be any more dragons left in the empire."

"Too long, young king. I am the last of my kind in the land — all the rest had been driven to the East by Obelevon. That treacherous king left me here, in the dark, as thy folk stretched their borders above. I had some visitors, at first; none returned, and soon none followed. There have been many years of darkness before thy foe found me. Dost thou know what he means to do?"

"Neiphorous? He wants to use you as a weapon. To conquer the elves. He thinks that by killing me and making himself emperor, he would be able to control you."

"And he knows this well. I would not want to war with the East, but the chains that bind me are deeper than the scales; if Neiphorous be king, I will never be free of his will." She rose up higher and stared me down. "No king shall rule over me ever more. I will aid thee in thine fight, but thou must set me free of the chains. If thou do not, then we shall both lose all."

I thought back to the promise I made to the *other* dragon — *you must free the hostage once the time comes.* It seemed like a lot of different forces were wanting me to free this dragon, and it was either I let her go, or Neiphorous used her to destroy the East.

"I will free you," I said with newfound resolve. "I will defeat Neiphorous."

"Then we are agreed. I will return thee now to thy fight. Be brave. Break the chains at once; if death comes to thee by the Neiphorous's blades, then we are both forever lost."

Her final words drifted away as the light filled in from the edges of my periphery, and I was once again on my back beneath Neiphorous's raised swords, exactly as I had been. As he brought them down, I rolled out of the way just before they made contact. His swords clattered against the stone and he groaned in annoyance that I was apparently still fighting.

I pushed myself to my feet and ran to Hythraga's muzzle. I had no idea how I was going to break chains that strong, but in the spirit of trying, I maneuvered my knife between a slit in its metal plating. Remius shrieked at me, suddenly more panicked than I had ever seen him.

"What are you doing?! STOP! IF YOU FREE HER NOW, SHE'LL KILL US BOTH!"

I froze, my hands shaking. Then, turning to Remius, I shrugged. "Better her than you."

With that, I grabbed the hilt of my dagger with both hands and threw my entire body weight into prying the muzzle apart. With a deafening crack, the plates split apart and clattered to the ground. As if spurred by the chain reaction, the rest of her bonds cracked and crumbled away.

Remius stood frozen as the dragon rose to its feet for the first time in more than a thousand years. At her full height, she nearly skimmed the ceiling, and she had to lean down to look at us. She spared a glance at both of us, lingering just slightly on me, before she winded up as if to pounce and launched herself at the ceiling.

The stone dome broke away immediately, sending massive chunks of the ceiling toppling to the ground like meteors. I fell to my knees and covered my head, my ears ringing from the mix of stone shattering and earth caving in and Hythraga's victorious roar as she took flight. Her massive wings clouded the air with dust and propelled her through the ceiling and into the open sky.

Once the rubble began to settle, I raised my head and looked around. The braziers were all extinguished by the gale of her wings, but the room was lit by sunlight streaming in from the jagged hole in the roof. There was no sound but the thumps of the last falling stones on the ground. Shakily, I rose to my feet. Neiphorous did, too.

And he was picking up his swords.

Chapter Forty

Remius took ragged steps toward me, choking on the dusty air. I stepped away, but tripped over a pile of debris and landed hard on my back. He made a sound halfway between a choke and a laugh, but it's not as if he was in much better shape than I was.

"You probably thought it was pretty clever, freeing the dragon, didn't you?" His voice was raw and full of contempt.

I pushed myself up, grasping frantically for my knife. I reached out, calling it, feeling for a connection… but nothing happened. As Neiphorous lumbered closer. I scanned the ground for my weapon. I found the hilt by a fallen fragment of the dragon's muzzle beneath a thick layer of freshly-settled dust.

I scrambled to snatch it up, but only stared in shock at my hand. The hilt connected to a jaded fragment of blade. The other half lay a foot away, no longer glowing, its dark silver painted black by the drying blood along its edges. A surge of grief overcame me, but it was quickly overtaken by fear. Remius, seeing that I was now unarmed and fueled by vengeance, hefted his swords and charged at me.

Mustering as much energy as I had left, I made a break for the stairs. Neiphorous ran after me, but I was faster, and it seemed like nothing stood in my way. Once I was free of the dungeon, I could find a weapon, or my allies—

I ducked away from the stairs at the last second as a figure stepped down onto the rubble. It was one of Neiphorous's elf soldiers, followed by a half a dozen more, each armed. Remius cackled at their arrival and brandished his sword at me.

"You see?! You never had a chance! You should never have come back — but I'm glad you did, because even while Hythraga is free, I can console myself by *killing you!*" Spit flew from his mouth with the last words, and I could see some of his soldiers exchange confused glances about the state of their leader. He seemed to notice, too, because he then turned on them. "Why are you all just standing there? Bring him to me! NOW!"

His soldiers immediately mobilized, making a wide formation to close in on me from each side. I knew I had to do something fast, but I was unarmed, exhausted, and still dazed from the chaos of the dragon's escape. With no other options, I closed my eyes and mouthed a prayer to whatever Elementals were still on my side.

Before I had even finished, though, I was drawn back to the present by one of the soldiers muttering a question to his comrades in Elvish.

I opened my eyes as the soldier pointed frantically at the sky. Following his gaze, I saw a figure falling down through the hole in the ceiling above me — no, not falling, *floating*. Even from below, I knew exactly who it was, his auburn hair catching sunlight in a way distinct to him.

Aeres landed in front of me completely unbothered by the two-hundred-foot leap through the collapsed roof. I thought about how much easier my history of falling would have been if *I* were an Elementalist, but I was too relieved by the reinforcements to be jealous.

He faced me, ignoring the elves. "I'm gonna guess you were involved in that dragon that just broke out of the ground, weren't you?"

Without waiting for an answer, he pressed the button on his rod and the copper blades shot out from both sides. Turning toward the soldiers closing in, he said, "I'll handle these guys myself. Once you see an opening, run and don't wait for me."

Before I had even given a response, he sprung forward, slashing out with his staff at whatever unlucky soldiers were nearest. As if broken from a stupor, all of them converged on him at once, the fiery warrior that just fell from the sky clearly more of a priority than me.

Per his instructions, I slipped past the fighting and bolted for the stairs, stumbling over fallen debris and stones as clashes rang out from the fighting behind me. I had almost made it when I was stopped by a sword swinging for my head from the side. I ducked just before it decapitated me, not even bothering to confront Neiphorous — I was unarmed, and there was no reasoning with him in any state. With Remius pursuing right on my trail, I passed the threshold and bounded up the stairs, away from the dragon's ex-prison and back into the castle.

I had no idea how many soldiers would be around now, but I didn't dare hesitate. The dungeon was as dark and silent as ever — blindly, I stumbled into a cell door hanging slightly ajar, but returned the favor on Neiphorous by throwing it completely open behind me. Judging by the echoing crash and his startled cry, it seemed to have worked to stun him for a moment, but I had only just made it to the next staircase when I heard him running to catch up with me.

I tripped over several of the worn steps, but it only made me push myself harder. After escaping into the open hall, I veered right, toward the main gate, where I assumed I could find more allies of mine. I rounded a corner, but staggered to an abrupt stop.

The hallway in front of me was half caved in, the wood beams that held up the ceiling splintered on the floor. Flames licked along the wreckage, sending smoke wafting up to the ceiling. I had to shield my face from the heat, barely processing what I was seeing, but had no time to weigh my options — Neiphorous didn't even seem to notice the wreckage as he came around the bend.

I reversed course and bolted in the opposite direction, through gilded halls filling with smoke as I was now running from more than just the sword-wielding maniac. The walls shuddered, and I had a sneaking suspicion that the castle's centuries-old foundation wasn't designed to handle a dragon breaking through the floor. A thunderous crash from an adjacent hall room launched more smoke into the air. I pulled my shirt over my nose.

I saw an intersection coming up ahead of me — behind me, Neiphorous was slowing as he choked on the smoke, but he was still pushing himself to catch up. Straight ahead was a window overlooking the river, and judging by the clouds of smoke coming from around the hallway to the right, that way would probably kill us both by suffocation.

With only one more option, I turned left, up a minor staircase most people wouldn't even notice. Our boots hammered on the steps as we rose to the second floor. The air was thicker and hotter than below, and I saw that the fire and carnage had also begun to spread upward: Directly ahead of us, a support beam gave out, sending a rafter plummeting down. The floor buckled under it, and large chunks of hardwood quickly began to cave in like sand falling into a pit.

Before the floor beneath me could give out, I continued further up the stairs. The smoke on the third floor was lighter for now, but the collapse of the second floor's ceiling had impacted this level, and I knew I couldn't linger any longer. Neiphorous just barely made it to the fourth floor before the stairs collapsed behind him. It occurred to me how easy it would be to just kick him down into the fire below if it didn't come with the risk of him slicing my foot off.

Though the fourth floor was in better shape, I needed to stay ahead of both the spreading structural damage and the bloodthirsty warlord. I continued up the stairs. My legs burned, but not because of the heat from the flames. The entire castle shook, knocking us both to the ground, but I pushed myself to continue my ascent.

I realized after climbing two more stories that there was nowhere else to go. We had reached the highest floor of the castle, and the only way back down was the stairs which were being quickly devoured by the inferno. I fell back against a wall, unable to take another step without catching my breath. Neiphorous also collapsed at the top of the stairs, gasping for breath with his swords still clutched in his hands.

Though it seemed we had entered into a momentary truce, the smoke was slowly but surely filling the air. It wouldn't be long before the flames themselves reached us, if the whole building didn't collapse onto itself first. I needed to get outside. This entire floor was lined with a defensive balcony, so escaping the smoke was no problem, but there would be no way to get down to the ground without falling to my death. I stepped unsteadily away from the wall and walked to the arch leading to the battlement — Remius seemed in no rush to follow me, knowing that I had no way to escape.

I stepped outside. The wind whipped at my clothes, but I appreciated the fresh air. I walked to a crenel and took in the city. Streams of smoke rose sporadically throughout, the echoes of the battle far below muffled by the wind. I wondered where Cedric was down there, and how Aeres was holding up against Neiphorous's soldiers.

"Ready to finish this?" a voice called from behind me. It was so raspy and hoarse I barely recognized it as Remius's. "You better be, because there's no more running."

I turned to face him. He leaned on the arch, one sword in hand, the other sheathed. His free hand was holding a piece of fabric to the wound in his thigh, and I saw as he threw the cloth away into the wind that it was stained dark red.

"Oh, that? Uncharacteristically clever on your part, since the only way you'd ever be able to strike me was with *magic.*" He spat the last word like it was a slur. "But I'll survive. I always survive. The pain is just the price of power. You wouldn't know anything about that, though, would you?"

I knew he was taunting me, but I couldn't stop myself. "I've gone through worse than a stabbing to get where I am right now, and I'm still standing." I was going to leave it there, but figured if this was going to be my last stand against Neiphorous, I might as well make it count. "But I'm not sure *you'll* be able to say the same — I mean, Acturas sure isn't."

For the briefest moment, I caught his smugness falter. "You…" he started, but caught himself. "Acturas was never capable of achieving his goals. He was too ambitious with nothing to back it up. I taught him as best I could, but he didn't have it in him to be anything but a servant."

"You taught him as best you could, but I still killed him. Maybe I'm stronger than you think."

"*Then prove it*," he hissed.

He raised his sword and charged at me once again, ready to impale me. I threw myself to the side, but he slashed at me, leaving a streak of pain along my back where it made contact. I whirled around just in time to avoid his blade as he lunged for my throat, but I lost balance, falling to the ground and scooting backwards as he swiped at me. Before I could return to my feet, my back hit the stone wall on the side of the balcony. With nowhere else to go, Remius raised his sword over me, but I kicked him in his wounded leg and sent him falling back, too.

"I guess that leg does hurt, after all–" I jeered, but was cut off by a deafening crash. The entire castle shuddered, and we both turned just in time to see a section of the roof cave in, massive stones toppling off the wall and splashing into the river as it free-fell through the lower floors. Billows of smoke erupted from the gap, snaking into the sky like storm clouds and sending ash drifting down around us like snow. The castle felt ready to completely collapse at any second.

Remius sat up, his attention returning to me. He had been too distracted to realize that I had already risen, and as he swung his sword once again at me, he was caught off guard when I parried. He felt for his sheath, but found it empty. The rumbling had covered for me while I slipped his spare sword off his belt.

He took a long moment to process what had happened, then immediately sprang into motion, pushing himself onto his knees. Now that I had the upper hand, though, I wasn't going to give him the chance — I kicked him hard in the shoulder, sending him sprawling down as his sword flew from his hand and disappeared over the side of the balcony. He almost went over the ledge himself, but grabbed hold of the crenel just in time.

I raised his sword to his face. He was hardly in a position to move, much less fight back, but I wasn't going to let myself underestimate him again.

His cleared his throat, his voice suddenly softer. "Damion– that's enough. Don't you see? You've already *won*, there's nothing more I can do. Are you going to kill an unarmed man?"

When he saw I hesitated, he pressed more. "You know if you kill me, there will be no difference between us. You'll be nothing but a merciless killer. Is that what you want? Is that who you are? Go ahead, kill me, you'll only *become* me. And–"

"That's enough," I interrupted. He didn't stop.

"I always thought you to be nobler than your father — more merciful, much like your mother–"

"Remius, stop."

"And that elf in your company, what would he think–"

"That's *enough,* Remius!" I snapped, and this time, he fell silent. My hand shook as I kept the sword raised, his words echoing in my head. Was I really going to do this? I had to do the right thing. I looked into his eyes, searching for anything that would change my mind, but found nothing but fear. That settled it.

I lowered the sword. "As long as you're alive, nothing I care about is safe."

With that, I placed another kick against his chest, breaking his grip on the stone walls and sending him plummeting down to the river. I watched with grim relief as he fell, his screams drowned out by the rushing wind and the knowledge that I would finally be safe. A second later, I noticed a flicker of gold in the early evening light above me. I looked up toward the ashen sky just as Hythraga's shadow passed over me, diving down after Neiphorous. His shrieks ended abruptly with the decisive snap of her jaws.

I watched as she rose up over the castle once again, paying me a silent glance before she turned away and soared toward the mountains, soon nothing but a gold glint in the western sky.

Epilogue

By summer, it was over. I stood outside the
courthouse door, backed up on all slides by imperial
guards. An attendant adjusted the crown on my head
— I still wasn't used to its weight, but I was getting
better at keeping it upright. I silently recited my speech
to the closed doors, waiting to be called inside after the
lesser business was finished. I was interrupted by the
declaration inside.

"All rise for the emperor."

The guards pulled open the doors and followed
me as I stepped through. I kept my eyes fixed ahead,
ignoring the pews lined to the brim with standing
spectators eying me as I strode to the end of the room.
I stepped between my podium, Cedric to my left,
Commander-in-Chief Mauria to my right. I had offered
the role to Aeres after he saved me from the collapse
of the castle, but he turned it down to lead the Hall
of Elements instead. At least under his command, the
Elementalists wouldn't let the city get conquered again
under my rule.

"Lords, diplomats, citizens," I began, still
not used to the sound of my own voice resounding

off the walls, "thank you all for being here. This is the first imperial audience since the end of the war — unfortunately, it must be held here as the castle's reconstruction is underway, but there is lots to discuss. First, I–" I cleared my throat to cover the misstep. I didn't dare glance at Cedric, but I knew he was suppressing a laugh knowing how much I struggled with the royal 'we'. My father used it so effortlessly, but I seemed incapable of adjusting to it. "*We* want to make clear to all of Excutatem that the worst is behind us. The Continental War is finished, Remius Neiphorous is gone, and thanks to the diplomatic efforts of Princess Rema, Minesra has lifted our reparation debts. Now, we can finally mend our empire."

I paused for applause, and the crowd delivered. Echos of cheers and applause amplified off the walls and carried the energy up to the court's high ceiling. I couldn't help but grin. Maybe I could do this after all.

Once the audience naturally calmed, I continued. "That said, the coming years won't be easy. There is at least one dragon free in the West, and there are reports from the Pass of more nearing our borders. What's more, Arrat Neiphorous is still at large, and the sorceress Meca Khumalo is believed to have fled back to the Ghânt. We cannot know what will become of any of this yet, but we *can* assure all of Excutatem that we will be here to face it when it comes."

I was cut off by another round of applause, this time offered freely by the rows of spectators. Despite the danger of what I had just said — dragons returning and vengeful enemies plotting — it seemed nothing could overshadow the hope of a new era, a breath of peace between the continents, a new normalcy. We all understood that the world would never be the way it was before all of this, but if we were going to face the future united, then maybe there was a chance it wouldn't be that bad.

I held up my hand and the crowd fell silent. I glanced at Cedric; he knew what was coming. He had been waiting all day.

"Speaking of moving forward, there are some things that are best left in the past. Some history that Excutatem is better off without." I gave the signal to Commander Mauria and she passed it to the guards. They pulled open the doors, and a set of elven soldiers marched into the room, a prisoner in tow. His wrists and ankles were bound in chains, and his mouth was held closed with a leather strap. His hair was unkempt and grayer than when I last saw him, but it had been a long time. I met his gaze, his eyes wild with anger. One of the soldiers had to yank on the chain to get him to continue to the floor.

"May we present *former* general Acturas Assix. Forgive his appearance; he's been held in custody at a Minesran embassy in the South for about four months now. We truthfully didn't think he had survived — it was so disappointing to learn otherwise."

Chuckles broke out among the audience. Acturas wasn't as much of a beloved figure after word broke of what he'd done, or *tried* to do.

"While he no longer has enough influence to pose any sort of danger to the empire, we believe he represents the worst of us. His philosophies are the same that led Excutatem down its dark path in the first place, and we think it's time to put that philosophy to rest. It's been a long time coming." I turned to Cedric, his satisfaction clear on his face. "Would the King Consort like to do the honors?"

I stepped aside as he rose from his throne and took my place behind the podium. He ignored the cards with the script, not far enough yet with his reading tutor to have any use for them, but it had been ingrained in his memory after he repeated it all day.

He cleared his throat and locked eyes with Acturas. "On the charges of conspiracy to kill the heir, desertion of duty, heresy against the Elementals, high treason against the empire, and the theft of a horse and wagon in Ramethus…" he listed each one with an edge sharper than my knife had been outside Sitika, "… Acturas Assix is forever banished from the realm of Excutatem and all allied realms on the continents." He looked at me. I nodded. With a deep relief, Cedric ordered the guards: "Take him away."

He fought against his restraints as the guards seized him. I sat back upon the throne, Cedric at my side, as Acturas was dragged away to yet another exile.

Acknowledgements

This book's earliest forms were spawned almost eight years ago when I would imagine elaborate worlds in my basement. Though the story, characters, and locations have transformed completely since their earliest forms, my love for the process of creating has only grown along the way. And while the foundations have been with me for as long as I can remember, the finished story wouldn't have been possible without the effort and dedication of the most resilient people I've ever met.

Of course, the first one I have to recognize is Claire Denny, my head editor, advisor, and voice of reason. You subjected yourself to more of my pure, unrefined writing than anybody should ever be forced to bear witness to, and all purely for the love of the game. My only regret in the writing process is that I didn't ask you to be a part of it sooner, but even though you joined late in the race, I couldn't have gotten over the finish line without you. You've truly earned the title "*#1 exwarrior*".

Thank you as well to Emlyn Monti, Kait Hsu, Erika Tross, Cailyn Burks, and Mars Moorhead for generously proofreading and offering comments on excerpts; Princess Opoku-Anarfi for helping me maintain sensitivity while representing as many groups and cultures as possible in this world; Abby Mauney for emotional support; and, last but not least, Ms. Dyche — the greatest guide, mentor, and teacher I could have ever asked for. You've all contributed to this project in ways I could never begin to pay you back for.

Thank you to my mom: you were the first supporter of my writing, and I'll forever appreciate how you always encouraged me to reach skyward and achieve all that I wanted. Thanks to you, I never once doubted myself, no matter how ambitious it seemed, no matter the obstacles it presented, and no matter what other people said. I wouldn't be where or who I am today without that mindset.

And, finally, thank you to everybody else who had to put up with me talking incessantly about this for the last three years. This project has meant the world to me, and I'm overjoyed I finally get to share it with you all!

About the Author

Alex is a 16-year-old author from Northern Virginia. He has been an avid writer since his early years, eventually studying creative writing at a selective high school arts program. His works have been published multiple times in state-recognized literary magazines, earning awards and recognition. Exile is his debut novel, with many more to come!